Destination:
TAMAKWA TERRITORY

Destination:
TAMAKWA TERRITORY

PHYLLIS A. HARRISON

DESTINATION: TAMAKWA TERRITORY

iUniverse books may be ordered through booksellers or by contacting:

iUniverse
1663 Liberty Drive
Bloomington, IN 47403
www.iuniverse.com
844-349-9409

ISBN: 978-1-6632-2833-8 (sc)
ISBN: 978-1-6632-2834-5 (e)

Library of Congress Control Number: 2021917917

Print information available on the last page.

iUniverse rev. date: 10/06/2021

DEDICATION

For June Mackey and all those who
make our voyages a little easier.

Destination
Tamakwa Territory

Autumn 1643, Somewhere
on the Atlantic Ocean

"How much longer do you think, Gilles?"
In the darkness of the ship's hold, Elsje searched her husband's face, looking for any indication of optimism or pessimism. His usually open and expressive face was completely blank for a brief time until the shadow of irritation passed over it.

Gilles took a moment to gather his patience so he wouldn't lose his temper with his wife. Of course she had never been on a great ship on the ocean before, of course she had never been confined in a cramped, dark space for weeks, of course she had never lived for so long in such conditions, and she probably had never before known this kind of insecurity about the future.

He knew that Elsje hadn't been feeling well, ever since the first day they had boarded the ship, and he knew that this had made the voyage doubly hard for her. Still, she had endured this with him, both of them on the same journey, but each alone with their own personal struggles during the long days and the dark nights. Neither one of them would have ever believed that their lives would lead them here, to the great unknown that it was at this moment in time, endless time upon the sea.

Gilles had not shared his thoughts with his wife, something that might have made the journey a little more bearable for both of them, but he was not inclined to do this, even under better circumstances. He knew that over the past weeks he had retreated ever deeper down the dark hallways of his thoughts, into an inner place that held only one person, himself. Unfortunately, he was not entirely alone here either. Fearsome dark shapes

1

waited for him in the murky corners of his mind, creeping up behind him again and again.

He had tried, a time or two, explaining to Elsje that there was no way for him to have the knowledge of when they might arrive, even if it was true that he had been born into a family whose main financial interests and accumulated wealth were from shipping. He had never bothered to tell her that most of his experience with sea-going matters came from overhearing his father's conversations as he interrogated the shipmasters, argued loudly with accounts keepers, or engaged in heated discussions with trade partners regarding the minutiae of contracts. In fact, most of Gilles' education in this area came second-hand, from studying the pages of the accounting books his father had forced upon him, endlessly long pages filled with tiny numbers, the repetition only interrupted by brief smudges of the ink. In actuality, Gilles had experienced very few journeys at all upon the water.

He had tried a few times to tell Elsje that he, too, had lost count of the days and that she would know when he knew. He had even hinted broadly that she was fast becoming another one of the people he was avoiding in what was becoming a smaller and smaller prison floating on the water.

The nights were different than the days: In the darkness and the quiet of the evening, when there were rhythmic snores, regular coughs and the creaking of the ship all around them, he went to Elsje for marital comfort, for physical relations, one of the few opiates of life left to ease his malaise and ennui. There was not nearly enough ale supplied to them to eradicate or even soften the ever-present harsh reality of their situation. Elsje would shift the baby over to her side as Gilles positioned himself over her on the bunk, moving under the blanket and using the wooden posts, the demarcations of their small allotted space, for leverage.

The nights gave him some brief transport to another place, but the days were far too long. Perhaps they would just die here on the sea, and he shouldn't even worry about a future that was never going to come. Maybe he should just take whatever small joy he might find in each day and be satisfied with that, the occasional chance to go up on the open deck into the fresh air and sunshine, having food enough during a meal with no trace of mold on it, or an unexpected extra ration of herring or ale.

No, his life was not going to end on the water, he kept telling himself that. He had survived much worse, and they would survive this too, just as long as they could keep their sanity. Gilles took another deep breath, striving for calm and readying his reply. Pulling himself together, he reached deep down inside to find the last measure of patience he had. What could he do for his wife? What could he say to her? He was the head of the household and was supposed to be the strong one, the confident and reassuring one.

"When we are allowed back up on the deck again, I will see who else I might ask and what I can find out."

He managed a small smile for her. He had already asked everyone at least half a dozen times, and they were as tired of answering him as he was of asking. He had asked the shipmaster, the other passengers, and even some of the sailors. There were no birds around, but perhaps he could ask the sun, the clouds and the wind since he had not asked them yet. In reality though, no one could truthfully say that they knew how much longer it was going to be.

Elsje guided baby Jacomina back to her breast and Gilles tried to relax, breaking his eyes away from hers and moving them out into his dim surroundings, over the system of wooden berths built into the sides of the ship, a strange trelliswork with vines of living fruit clinging to them. The racks reached from floor to ceiling on either side of this middle deck of the ship, and now the thought occurred to him that the passengers were billeted very much like crated chickens being transported in the back of a farmer's wagon on their way to the big fall market fair in old Amsterdam. They were not livestock though, they were human beings, and this wasn't a wagon jolting over solid and familiar roads. This was a ship on the great open waters of the Atlantic, and there were no signposts or landmarks that people always expected to see along the way.

Gilles supposed he should be grateful that they had a place to sleep that was up off the floor and that they were not spread out like animals in one great enclosed barn. He knew that these miserable and crowded quarters were fitted with these berths, not to provide comfort in lifting them up to a higher, dryer perch, but to stack the maximum number of paying passengers in the hold. The owner of the ship may have begrudged the cost of the additional lumber needed to build these racks, but it was simply a matter of maximizing profit. Each four by five-foot section held between two and six people, without mattress or pad offered as a concession to their

3

humanity. There was only a small bit of hay for cushioning and absorbing the human odors and waste that might be accumulating there, along with the fleas, during the long weeks they would be living in the space.

If this ship had been seaworthy enough to carry more valuable cargo, it wouldn't be used in this way and relegated to carrying two-legged livestock, the unwanted discharge of old Europe. Now showing her age, worm holes at the waterline plugged again and again with pitch and having a patchwork of repairs here and there, the vessel was moving toward the end of her useful life as anything except firewood or a breakwater, the last humiliation of a once-proud vessel. Den Eyckenboom, The Oak Tree, had no glorious and illustrious life ahead as a fighting ship in a great navy. She would no longer be used as a trade ship, a purveyor of wealth with her own supercargo, a company representative whose sole employment and responsibility was to oversee the welfare of the goods she carried. Now Den Eyckenboom just carried the human overflow and refuse of the Netherlands, hauled it away to be dumped on the other side of the ocean.

They might not be chickens on their way to market, but Gilles knew they were headed toward some kind of an appointment with fate. A few of them were individuals of significant means, but most were those whose last coins had been invested in the journey, seeking refuge, fleeing whatever it was that they tried to leave behind. Some of them, Gilles' wife Elsje included, still clung to the delusional belief that they were going to the Dutch claimed territory to seek and find great fortune, then someday return triumphantly to their old homes.

Feeling a stab of sympathy for his wife now, and also some guilt that he had been unable to provide a more stable life for his young family, he thought he should try to make more of an effort to ease her mind. Gilles would start over again and try to speak to his wife in a more compassionate way. After all, it was really not her fault. He knew that she wrestled with her own demons every day, just as he did with his own.

"I don't know how much longer, Elsje. We are still in the middle of the ocean but I imagine we must be more than halfway there by now."

He always told her that, although he really had no idea where they were. Elsje saw the direction of his eyes, fixedly turned away from hers now, avoiding eye contact by looking over to the bunk across the way, on the other side of the ship.

"She constantly watches us!" Elsje hissed, inclining her head in that direction.

Gilles looked at the three pale women staring intently at them, without shame or embarrassment for their blatant eavesdropping, without averting their eyes, listening, looking, and as always, prying hungrily into the family's everyday lives. The two daughters traveled with their elderly mother and an elderly dog that was as pale in color as the three women. The younger daughter, silent and wide-eyed, clutched a doll to her chest, never uttering a word, so Gilles supposed she must be feeble-minded. The mother just rocked back and forth, constantly humming to herself, but was otherwise silent as well. It was only the older daughter who sometimes spoke. With one blind white eye and an outcropping of boils across her face and hands, she was repulsive enough to behold, but her demeanor was worse than her appearance. In between racking coughs, she snarled a constant stream of curses, some directed at her sister or her mother, and others targeting any passengers who might be unfortunate enough to cross her path. Elsje had discovered this on their very first day out when she tried to be kind, to engage the creature in conversation.

Elsje's charitable attempt at civility had been a big mistake. The pale woman growled like a street dog with a newly-discovered bone from a rubbish heap, lashing out at Elsje and her family, delivering an unending stream of curses in her diatribe. The hag snarled that she was a great and important personage who was going to join up with the patriarch of the family, a man of significant means who would avenge the family honor for the many wrongs that had been done to her by the other passengers. Gilles dismissed this version of reality completely since the woman's vituperations had started on the first day out of port, and Gilles had not yet had an opportunity to even the score, to insult her as thoroughly as he would have liked. On some days it was harder than others to hold his tongue, but then he reminded himself that it was going to be a very long journey and would be longer still if there was an insane woman just across the way who was lying in wait for an excuse and opportunity to attack his family. Unfortunately, they were stuck inside the ship with the crazed woman and all of the other passengers for the duration of the trip, however long it might be.

Another nearby family leaned over on their berth to listen in to what

5

Gilles had to say to Elsje, to see if he might have any inside information as to how much longer it would take. Gilles wasn't blind. He saw those faces and ears turned to him, but he ignored them all, staring down at his hands now, examining them and wondering how they came to be so dry and so dirty when all he did every day was ride inside the ship. Maybe the other passengers had heard gossip, in all probability from Elsje herself, that Gilles' family had some connection to shipping and the sea. They might have thought that Gilles heard some news from the crew or knew something that they didn't, but this was not so. Gilles didn't bother speaking to the other passengers, and it wasn't only that he considered himself to have been born superior to everyone else on this wretched vessel. Family and fortune seemed to have deserted him in recent years, but he felt no pressing need to set the record straight and share the details of his life with anyone, not regarding his past or the reason why he was traveling with them, running from country to country for his life.

It had not been his idea to leave his homeland. France had picked the fight with Gilles, and he had been sentenced to death in his home country when he was just a teenager. This was no idle threat if the king's soldiers ever found him. There was a generous reward that was still being offered for his capture and return for public execution. His charged crime was for being a secret protestant, a Huguenot, and not being a good and faithful Catholic who was obedient to the official religion of France's king and country. Gilles didn't know anything about these Huguenots, even though tens of thousands of them had already been put to death by fire, sword and gallows. There had been some written legal protections for these people, but their reality did not always coincide with the laws that were on the official documents. His true crime, what Gilles had been guilty of, had been to come from a family that was a nice plump target.

During the French king's quest to find new ways to finance his opulent life style and the ongoing wars that continually drained the government coffers, the monarch seized upon a reliable method of extracting any excess wealth from his citizenry and replenishing the royal funds. Wealthy families and individuals were accused of being protestants and quickly sentenced to death unless they turned over their money and their property and begged forgiveness, the latter being the least important of the three conditions for absolution. Not coincidentally, the head of the Catholic

Church in France was the King's collaborator in this endeavor. Cardinal Richelieu took personal pleasure in overseeing the deaths of anyone who questioned his authority. Many French citizens fell in line with the proclamations, changing their beliefs and morality as it suited the king and the church, but many more fled the country. A few resisted. The French citizens living in the city of La Rochelle, including Catholics, separatists and others whose beliefs were not openly declared, were promised freedom to worship as they pleased, but this did not last for very long. Inspired by the love of their country, their city and their liberty, they had stood together, shoulder to shoulder in the name of freedom when they came under attack by the king's army. After months of resistance, the cardinal stepped in and personally oversaw the final slaughter of almost all of them, men, women and children.

What Cardinal Richelieu did not know was that these citizens were ready and willing to give their lives for the cause. It had ended badly for both sides, with most of the rebels starving, having eaten their leather shoes and belts after the supply of wild rats, domestic animals and, it was rumored, corpses ran out. Those few girl children who were found alive were given a quick conversion to Catholicism and then sent across the ocean to be the brides of strangers chosen for them, transported to the lonely men in the lands of New France. These men had been waiting long years for these fresh supplies. The "King's Daughters" as they called these girls, were ordered to bear as many children as quickly as possible to populate the territory and help the king retain possession of the French-claimed lands around Quebec. They were Catholic placeholders in the land the savage aboriginals called Canata.

Surprisingly, the French king's destruction of La Rochelle did not put an end to any further resistance. The name of the old city just kept cropping up in new settlements across the world as it had become a synonym for freedom and resistance to tyranny. La Rochelle took her revenge in other ways, too. Trade across France and all of Europe was severely damaged with the loss of the best sailing canvas in the world and the superior wine that had previously been made by the inhabitants of that ruined place. These industries had brought financial bounty to the king, but those who had previously lived there and had the knowledge of how to create this wealth were now dead or had fled the country. Even now, a generation later, the French economy had not recovered from the assault that had come from within, from their own sovereign.

The people of France briefly had renewed hope when both king and cardinal had died very recently, within the past year. The old king, Louis XIII, died a short time after the cardinal, his dog of the hunt, met his heavenly maker. While the old king might have thought the cleric a useful tool early on, it was whispered that he, too, had come to fear the cardinal in later years. The king was worried that he might not be able to die a peaceful death in his own bed, especially after seeing what so many of his subjects had endured at the hands of the church's inquisitors. He kept a close watch on the cardinal, waiting for the cleric to die first before he gave up the ghost a short time afterwards.

Unfortunately, there was no hope in a new king. The old king's son and heir could not ascend the throne yet, not even the steps to the throne without some help, because he was only four years old and could barely reach them. The machinery of state had been so well-constructed though, that it continued to function without the old king who was barely remembered by anyone after the requisite period of mourning. The next regime carried on business as usual with the new king's widowed mother taking up her dead husband's work, acting as regent for her young son under the direction of a new cardinal, Mazarin. It was rumored that Cardinal Mazarin was the widowed queen's lover and so things seemed unlikely to change for a very, very long time.

Those who held the power in France were not listening and did not want any negotiation or reconciliation with the unhappy citizenry. Along with the other spoils the French government had taken from the victims, hope for their future had been stolen from them too. In the eyes of the old, and now even in the eyes of Gilles' young friends, he had seen this light grow steadily dimmer until it was almost entirely extinguished. This dark night of the soul had been ushered in and firmly established by a small circle of men in a relatively short period of time. Those who realized the futility of fighting this state of affairs gave up on life or gave up on France. When ale and other alcoholic spirits failed to make men forget the misery of their lives, those who still had the will and the means to do so left their homeland, leaving much behind, including their Catholic faith.

Gilles had no interest in politics or religion and no time or patience to concern himself as to whether this state of affairs would come to an end any time soon. It could happen in the next year or in the next five hundred years, but it seemed doubtful that much would change during his own lifespan. He moved on with his life, knowing that he personally did not have hundreds of years to wait for sanity to return to his homeland.

Escaping to the Netherlands had saved his life but not his birthright. Just as the French government had done after the old king's death, Gilles' family had gone on with their lives without him, now just a little less wealthy and with one less son than they had before. With the reward still being offered for Gilles' apprehension and French bounty hunters asking questions about him in Amsterdam, his city of sanctuary was no longer safe.

Seeing the reality of his situation, Gilles had willingly stepped onto this ship and started his journey toward a new life in a new skin. If he had been alone on this journey, it would have been a very different adventure, but with his new family in tow, it was difficult for him to drive back the worries he had regarding how they were all going to survive. In time, he hoped he would come to a place where his life would be something more secure, more akin to the way he had believed his future would be when he was a wealthy and privileged child in France.

Gilles' home country was not alone in this great upheaval, and now it seemed as if the entire world was on fire. Spain had led the way with the great inquisition, but France and England soon followed suite and succumbed to this madness as well. One group of English protestants had sought refuge in the Netherlands, but when their new homeland proved to offer less than what they had hoped for and a decade-long military truce between the Netherlands and Spain threatened to come to an end, they decided on a more radical course of action. After making some inquiries, promising financial return to their investors and downplaying their spiritual inclinations, the Pure Ones, or the Puritans as they were called sometimes, secured an English patent in the wilderness lands of the newly-discovered continent across the Atlantic Ocean. They refitted two leaky old trade ships to accomplish their mission. Strangely enough, one of them, The Mayflower, had been well-known to the ill-fated city of La Rochelle. Along with a few adventure-seekers who joined up with them, they headed west across the ocean to build a city on a hill where they could practice their own brand of civilization with their religion at the center of their lives. The Mayflower managed to reach the other side of the ocean late in the year, dropping anchor next to a sandy and desolate piece of land. They spent their first winter on the ship, freezing, terrified of their wild surroundings and dying in large numbers before they finally disembarked in the spring. They called the place New England, and every time the name was spoken aloud, it was a wish and affirmation that it would be a safer and saner version of their old homeland.

These English wanderers had originally requested settlement in the Dutch- claimed territory, knowing that the Netherlanders were generally more tolerant of individual freedoms than their own government, but this request had been denied. Always on their guard, the Dutch had probably been worried that allowing a large group of religious fanatics in their midst would only be asking for trouble. They had some previous experience in that regard at home when they had to deal with the bothersome Mennonites who settled among them there.

The Dutch settlement of New Amsterdam had not been started with any such lofty ideals. In a way, it had been an accidental colony. There had never been any intention of planting anything permanent there. The practical but adventurous Dutch were always on the lookout for profitable new opportunities, even though difficulties in their Malaysia and Brazil colonies had recently made them a little more cautious. The government of the Netherlands was not willing to risk another expensive investment venture, so they turned everything over to one of their major corporations, the Westindische Compagnie, usually just referred to as the WIC. The company assumed the financial risk of the venture in exchange for the profits while the government collected the taxes and distanced itself from the West India Company's sometimes questionable actions and behavior. The eager European markets for beaver skins and the pelts of other wild animals from the newly discovered continent brought new wealth from this trade to the Netherlands. The fort and growing settlement at New Amsterdam provided the added bonus of a home base and safe harbor where the Dutch ships could hide out between forays to plunder the trade goods of other countries as their ships sailed by.

Not everyone was eager to go experience the new continent. Given the savage conditions and the settlement being so far away from civilization, the West India Company found few tradesmen who were willing to leave the safety and comfort of the fatherland to go there. After some searching, the WIC had found this much-needed labor among the restless English. Recognizing the necessity, the company had permitted a few Englishmen to come to New Amsterdam, but this was only if they practiced a trade that was in short supply there. Letting in a few of these Englishmen probably would not cause too much trouble, especially if there were no English houses of worship in the colony, only the Dutch Reformed Church. The local administrators in New Amsterdam had no objections to letting the English and others worship as they pleased, just as long as it was inside a building with no crosses on it or other signs of religion visible on the outside.

More and more of the English were coming into the colony and it was not just the laborers: Others were bringing their families with them and now they were multiplying faster than rats on a grain ship. Their loyalties were suspect, and this worry persisted because they continued to speak English among themselves. For all anyone knew, they might be plotting to seize the colony for England and no one would know this until it was too late. These English families weren't just confining themselves to New Amsterdam and staying on the tip of Mannahatta Island though; they were becoming a larger and larger portion of all of New Netherland's population. They were planting themselves on the lands across the East River around Breuckelen, the westernmost part of the Long Island, and in small settlements like Heemstede, further out on the island. If this wasn't concerning enough to the WIC, word had spread across the world and now more seekers of freedom and fortune had started coming in from dozens of other countries. Gilles knew he was headed to a most unusual place and into a most unusual situation, but the more he thought about it, the more he understood why the West India Company believed that he was exactly the right man to send in there.

"It's so hot and sticky. I had no idea it would be so warm this late in the year or I wouldn't have brought so much wool to knit stockings, hats and mittens."

Elsje's voice interrupted Gilles' thoughts although she directed this comment not at him, but at the family members traveling with them who occupied two nearby berths. Gilles knew his wife was keeping her sanity and making her own contribution to the family by knitting and trying to keep their morale up with happy conversation. He reminded himself that he should really try to be a little more understanding. In addition to the motion sickness, every day she had to deal with fussy baby Jacomina at her breast, their toddler, Bruinje, who needed two people to keep an eye on him on his quiet days, and Elsje's miserable old widowed father who contributed little besides complaints and proclamations of future doom.

Like poor quality wine that was only good for use as vinegar, old Hendrick only grew more sour and bitter as he aged. Gilles would have liked to leave the old bastard behind in the Netherlands, but unfortunately, Elsje wouldn't hear of it. Hendrick shared his berth with his teenage son, Heintje, and occasionally with little Bruinje when he happened to fall asleep there. Because Hendrick made no serious effort to get along with Gilles, it was a good thing that he was two berths away, with Elsje's young sister Corretje and their servant Aafje Vander Cloot occupying the middle berth. This buffer between Hendrick and Gilles had only limited success in keeping the peace between the two men though.

Loud voices from the other side of the ship rose above the hum of everyday conversation and the ship's creaks and natural noises. It had suddenly become quiet around them as everyone listened, trying to find out what was happening.

Had the ship sprung a leak?

Were pirates boarding them?

Gilles heard the smacking noise of fists, flesh connecting with flesh, screams and shouts from some of the passengers closest to the disturbance, and there was the crashing noise of a large body connecting with one of the wooden posts that delineated the berths. Two of the passengers were in a fight. Gilles just hoped they would not come near his family and that they had no more dangerous weapons with them than their hands.

"Help! Help!" a woman cried out from near the melee, but no passengers moved to go to her, all of them shrinking back into the safety of the shadows. Running over to the stairs, racing up the ladder and pounding on the closed hatch with her fists, she called out to the crew.

"Help! Help me!" she cried out again.

Up above, they had already heard the commotion and four sailors flew down the steps with capstan bars in hand, pushing the woman roughly out of the way. The sailors separated the two bloodied men, then dragged both of them back up the stairs by their collars, ignoring the cries and protests of their respective families. Gilles did not know what they might do to the men, or when they might be returned below, but he hoped it would not be very soon.

Given the frustration of their situation, it was no surprise that fights frequently broke out. All manner of crimes had been committed on the ships as they traveled, everything from petty theft to murder. The shipmaster would have had enough to deal with, in terms of navigation and keeping the passengers fed, but there was also the peacekeeping needed between members of his crew and the voyagers as the journey grew longer and tempers grew shorter. If Gilles ever had thoughts of becoming a shipmaster, this voyage had succeeded in putting those thoughts out of his mind permanently. Often these days, he thought they had come to be living like frightened house mice trapped under the floorboards, scrapping and squabbling with each other over nothing that would be of any consequence out in the greater world they had left behind.

If he hadn't known it before, he realized with sudden clarity now that he was not actually heading from one great civilization to another. After all, these were not the most illustrious of citizens that traveled with them, and there would be many more of the same kind that had already removed themselves to the colony. The poor and pathetic Dutch settlement grandly named New Amsterdam would be nothing like the cultured and prosperous city they had left behind in the Netherlands. They were headed toward what was perhaps the last place on earth for many of them to run to, the last place most of them would want to go to, frantic and bedraggled rats swimming away from the burning and sinking ships of their past lives.

The rest of the hold was very quiet now, quieter than usual, except for the old woman across the way. The mother of the crazy woman continued to hum to herself, the same tuneless hum that never stopped, not during the day or during the night, not even during the fight. Gilles believed he would have already gone mad from the old woman's incessant noise if it had not been for the constant talk of the other passengers drowning her out. Finally, someone on the other side of the ship laughed and then, little by little, conversation resumed, except for where the fight had started.

He supposed the sobbing noises he heard were coming from the wife or child of one of the combatants. He tried to relax, noting that his body had tensed up completely and his own fists were clenched. At least this time no one had died or been badly hurt. Gilles recalled hearing the story of a young woman whose husband had been killed in a knife fight on board one of the ships, leaving her a poor, pregnant widow, arriving alone in an alien and hostile land. There would be gossip and stories in the days ahead regarding who had started the fight and what they were fighting about. There would be sides to be taken and cases to be made for justice. At least it would offer them all a temporary diversion, something new to think and talk about. Many of the passengers were grateful for the distraction, although they might not want to admit this, even to themselves.

"I want some carrots and apples, a roasted chicken, apple crullers and apple dumplings when we get there," Elsje offered loudly.

She smiled at Gilles, and he knew she was trying to offer a better distraction, to lighten the mood and cheer the rest of their group. He knew that she couldn't really be thinking about food: She still had that green tinge to her face that told Gilles all he needed to know, that her stomach fared no better on the quiet seas than on the rough ones. Elsje liked to cook and occasionally recited her shopping list to bolster everyone's spirits, but for Gilles, it only raised the specter of possible starvation that was ahead of them. She had to be as disappointed in the limited fare on the ship as Gilles was. He was eternally tired of eating salt cod and peas, day in and day out. The small rations of ale, herring, and occasional salt beef or ham did not placate him, but he supposed he should be grateful that they had any food at all and had not run out.

They had already been fed both of their meals today, and, at Elsje's insistence, Gilles had dutifully finished his. He tried not to even taste it anymore, just to let it move as quickly as possible from his lips to his stomach without lingering anywhere for too long in between. He longingly thought of what he would give for some freshly roasted beef, a delicious pheasant or some onion soup with hunks of hot buttered bread to go with it. When he had the opportunity to have those once again, he was going to appreciate them anew, smell and savor his food for a long time before he even tasted it, and then let each bite linger in his mouth before he swallowed it. He decided, that for now at least, he needed to come out of his bad humor, out of his melancholy and the dark mist that perpetually

14

seemed to surround him, to join his wife and indulge in some fantasy of his own, to escape for just a little while.

"Do you want all of those in one meal, in that order?" Gilles asked her.

Elsje laughed, a small laugh, but it was good to hear.

"Maybe I will, but I'll save my apple dumplings for last!"

Gilles had never said so aloud, but he resented the fact that he was far too young to bear all of this responsibility. It was not as if he had been raised to understand how all of this was supposed to work. When he was growing up, his father made the fortune and the family servants took care of everything else. The burden of finding shelter and food for his wife, his two small children, his father-in-law, his wife's teenaged brother and sister and the two servants in their family group weighed on Gilles before he had even arrived in the new world, weeks before he started to tackle this task. Barely of majority age and not so long out of his teens himself, Gilles had the devoir of feeding them all.

The two servants had been recruited for two reasons: It was true that they were part of the requirement for Gilles' receiving his land grant in the new country, his patroonship, but they were also needed to help the household survive by bringing their skills and abilities along with them. The girl knew about farming, and the man was tall and strong. Gilles was strong enough, but he was only one man. Hendrick, being old and crippled, was unable to contribute very much besides aggravation. There had been a fight back in Amsterdam, the indirect cause being Gilles and the direct cause being the bounty hunters who were looking for him. When Hendrick was caught in the middle of the altercation while trying to save his tavern from the destruction, he had been injured. After infection set in, the chiurgeon had saved his life by amputating Hendrick's arm. This reality hung heavily between the two men, unspoken blame on Hendrick's part and unacknowledged guilt on Gilles'.

When he did engage in conversation with the rest of his family, Gilles told them that their table would always be filled with wonderful food, embellishing his tales by describing large fish that jumped out of the ocean and into their waiting baskets, great quantities of wild game that overwhelmed the snares in their fields, apple trees so laden with fruit that the tree branches broke and wheat that came up through the rich earth of the new land as fast as it was planted. In actuality though, Gilles had only a vague idea of how he was going to feed everyone. A verse from something he read somewhere long ago came back to him: "What did I do to deserve the burden of all these people? Did I give birth to them? Did I bring them into the world? Where am I supposed to find food for all of them?"

The lie of his cocky confidence would probably be known only too soon after they got there, when true hunger set in. The best he could do for them now was to put up a brave façade, to keep their spirits up and feed them with hope for the future. The weight of this responsibility would have been difficult enough for anyone to shoulder, but to seal the bedevilment, Gilles was cursed with a spirit that wanted something else in life: He wanted to be free to explore the wide world and to restore his lost fortunes. These two innate lusts drove him forward, much more than any sense of urgency regarding mere human needs like food or shelter, but now he had the others to consider. At times he found it difficult to stop thinking about running away from them all when he reached the other shore, running straight into the wilderness and abandoning them to fend for themselves.

"So do you think it will be *very* much longer?" Elsje's voice interrupted his thoughts once more.

"Not so long I think."

He patted her hand, restraining himself from patting it rather harder than was necessary, feeling the frustration rising back up inside him again.

The overhead hatch was still closed, sealing them in below the open top deck of the ship. Passengers were only allowed up, a few at a time, on days when sailing was easy and the weather was peaceful, so Gilles had to rely on other methods of preserving his inner calm while he was locked up. Elsje planned dinners and shopping lists while he tamped down his own rising panic about their uncertain future by taking stock of his assets. Dreaming about his future plans had become the chief armament he used to fend off his worries and his fears. Because his education had mainly been in accounts, he often viewed situations, relationships, and even life as being simply two opposing columns. On the asset side, he had a modest job waiting for him, the position of company clerk and translator for the Dutch West India Company. Some would have considered it a great position to aspire to in a lifetime, but not Gilles. He had been born into much better circumstances and considered it of little consequence, maybe even his due owing to his superior family bloodlines and his education.

There was the little house he had in the settlement of New Amsterdam, a house he had never seen. Based on the drawing the surveyor had made on the deed margin, Gilles could see that it was a very small house, humble, not much to brag about really, but it was a start, a shelter for them to go to. No one had been more surprised than Gilles when he had become the owner of this plot of land, a wedding gift from his best friend, Jean Durie. Gilles never asked Jean how he had come into possession of it, and he wasn't really sure that he wanted to know the details. If he had asked, his friend would probably have replied with a wink and a smirk. Knowing that Jean had not only a love of gambling, but also a talent for trade and somehow always coming out the winner, Gilles had a pretty good idea of how the deed had changed hands. He just hoped that some former owner wouldn't come looking to repossess the property after they had settled in there and planted their crops. Land ownership for most people in the world was unusual. Until just recently, the land in New Amsterdam had mostly been the property of the West India Company, to be rented out for profit or used as the company elite saw fit. Things had not been going well for the colony in a number of areas lately, so many of the laws and rules had recently been relaxed in the interest of keeping their business concern going. Although there would be a few more landowners than there had been previously, many of the local denizens still had the challenge of finding shelter. They might rent from the company if they had the means to do so, find a house where the family would provide them with bed and board in exchange for work, or as a last resort, live like an animal in the wild. If many of the settlers were hardy young men with no families, maybe it didn't matter so much if they found accommodation in the woods with other creatures of the forest.

His greatest prize so far, the repository for most of Gilles' hopes and dreams, was his patroonship. With certain conditions attached, this property had been granted to him by the Westindische Compagnie. It consisted of eight miles of land on either side of the North River, a day's journey north of New Amsterdam and a day's journey south of another patroonship, a piece of real estate that was becoming very well-known back in the Netherlands and around the world. This other patroonship was called Rensselaerswyck, and it had brought both wealth and fame to its owner, one Kiliaen Van Rensselaer. Gilles had been given his choice of

17

locations and selected this place in the wiltwyck, reasoning that it would make a good stopping-over place for ships needing refreshment for their crews, resupply, or maybe even someday, an inn for weary travelers.

Gilles dreamed about making these wilderness lands of his into a great plantation that would one day rival the kingdom of Van Rensselaer. With tenant farmers working for Gilles and cultivating his forty acres of land for him, he could enjoy his wealth while he and his family lived many miles south of it, in the comfort and security of New Amsterdam, at the mouth of the river. He could just collect his income from ships as they brought goods up and down the river, to and from his own private colony, trading in furs, wine, timber and wheat. He knew that there was already a small trading post near his land, so he surmised that the Esopus tribe of savages living nearby must be on good terms with the West India Company. With the income from his clerical position and the little house in New Amsterdam to get them started, Gilles and his family would have some security while his patroonship was getting established.

His associations with the West India Company in the Netherlands had secured his land grant, something that would not have been possible before the company had changed their rules and regulations. From the very beginning, few shareholders had the capital to invest and fewer still had the inclination to take the risk in the new world. Gilles had only been a small investor, not actually a full member of the WIC at the time, but maybe the timing had been exactly right for him to take advantage of new opportunities. To secure his land forever, the terms of the contract required that Gilles start by finding six souls over the age of sixteen and pledge to settle one hundred more there within the first year, otherwise ownership would revert back to the company. If all went well and the patroonship was profitable, Gilles would stay on with other colonists even if the company were to pull out of New Netherland someday, leaving it behind for more lucrative ventures. Gilles took heart from this thought, that he was still very young and had not just one, but two pieces of property waiting for him. He only had to cross an ocean to get to them.

Gilles also counted on the asset side of his ledger, somewhat guiltily, the money from the sale of his father-in-law's land in old Amsterdam. Although it was not really Gilles' money, he would be sheltering the old man and most of his progeny, so he reasoned that he was certainly entitled

18

to the use of it, at least to feed them all until his own success arrived. It was likely that the West India Company had been eyeing Hendrick's tavern for many years due to its location. When it was destroyed by the fire, it seemed that providence had given the company an ideal site for building their new warehouse, one that was already mostly cleared except for the charred rubble. Gilles had convinced Hendrick to sell his Amsterdam land to the WIC, and this might have been another reason why the company men had wined him and dined him, offering him the clerical job and then sweetening the deal with the offer of a patroonship.

Gilles lived with the nagging fear that all would not turn out as he had hoped. He was anxious for this journey across the ocean to be over, to get started on his new life, but he was also afraid of what he would find when he got there. He was afraid of all the work that would need to be done and afraid of all the ways his dreams could miscarry, due to known risks as well as unforeseen circumstances. Whenever he was overwhelmed with this anxiety, Gilles always went through his mental ledger, particularly in the middle of the night and in the early morning hours when he woke in a sweat that was not caused only by the sticky, humid weather and the mass of human bodies clustered together in the ship's hold.

When these thoughts were not enough to slow his racing heart, Gilles turned to his greatest reassurance of all, the magic charm that always restored his peace, his balm of Gilead, his friend Jean. A relict of Gilles' last days in France, Jean had fled France with Gilles, and together they had started new lives in the Netherlands. Jean was always there for him, wise and ready counsel whenever Gilles didn't know what to do next. He had boarded an earlier ship, gone ahead of them by several weeks, so Jean was probably settled in New Amsterdam already. Gilles would not even consider the possibility that his friend's ship had not arrived there safely, although shipwrecks were all too common an occurrence. He didn't know what he would do if Jean was not there to help him through the struggles that were certain to lie ahead. Because the thought of losing both a best friend and the security that Jean personified was just too overwhelming to think about, Gilles always pushed those thoughts out of his mind when they tried to get in.

Gilles was not naïve: He knew that the challenges and dangers before him were formidable, but he always reminded himself that so, too, was the

19

opportunity. He clung to his hopes with a tenaciousness born of his own will-power and his anger at those who had attempted to take from him not just his inheritance, but also his life.

"Only another couple of weeks," Gilles told Elsje once again, trying to control his voice, knowing full well that his wife heard the hollowness of the promise.

Gilles knew she had already resisted asking him once again for as long as she could. He really didn't know, had no idea at all how long it would take, although Elsje seemed to believe that he must somehow possess this knowledge. He marveled at this woman of the world who actually believed in him when he himself felt so much like a lost child.

"When we get there, you will be a grand lady of New Amsterdam, a company man's wife! You will be out shopping every morning for fine delicacies for our dinner table and have tea with all of the important West India Company wives every afternoon. Of course, you will have to have some new dresses made."

Elsje smiled at him, reassured for the moment, sighed a little and leaned back against the wooden post of the bunk. It made Gilles happy too, seeing her satisfied and quietly hopeful, at least for the moment.

Den Eyckenboom did seem to be sailing to the ends of the earth now since it was taking so long. The ship traveled on, in the daylight and in the darkness, under starlight, under moonlight, beneath sunshine and clouds, leaving far behind the city of old Amsterdam with all of its civilized pleasures and happy pastimes. They were leaving behind musicians and plays, markets filled with anything imaginable, fine art and books, shops full of books. The West India Company's distant fortified outpost on Mannahatta Island was somewhere up ahead in the darkness, just a spot on the map of the new frontier, a God-forsaken, and as rumor frequently had it, soon to be company-forsaken colony.

With so many concerns weighing on his mind already, Gilles would not have even considered taking on the responsibility of feeding the two strangers if they hadn't been a requirement of the West India Company's to get his land grant. Because he had been so excited about his new venture, he hadn't expected that it would be so difficult to find workers who would accept his proposition. He didn't understand their reluctance until he realized that they might not consider it as great an opportunity as he did. It seemed that no one wanted to give up all they had ever known to go work in a wilderness that had become infamous for difficult living conditions, savage animals, and the brutal wild men who occasionally swarmed the settlements and killed indiscriminately, sometimes even eating their victims. Gilles was so desperate to fulfill the initial quota, to obtain his land, that he took the two servants on without knowing very much about them at all. Now that he had fulfilled the first part of the bargain, he needed to find the additional one hundred men and women within the next twelve months. As soon as he arrived, Gilles needed to find those pioneer settlers and find them fast, since he had already wasted at least two months on this ship. He had found no prospects on board, not among the passengers or crew, and unfortunately, he could not even include Elsje's young brother and sister because they would not be old enough to satisfy the requirement.

Besides the maidservant, Aafje, there was the Blackamoor, a very long way from his origins in North Africa. He had accommodations for the voyage on the same deck as the other passengers, but behind a wooden grating that was the divider between the single men's quarters and the family section. Some of the passengers in the family area were young girls, traveling alone, orphans sent over to work as servants for the company. The master of the ship had installed the grating as a reminder and deterrent, as it was certainly not strong enough to be a truly effective barrier between the two groups. The man had been working in Amsterdam and Gilles had only known him for a very short time. Now Gilles barely remembered what he looked like, except that he was very tall, very strong, and didn't have much to say. Aafje, the hefty farm girl who had signed on with Gilles and shared the bunk with Elsje's sister Corretje, took up space that might well have served two people of more ordinary proportions. She presumably knew about country things like crops, midwifery, animal breeding and cooking, so Gilles considered her an important asset and someone who could be a great help to him and to Elsje.

Because he had so little success in finding anyone else so far, Gilles only hoped he could find the remainder of his settlement quota in the New Amsterdam colony. He wondered if the company would accept the foreigners living there in the required head count. He supposed they

21

would, because Van Rensselaer had been allowed to stock his patroonship with people from every country in Europe.

Gillesville.

He liked the sound of that, but if he had a ragtag group of formerly homeless outcasts for settlers, it might become a joke, or even a disparaging epithet. Gilles looked over at the farm girl now. Aafje Vander Cloot, she said her name was. That was nearly all he knew about her. She had been selling produce in the Amsterdam square market and Gilles didn't know what she was running from, but given their fast departure and the few belongings she brought along with her, it was highly likely that she had not bothered to tell her family that she was leaving. Gilles assumed she was illiterate, as most farm people were, so her people would never hear from her again or even know what had become of her. She had just disappeared one day at the market and had never come home. He watched as Corretje and Aafje sat side by side, their heads together, both giggling, talking about whatever it was that young girls talk about. Gilles wondered if Aafje might have, under her freckled face and toothy smile, fears or regrets, but he certainly was not going to ask her: He didn't want to hear anything right now that didn't bolster his own spirits.

From the maps he had seen of the new continent, Gilles knew there were two other rivers, the South River and the Fresh River. Even if land had been offered to him there, he felt more secure in having his patroonship lands closer to New Amsterdam, on the main waterway that ran right by New Amsterdam's fort on the west side of Mannahatta Island. This river had many different names on the maps that had been made so far, depending on who the mapmaker was and which country he was from. It was called the Mauritius, Hutson's River, or the Noordt River, but it was always easily located, being the most prominent feature on any map of the Dutch-claimed lands. There was one very good reason why the great river was only called the "North River" on maps made in the Netherlands, and it was not simply because it flowed south to the ocean from somewhere up in the mountains of the wilderness. The Netherlanders, always precise, intentional and practical people, knew that both the French and the English were still laying claim to land that had already been settled by the Dutch for more than a generation. Although the contentious English always seemed to claim every piece of land they ever saw or even heard about, this particular claim just might have some validity if the river was ever called by the name of the Englishman who had explored and claimed it for the Netherlands, Henry Hudson.

Hudson, known in the Netherlands as Henrik Hutson, was an Englishman who explored New Netherland for the Dutch, mainly because some of his earlier exploration schemes for his own country had not turned out so well. The explorer had found no patron to finance his continuing ventures in England, but he was able to convince the Dutch East India Company to finance the voyage that gave them their claim to Nieuw-Nederlandt. Hudson had not been exactly truthful to his Dutch financial backers either, telling them that he was sailing to the east, to Scandinavia, to find a northern passage to China and the orient. He had not continued in that direction though; he had turned his ship around, sailing west when he was just out of sight of the company telescopes.

There was always a little concern hanging over the WIC regarding legal claims that could be made. It was feared that when England's violent domestic troubles and religious distractions settled down, when they were able to deal with other matters, the English ships might come sailing in one day to collect what they still considered to be rightfully theirs. England claimed not only the island of Mannahatta, but every bit of land on the eastern coast of the new continent, everything from the never-melting ice fields of New France, north of the St Laurent River, to the tropical Spanish lands in the south. The English maps called almost all of the new continent "Virginia", after their virgin queen, Elizabeth. The Netherlands, supremely conscious of England's recent past military help against their mutual Spanish enemy, did not want to do anything overtly that might upset this fragile alliance, but printing up maps seemed a good alternative way to stake their claim.

The little village of New Amsterdam had come a long way from the days when a few company men and some French-speaking Walloons had set up the first trading post and shelters there, pledging to live under the laws and jurisdiction of the Dutch West India Company. The company sent the Walloons over as the original workforce, complete with females selected for them so they could continue to breed while they worked the land and wove cloth for the company.

Gilles believed that the Westindische Compagnie had offered him the position of company clerk in large part because he spoke several languages, French and English included. Thinking ahead to his probable new duties, he could already see that there were going to be challenges and headaches with the legal documents as well as in language translations. He wondered if he had made a mistake in agreeing to accept the position at all, but what choice did he really have? He needed a way to feed his family and he needed to go somewhere that was safe. The company needed someone willing to work for them in far-away New Amsterdam, someone who could speak a few languages and was loyal to them. The WIC men were powerful and revered men, but they were not especially known for their generosity or for their stupidity when it came to making any deals, from international trade to buying a simple loaf of bread. Maybe it was just Hendrick's land they wanted, maybe they liked Gilles personally, or maybe he had the exact skills they needed at the right moment in time. For now, he could come up with no other apparent reason for his good fortune in securing both a paying position with the company and the patroonship.

Gilles had to wonder how he was going to keep accounts for the company when much of it was for conducting trade with the savages. Were there translators there who could help him? With not just one, but dozens of aboriginal languages, would he be able to learn them, to communicate in them all? He hoped they didn't expect him to work with legal documents. Gilles knew nothing at all about deeds, surveys, or the law, only about accounts. He hoped there would be some capable and experienced people there who could help him with his new position and translators who spoke the languages of *les hommes sauvages*.

One of the many laws that had been changed lately was the earlier decree that the colony would only allow the use of the Wilden seashells, zewant or wampum as it was called, for currency. They had not previously permitted the use of guilders, stuivers or anything else from the civilized lands across the sea. Were the financial record entries all in terms of seashells? The very idea was ridiculous, but if it was still legally in use, maybe Gilles could just pick up some shells off the beach and collect himself a fortune on a sunny day.

Just thinking about the possible scope of his new duties was overwhelming. When he thought about all of the details, the intricacies and the challenges that lay ahead, it seemed hopeless that he would ever be able to do the job they were asking of him, and equally hopeless that he would be able to make a great plantation out of a piece of tree-covered land that was far up the river in a wilderness surrounded by savages. He had to keep going forward and believing that somehow it would all work out, just as long as he was not overwhelmed by the obstacles that he was certain to encounter along the way.

A third possibility, one besides success or failure did exist: It was entirely possible that New Amsterdam was such a chaotic and corrupt place, for all of the strict regulation he had heard about, that the only rules that mattered were those of the company. Maybe everyone did what was ordered by the governor, whether it was legal in the fatherland and the way it was done in civilized countries or not. If no one else could do any better, or maybe if no one else even wanted the position, then maybe Gilles really was the best man for the job, possibly even their last resort. In a way, it was the very best kind of job security: No one would be the wiser if he was a dismal failure at the position, just as long as he kept the men in power happy.

"I hope there is a good market, a big market there," Elsje said, interrupting his thoughts once again, a worried look coming back into her eyes.

"We won't need a market, Elsje! It is a good land they say, a land of plenty, filled with apple and peach trees, fish, wild game, flocks of wild chickens and great herds of deer, all there for the taking. We will also have a vegetable garden, a very big one, and we will all have to work in it, isn't that right, Heintje?"

Gilles tossed this remark loudly over to his young brother-in law, drawing the boy into the discussion.

"Um-hm."

The teenager didn't look too sure about that. He had been sitting in glum silence for most of the journey, and Elsje had worried aloud more than once that perhaps he might have worms. Gilles thought there was little wrong with him that some hard work wouldn't cure. Old Hendrick offered that a good beating wouldn't be wasted on him, either.

Around them were the everyday sounds they had become accustomed to hearing, the ship creaking as it rocked slowly back and forth, the low buzz of conversation and the old woman across the way humming to herself. Some of the men gossiped with the women or played games to pass the time, but Gilles wasn't one for playing cards, dice or Tric Trac. He wasn't inclined to talk with anyone at all unless it involved opportunities for finding settlers for his land, making money in trade, or learning something new about their future home. Too many thoughts had been running through his head today, thoughts of the past, present and the future, memories of the old land and worries about the new one. Because there was nothing else to do to pass the time, Gilles decided he would try to go to sleep. Another day had come and gone. Hopefully they were one day closer to their destination.

he constant rocking motion of the ship had become so much a part of normal life during the voyage that Gilles no longer even noticed it. Unfortunately, this was not Elsje's experience. She was only too aware of it, was startled and alarmed with every change in course or speed, and was certain she would be sick for the entire duration of the long journey. She had tried to prepare for it by bringing some dried ginger slices to ease her stomach complaints, but those were long since gone. Although she tried, Gilles could see that she spent much of her time with her head resting in her hands. She was not eating very much and giving the rest of her meals to the others when she could no longer force down another bite. She had definitely lost weight. The rhythmic slap, slap, slap of the water against the sides of the ship that had been so apparent, even comforting to Gilles for the first few weeks, was no longer noticed by anyone except for Elsje who complained that it gave her a constant headache. There were times when the fear came over him that she might not live long enough to see the other shore, but Gilles told himself that this was ridiculous. It was only sickness of the sea and it would pass eventually. He couldn't imagine his life without her or living it as a very young widower with two small children.

Being confined like an animal below the deck of the ship, the darkness and sensory deprivation made Gilles even more restless than usual. Whenever he had sailed in the past, Gilles spent most of his time on the upper deck, reveling in the open air. Those voyages had only comprised short distances of travel, and back then he had usually been within sight of land. During those trips the rough sailors had mostly deferred to Gilles, the shipping company owner's son, in spite of Gilles' ignorance of all but the most basic duties of the crew. The men had occasionally baited and teased him as they did the bears in the marketplace, but Gilles always put up with it, knowing that it would be a short journey, and they would stop short of doing him any serious physical harm. He also knew that his father needed able seamen and would be loathe to get rid of any one of them, even for good reason. Experienced sailors were hard to replace, especially if it was on short notice.

The passengers had not been let up onto the upper deck for two days now, even though the seas seemed calm enough. Gilles wasn't sure if he could take one more day without seeing any daylight. When they were below, the only light they saw was what came down through the grating at the top of the steps and the light that seeped in from cracks in the sides of the ship. A mostly successful attempt had been made to seal the places where age, rot, and sea worms had been, but there had been somewhat less success in sealing the areas around the old gun ports during Den Eyckenboom's conversion from a fighter to a freighter. These openings let in a little light, and occasionally, some fresh air and seawater.

The two men who had been fighting the day before were escorted back down the stairs after spending the night somewhere on the upper deck of the ship, probably out under the stars. It seemed to be not a very serious punishment, although their families were grateful to have them returned. Gilles wondered if he should start a fight with someone in order to get some time out of the dark hold, but there were too many variables in that plan, too much that could go wrong. He began to wonder if the perpetual darkness was affecting his mind in some way; his patience and temper did seem to grow shorter with each passing day. He was locked away now, removed from the sights and sounds of the outside world and the fresh salt air, but still he could tell from the quiet, even rhythm of the water outside and the ship's nearly-horizontal orientation that the winds were calm. The sails rarely seemed to change at all anymore and there was nothing putting an edge or a boundary on the daily tedium except for the rare, occasional variation in the speed of the ship. Their progress was painfully slow, barely enough for the Dutchman's Log to register much movement of the ship at all on some days.

When the passengers were allowed up on the deck, a few at a time, there was nothing but the open water to see, no land in sight in any direction, and there hadn't been any for many weeks now. The fate of the forty-some-odd passengers depended now solely upon the whims of the wind and the skills of the crew. There was nothing that could be done to change this reality; it was singularly frustrating and the daily repetition was broken only by gossip and occasional events like the fight between the two men. The same dull colors gave no stimulation or challenge to the senses, and at night, as if his mind was in rebellion, Gilles began to dream of fields of brightly-colored tulips, shape-shifting in the wind, beautiful bejeweled women in brilliant ball gowns twirling around under golden lamplight, and the bright, freshly-greened trees of early spring, their branches burdened with flocks of birds spreading their wings to reveal magnificent multicolored plumage.

During the first early days of the voyage the wind had bellied out the sails, filling them with energy, just as Gilles had been filled with the excitement of this great change in his life, this turn of events that he had never seen coming. His life in Europe had been difficult these past few years, a terrible reversal of fortunes from wealth in France to street beggar in Holland, but Gilles had refused to give in, refused to starve or die, and made his way back, day by day and guilder by guilder, slowly building a better life for himself. There had been successes and setbacks, the most recent troubles taking him here, to this voyage.

In spite of his having to make a fresh start all over again, Gilles would not relinquish hope for the future. He gripped tightly his trust in the stars and his belief in this new beginning for himself and his young and growing family. He had to keep believing that it would work out well, that it would bring them on the trade winds of change to a new world, not just to a place of survival, but to a better life. They had left their previous lives behind with the foaming wake of the ship, jettisoned all of it as debris and discarded refuse on the waves of the past.

Den Eyckenboom had started the voyage by skimming easily over the water, dipping and dancing on the waves like some frolicking gull on the wind or a new lamb just discovering the joy of youthful legs in springtime meadows. They had moved easily out toward the ocean, starting from Amsterdam in the Netherlands and then sailing north through the Zuyder Zee to make their way out to the northern Atlantic. They made their last stop at the island of Texel to take on the final few passengers before continuing on their westward voyage, easing through the channel between France and England, where Gilles had sailed once before. This time there had been no opportunity to see his home shores, no chance to say goodbye before he left that part of the world behind forever.

Once out on the ocean, the ship had traveled only slightly south before following the compass heading due west across the waters, trying to outrun the fast-approaching autumn storms before they arrived. It would be unfortunate if the ship was caught out in a storm on the open sea, an innocent traveling all alone and unprotected in a wild and dangerous place, a girl-child passing by disreputable taverns as evening darkness and wide-spread drunkenness closed in. If the ship was not totally destroyed at once, there was always the possibility of dismasting, violent storms tearing the masts off the ship before finishing the job, or worse, just leaving it to drift into eternity, the voyagers having to pass first through long days of thirst and starvation before death delivered them from their final agonies.

In the beginning, Gilles had believed that it would be an enjoyable journey, that they would make good time and arrive before the anticipated date two months away, but those early days, so full of hope, had now turned into long weeks. His fears regarding their future constantly circled around him, sometimes like persistent fruit flies and sometimes like vultures with stabbing beaks, crowding in on him during the day and striking ferociously in the darkness of the night. As the days went by, these worries had become increasingly difficult to turn aside and hold at bay. He knew he was not alone in these thoughts because he heard the whispered prayers of his neighbors in the darkness. He had observed that some of his fellow passengers were in nearly constant prayer these days, even those who had less than an avidly religious orientation before they set sail. There were others on board who already had the habit of praying every day instead of once a week, further confounding Gilles' sense of time.

They had left Amsterdam at the very beginning of autumn so they had been expecting the days to get cooler and the wind to pick up, but summer had so far refused to relinquish its hold on this year. The crew kept the sails pulled taught, but progress was slow. They had to wait for the situation to change, to call upon their inner fortitude for more patience or call upon the Almighty, whichever seemed the best course of action at the time. Given the unusually hot weather, the airless compartment they traveled in was often so putrid that it burned Gilles' nose and throat. It was no surprise that Elsje and many others did not feel well. Most of the passengers were unaccustomed to the heat, having lived their entire lives in the Netherlands where it was never too hot and never too cold, except for unusual hot days in the summer and occasional rare winters when the canals froze over and everyone dug out nearly-forgotten ice skates to run outside and enjoy a very short winter.

The passengers sweltered in the stuffy hold, the smells of their bodies mixing with those of the human wastes accumulating in the corner collection buckets, as well as with the careless deposits of the urinating and defecating dogs that traveled on board with them. Twice a day the refuse was gathered up and dumped overboard, but the lingering stink challenged even the strongest of stomachs, adding to the already sour aroma of past voyages' farm animal occupation and human sweat, nausea and fear. The stench seemed to grow in pungency while the days passed and the heat in their quarters grew. As Gilles sat watching today, the old woman's dog urinated loudly on the floorboards at the feet of the three gray ones.

"Damned cur!" the snarling daughter raged as she kicked at the dog. The old woman cried out as though she herself had been kicked, grabbing the dog and holding it close to her. Gilles pulled his feet up from the floor as the stream of urine made its way across the planks, creating a slow-moving channel that ended somewhere under one of the three family bunks. He was tempted to go kick the dog and the woman as well, but instead he clenched his fists and his teeth, got up and walked slowly over to the privy area to relieve himself. He did this, not because he had to, but just to take some time alone to let his anger pass. He hadn't been over there in a few hours, so it would also give him something to do, another way to pass some time. He took a good long time behind the curtain, breathing slowly, taking a few minutes for himself away from everyone else.

"It's not so bad, I think," Elsje said to Gilles when he returned. "I was worried mostly about storms, but it's been very quiet."

"This is a good ship and Jean recommended the shipmaster," Gilles agreed. "He has made a good name for himself and is surely the best ever."

Gilles knew that his wife had dealt with men of the sea every day in her father's tavern, so of course she would know of this shipmaster and his reputation. Gilles had heard of him as well, so he wasn't as concerned about safe passage as some of his fellow ocean voyagers might be. There were plenty of reasons to spend the entire voyage in prayer, but Gilles believed he had hedged his bets sufficiently for them to make it alive to their destination. Taking his friend Jean's advice, Gilles knew he had picked a good ship, but much more importantly, a good master. He had witnessed with his own eyes the all-too-common dangerous and leaky ships and the arrogant shipmasters who were often the younger brothers in wealthy families.

Only the oldest son inherited most of a family's wealth and so these second, third or fourth sons had to find their own place in the world, either through a life in the church, the military, or on the sea. If the family had some money to spare and some trust in the young man, they might take a chance on the investment in a ship, on the wager that it was a money-making proposition in spite of the risks of weather, pirates, and incompetence. Other young men, determined to have their own ship without family backing, were occasionally able to seduce other patrons into financing their ventures and thus were able to come into command of a ship on their own. Many of these young shipmasters had no knowledge of the sea at all and even less concern for passenger safety. Their sole desires were to accumulate riches, to prove themselves to a family patriarch or to best an older brother, preserving whatever cargo a ship carried only because of the impact it might have on their personal wealth and fortunes.

Daughters in wealthy families sometimes had more of an idea of where they would end up than the younger brothers, even if they had no say in the matter. Sometimes they were even more valuable than the second sons since their marriages, occasionally arranged from birth, were carefully planned to bring in a desirable son-in-law. A good dowry would seal the bargain, making daughters a much better investment than a second or third son, buying the patriarch a son-in-law of his own choosing. Gilles understood the logic of these methods of family wealth transmission, a tradition that had served men well for centuries. He had been a second son and accepted it as the way the world was, simply a reconciliation of black and red in an accounts book, of gold and blood in a lifespan. It was very simple: Life was only a ledger.

Once the fare for a sea voyage had been paid by the passengers and the money stowed away in a personal purse, safety of the travelers was no longer as much of a concern for many of the shipmasters. People were a constantly renewable source of wealth for the shipping trade. There were always more of them to be found, desperate souls willing to sell all they had accumulated in a lifetime for the chance to travel away from trouble and death. The passengers put their money on the bet that they would be able to stay alive and keep living. The third-rate shipmasters, braggart fools on the loose like evil spirits on a storming night, roamed the port cities in search of paying passengers who were willing to take the risk in spite of the news accounts of the missing or casualties. The grim phantom of death was always standing just at the elbow of each traveler, waiting, breathing in the intoxicating anticipation of the next soul it waited to claim. The end could come from a fatal mistake or just a simple happenstance that would set into motion the collection of a life, of men, women, and children, old and young, hardy and weak alike. Travelers might be trapped beneath the decks to drown, to gasp their last breaths in icy, stinging salt waters as a ship went down. They might have their throats sliced open expertly by practiced pirates roaming the seas, each one of the outlaws being his own shipmaster on someone's route to eternity. Alternatively, a passenger might suffer a minor injury resulting in an infection that crept through the body, eventually laying claim to the heart, lungs or brain. Without benefit of onboard physician or chiurgeon to treat the injured, there was generally nothing to be done to change what fate had ordained.

In death though, these spent lives burdened neither the clergy's time nor the cemeteries' finite green spaces in the home ports. The bodies were rarely recovered or returned, and so the passenger names, dozens at a time, were simply listed as dead or missing if anyone had bothered to record the names before the ship left port. Often the masters didn't report incidents because it would only be bad publicity, hampering efforts to finance their future enterprises. It was much more important to salvage their ships, their cargo and their reputations than to concern themselves with the people on board. Those left behind on the land, if they inquired about missing relatives, often couldn't read enough to discern the names on the posted lists. People frequently just disappeared and anyone they might have left behind in the home country would always wonder what had become of them. At least Gilles had the cold comfort of knowing that Elsje's aunt, uncle and younger sister Jannetje, all left behind in the Netherlands, knew that the rest of their family was headed to New Amsterdam.

The crew members who were swept overboard during storms often met a quicker and more merciful end than the passengers, and they always had a family of sorts. Even if they were orphans or unmarried, they had the brotherhood of sailors. Gossip among the crews in the different ports provided their word-of-mouth obituaries. A tankard or two was lifted in their honor with a fast, liquid-accompanied eulogy as news of their deaths traveled up and down the shipping lanes.

Den Eyckenboom was different, a cut above, mainly due to her master's experience as well as his humanity. Her reputation, though not exactly one of luxury, did give a passenger some expectation of arriving alive at journey's end. Gilles was reasonably sure that all of the requisite precautions had been taken, including thorough inspections by knowledgeable ship's carpenters, competent repairs and new tar and hemp, both below and above the water line where the sea worms from exotic ports had drilled thousands of small holes through the wood. She carried with her a prudent load of cargo, an excellent navigator, the most up-to-date maps and navigational equipment, prayers from the domine of the local church at her initial launch, and of course the lucky coin that was always wedged in between the keel and the sternpost at the completion of a ship's construction.

The anticipated physical challenges of the voyage had been meticulously prepared for with sufficient provisions and carefully allotted space, which was beyond what one could expect in the way of creature comforts on other ships. They even had hot food, although the bricked fire pit on board only promised warm meals for as long as the cook could keep the fire going. Often the cook was the youngest member of the crew since it was desirable that he be the most sober one. Carelessness by the cook could result in the ship catching on fire, resulting in the terrible choice each person might have to make, to choose his own death by fire or by drowning.

For the seamen and the fortune-seekers traveling alone, it was their own risk to take, but Gilles carried the additional worry of the safety of his family. They were now hundreds of miles from any port, and it was unlikely that there would be any friendly passing ships within sight of a needed rescue. Den Eyckenboom carried a small compliment of guns on the upper deck to dissuade the privateers and pirates who were as much of a hazard as the natural forces that challenged their safe arrival. In truth though, her guns were there mostly for ornamentation and the crew would be no match for any serious challenge. Gilles knew this, breathing not a hint of it to Elsje, but maybe she already knew. It was probably best that they traveled in the autumn, when the pirates might be more inclined to stay in the warmer southern ports of the West Indies, enjoying an enduring summer there, placated with plenty of rum.

It was a peculiar irony: Gilles had not even intended to marry, let alone to collect such a large family, at least not until he had traveled a few more years down the road of his life. When the opportunity for marriage first presented itself, neither Elsje nor her father had entertained the idea seriously. It had just seemed like a reasonable course of action to Gilles at the time. To his surprise, Elsje had proved to be a strong and reliable partner as well as an enjoyable wife. She was not only a sharp business woman, she was an enthusiastic lover. Even better, she was an anchor of security, a champion of Gilles and his dreams in spite of the difficulties they had endured in the few years they had been together. Now here she was again, at his side, following his lead into yet another unknown.

Gilles had made the deliberate decision not to think of past difficulties and tribulations. He refused. They were still too fresh in his mind, too painful. He slammed shut the door to these thoughts, pulling the cross bar down into the holders to keep those memories of past miseries from invading the present, from getting into his mind and polluting the future. He would not waste his time wondering if the harsh past events had been a punishment from the Almighty, the evil of men, poor judgement on his part, or just simple bad luck. Having already survived several attempts on his life, Gilles was not going to be beaten by his own fears, not now that he had come this far.

As he had been thinking briefly about the lost fortune of his childhood, a strangely comforting thought, an ironic one, came to him now: It may not matter at all that he had very little money because there would be few luxuries available to buy when they arrived at their new home, food included. His lack of income and savings might not be any greater impediment to survival than having it. The company would pay him at the end of each year, in exchange for his services as company clerk, but they had promised to furnish basic food and necessities for his family in the meantime. He had experienced first-hand that the WIC officers in Amsterdam ate like kings, and gluttonous kings at that, but the situation was very different in the colony. Gilles didn't trust that the quantity and quality of food provided to his family would be sufficient. If there really was a bounty of wild food in the new land, maybe he wouldn't have to worry about getting enough to eat and could just invest all of his funds in the fur trade.

Gilles didn't want to admit it, even to himself, but he was relying on the abundance of fish and wild game that he was told would be there. He didn't concern himself with the fact that he had never before done anything toward securing his own food besides ordering servants to go and get him some, buying it from an innkeeper, or helping himself to what was in Elsje's kitchen. It had only been in the past year that he had learned how to kill a chicken with an ax. All of the family members had been city dwellers, but now they would have to learn how to farm, fish and trap wild game. Young Aafje, having lived on a farm her whole life, might prove to be more important to the family's survival than anyone else in their group.

In the column of other assets, and something that Gilles didn't want to count on, was Elsje's newlywed sister, Tryntje, who was already living in New Amsterdam. Tryntje and her husband, Adriaen Ver Hulst, had only been living there for a short time. There had not been much communication received from her, only one letter that had arrived shortly before they left Amsterdam. As Gilles had expected, Tryntje supplied very few helpful details about life in New Amsterdam, the missive being short on information and long on local gossip. Given the family connections, it was possible that Gilles had been offered the clerical job due to Ver Hulst's political influence, although he had never met the man. Tryntje had married him and moved to New Amsterdam the year before, while Gilles and Elsje had been living in the German Palatinate. All Gilles knew about him was that Ver Hulst was wealthy, influential, and a member of the West India Company in good standing. Gilles was determined that they would not be asking for his help, like some poor relations or beggars. He wanted to appear as wealthy, prosperous and suitable for promotion as possible, making Ver Hulst's acquaintance and getting into his good graces as soon as he could after they landed. It was unfortunate that Gilles' title was only "clerk", but perhaps family ties and owning two pieces of property there would be enough to get him into Ver Hulst's social circle and secure faster promotions.

Gilles had to wonder how old Hendrick had managed to make such a good match for his second daughter when he knew there was no dowry. Tryntje was a flirtatious beauty, but company men generally took such women as mistresses and required much more than that in a wife and something more substantial in the way of a dowry than a pretty face and a child on the way. Although they had been busily preparing for the voyage before they left, Gilles did take the time to write a letter for Elsje, to let Tryntje know that they were coming. He also wrote a letter to his friend Jean, asking him to evict the tenant who had been living in his little house, sending both letters out to New Amsterdam on the Wapen Van Rensselaerswijck that had set sail shortly before Den Eyckenboom.

Gilles knew the family would have to get through the winter and the spring months ahead, staying sheltered and fed until his first crops could be planted and harvested the following summer. He knew there were people in the world who lived by eating squirrels and he hoped he wasn't going to be one of them. Pigeons might not be too bad though, as long as he could get some nets to catch them and some cream to serve with them. Certainly there would be pigeons there as they filled the cities of Europe.

"Gilles!" Elsje elbowed him.

"I told you, he spends all of his time daydreaming! What good is he?" Hendrick shook his head, dismissing his useless son-in-law once again.

"What? I'm thinking of all the things I need to do when we arrive."

"Father wanted to know if we can grow our own tobacco there."

"Ja, of course we will grow tobacco. It's a good land for it, and you know that a lot of tobacco shipments are coming out of New Netherland. We'll grow other crops too, all kinds of crops, and grapes for wine."

"Always wine with him!" Hendrick shook his head again. "All he does is drink wine and daydream. I should have found a good husband for you like the one I found for Tryntje."

"Father, don't start. We have days of travel left and we want to have them in peace, isn't that so?" Elsje fixed her father with a hard stare. "If Gilles wants grapes, he'll have his grapes, you will have your tobacco, and I will have my spice garden."

The old man grumbled something under his breath and rolled his eyes

37

at his daughter but said no more. Gilles was about to say something in reply to this, but the look in Elsje's eyes warned him not to. He closed his mouth and returned to his reverie.

When he thought about his future crops, Rensselaerswyck often came to mind. Gilles' dream was to build his own patroonship settlement into one that would rival Van Rensselaer's. He frequently reminded himself that Kiliaen Van Rensselaer had never even set eyes upon the new continent, and if he could bring forth wealth from across an ocean, then Gilles could do even better while living in closer proximity and managing his own project. Van Rensselaer's great-nephew, Arendt Van Corlaer, was only slightly older than Gilles and was successfully running Rensselaerswyck since the old man's sons were still too young to work in the family business. Van Corlaer had done very well as secretary and accountant for the venture, although there had been gossip that the nephew's ambition, lavish spending and free use of his uncle's money had been used to make his own fortune. Van Rensselaer had paid his young kinsman his highest compliments though, saying that Van Corlaer was "trustworthy" and "good with a pen". Higher praise was never heard from the lips of Kiliaen Van Rensselaer; the patroon never wasted words of praise on anyone, not unless there was something to be gained by uttering them to a specific audience or by putting it in writing.

Gilles' interest in this family was not simply an indulgence in idle gossip. A few years earlier he had signed a fur trade agreement with this same Van Corlaer and another with the Pelletiers, the father and son trading partners who lived deep in the wilderness lands north of Rensselaerswyck. From the earliest days the furs taken from the new world had made some Dutch investors very wealthy. The pelts of the beaver, or *tamakwa*, as Gilles knew that some of the savages called the creatures, were particularly prized above other fur-bearing animals. It had originally been hoped that there would be gold or silver found on the new continent, but so far, the greatest wealth that had been discovered came from the tons of fur exports along with the timber, tobacco, wheat and maize that had been grown there.

It would be nice if his modest investment brought a good return to him someday, but Gilles wasn't going to rely on the fur trade alone for income; it was really just a fun wager. Gilles remembered only too well the disastrous Tulip Mania that had brought great wealth and then financial ruin to many of the Dutch investors just a few years earlier. With the economy in the Netherlands booming from successful global trade, there were extra guilders in many pockets to put into the commodities markets. Many of the Netherlanders had invested in an exotic Asian import, tulip bulbs. Because a single one with brilliantly-colored flowers could sometimes be sold for a great deal of money, the market boomed for a short time before it completely collapsed. It had been a stark reminder that speculation in anything always carried with it some risk. Recently there had been some disruption in the importation of the beaver skins, leading to much rumination as to what might be causing this problem with the supply. Although a shortage might lead to a price increase in the short-run, Gilles didn't want to lose all of his investment, even if it was a small one. Now that he was going to be on this side of the ocean, he hoped to learn much more about the fur trade. It would be wonderful if his own patroon lands were full of beaver, muskrat, otter, mink and ermine.

Gilles knew nothing about furs except that they were valuable, warm to wear and soft to the touch. How did one find these animals, catch them, kill them, and make furs from the dead animal peltries so they would be supple, soft, sweet, and not crunchy, rotting or smelling like any other dead carcass on the side of the byway? He had absolutely no idea how to cure animal pelts, but that was not really his concern. He would just have his partners do this work for him. Gilles hoped to make contact with Van Corlaer, at least in writing if not in person, to ask for his business advice regarding the fur trade and management of his own patroonship.

"So Gilles, how long do you think we will be living there?" Elsje asked.

"As I said before, a few years to establish my patroonship, to save up for our return and to find Corretje a good company man for a husband."

Gilles smiled over at the little girl who blushed and looked away.

"She has a few years yet!" Elsje objected. "She needs to learn how to cook, keep house and also how to read first."

And also to have more to offer a man, Gilles thought, noting the girl's flat chest and baby face. "And when we have enough money to buy another inn in Amsterdam," he added out loud.

He said it, but Gilles knew that this was never going to happen. Even if it was possible someday, he didn't think the old world would ever divest itself of the old miseries. He knew that Elsje had latched on to this one idee fixe, either for herself or for her father's sake, otherwise she might not have boarded the ship at all. Gilles chose not to have this discussion about their return with Elsje, at least not right now. He had a little more time before it might be necessary. Who could say what was ahead of them in the coming years? This was the only door that had opened up, and seeing that this was the case, Gilles went through it, bringing his family and his hopes along with him. Today he took some additional comfort in the fact that he was not traveling alone. They were all on this great adventure together.

*V*ery early the next morning, even in his sleep, Gilles heard the sound of the cover from the overhead hatch sliding back. The dry wood screeched in protest and then he heard the sound of the grate being lifted. Without his even realizing it, his ears had been eagerly listening for that sound during every moment that he was penned in below. He was instantly awake as daylight flooded into the compartment from the opening, illuminating the ladder connecting the two decks. The stairway was a connection between the two worlds, one of survival below and freedom above. Shafts of light fell on clouds of floating dust, temporarily blinding the people in the darkness below, soft white creatures living perpetually under a warm, damp log. Although the aperture was at a distance away from Gilles, the sudden infusion of light was a shock to his vision. Blinking back the sudden, brief pain to his eyes and responding to the sound, Gilles moved quickly to his feet to seize this opportunity for escape since all of the captives would not be allowed on the upper deck at one time. Seeing that his wife was already awake, he spoke to her.

"I need some air, come up with me, Elsje!"

She smiled, barely out of sleep herself, and wordlessly waved him away.

They both knew that he wasn't sincere about this invitation. Gilles wanted the time alone and Elsje didn't like being up there: It was frightening for her to look out and see nothing in any direction but deep water. It made her feel even more queasy than usual. Her security had always been rooted in her home, and for the present, home was the small allotted space that the family occupied these many weeks. Her small measure of peace came from keeping things orderly, neat and tidy, and seeing that her family was

41

cared for as much as possible. Elsje disliked the sea intensely, although the men from the ships had delivered plenty of paying business to her father's inn and tavern over the years.

Not all of the passengers wanted to go up to the open deck, and Gilles was the only one in this family that found refuge there. The other family members didn't care for it, neither for the view nor for the few brief and unpleasant interactions they had with the crew. One sailor threatened to throw Heintje overboard when he played with one of the lines and several of the sailors eyed Corretje and Aafje in ways they found threatening. One of the crew, leering at the girls, suggested they could come up at night to see the stars when the rest of the passengers were asleep. Elsje wouldn't allow her children to go up either: She was afraid Bruinje would wander away and fall overboard and afraid that baby Jacomina would take a chill. Gilles believed it was just healthier outside than it was down below where they had to breathe in the heated and foul air that filled their living quarters.

Hendrick stayed below as well, reveling in his self-pity, being his usual miserable self, an irascible old codger and ongoing irritation to Gilles ever since they had left Amsterdam. Hendrick wouldn't go up on the upper deck at all, saying that it would only remind him of where he was. He was now almost completely dependent on his young son-in-law who was little more than a boy in his eyes, and an irresponsible, conceited and spoiled Frenchman at that. The old man's opinion was obvious to everyone in the disparaging way he addressed Gilles or talked about his daughter's husband. Gilles did very well to hold his tongue, but he could not keep out the visions he had of the old man falling overboard, and in spite of heroic efforts, Hendrick disappearing beneath the waves, his one remaining arm upraised in a plea for help as he sank slowly down into the depths.

Gilles had quickly grabbed his boots, pulling one on in his rush to the freedom of the hatch even as he heard his fellow travelers stirring in response to the wordless invitation.

"I'm taking the dog up!" the gray woman from across the way declared, grasping the old dog by the nape of the neck. The dog yelped and the old lady cried out, clinging to the small animal.

"It is not staying here!" the daughter stormed at her mother. "I'm taking it up the stairs for some fresh air."

She stamped off to the foot of the stairs, the small terrier cowering and shivering while tucked under her arm. Although Gilles wanted to run for the opening and push her aside, he didn't have his other boot on yet, and she had reached the stairs first. After he had jammed on the other boot, he ran toward the steps but stayed well behind the woman, out of arm's reach, just in case she decided to explode in anger once again or the dog had more teeth and life than it appeared to have. Gilles was right behind her though, taking his place at the front of the quickly-forming line. Other voyagers were still trying to get to their feet to join the group. This early in the morning, only a few others were awake and alert enough to scramble off their perches in time. Some travelers would be satisfied with just seeing a change of scenery while others sought fresh air for their lungs or a brief, refreshing salt sea spray on their faces and hands. Not always, but occasionally, this change of location and the brief misting of sea water was enough to temporarily alleviate the clinging stench that lingered in their nostrils or on their clothes, but it could not mitigate the smell that seeped out from under the caps or hats that confined their greasy hair.

As he ascended the steps, Gilles looked over to the other side, past the grating that separated the two halves of the middle deck. Over in the quarters that housed the unmarried men and sailors, Gilles noted that his servant was still there. The man was talking to another man but making no move for their open hatch. Later Gilles might go over to have a few words with him, just to make sure he was still healthy and ready to go to work as soon as they arrived, but for now, Gilles' only goal was to make it to the upper deck.

The steps going up were steep, and now Gilles remembered how difficult it had been for the children, the elderly and the infirm ones to come down those steps before they left, back when everyone seemed to be much stronger and healthier. He wondered if the old ones would be able to manage the steps again or if they would have to be carried up, perhaps in a shroud. If they were found to be dead one morning and already stiff in their bunks, he wondered if the bodies could pass through the hatch without breaking or dislocating any parts to get them up through the narrow opening. Their corpses couldn't just be left down in the hold for the remainder of the journey, not in this heat. He supposed the sailors might have had some previous experience with such a situation and would know

43

what to do. The thought occurred to him now that the ship was very like a woman's body, carrying life within, although there were the old ones as well as the very young inside, many more individuals than just the twins or litters when animals gave birth. The ship's interior was no womb though, being without very much creature comfort, only dozens of heartbeats, beating in unison as they traveled forward across the waters.

These days the seas around them had mostly fallen to sullen silence. There were never any other ships in the distance, leaving Gilles alone with his thoughts when he took advantage of these brief escapes from Elsje's questions and Hendrick's comments. If there ever was another passing ship and if they ever came close enough to have any communication between vessels, it might offer them the comfort of good news or desired information. They might find out exactly where on earth they might be at the moment or what the current living conditions were at their destination: plague or health, starvation or plenty, peace or war. It was equally true that an approaching ship could bring threats, flying the colors of bad news on a mast: enemy privateers, pirates, or the skull and crossbones warning of plague aboard the other vessel.

Some fifteen years earlier the Atlantic had been full of ships traveling back and forth, carrying throngs of Englishmen away from the religious and political strife in their country. Great flotillas of ships made it possible for many of them to escape the upheaval in the years 1625 to 1635. It was very quiet now, and not just because of the time of year. The steady stream of refugees from that island kingdom had taken flight, scattered like wild birds before an approaching storm when their king's government began to hunt them down, just as the Spanish and French governments had done. It had become a new national sport for them, on a much grander scale than a mere fox hunt. It was more like hunting partridge, pheasant, grouse or snipe since the quarry had to be flushed from hiding first and then captured as it endeavored to fly away. Occasionally they took the analogy one step further and roasted their prizes alive if the gallows didn't provide enough entertainment or failed to dissuade others inclined to follow a rebel's lead.

Many of these English refugees had stubbornly clung to their convictions, including their individual and unbending ideas on religious and other freedoms, especially if they had nothing much to lose, no land, wealth or any material stakes to keep them in the game. There was little incentive for them to continue living as tenants on land where generations of their families had been born into endless servitude. Those who managed to leave might have saved a little money or had a few valuables that were portable enough to bribe someone into providing passage away from their troubles. Lacking that, some just had will enough and legs strong enough to walk forward until they reached a better place. Mostly they traveled with what they carried within them, the knowledge of a craft or skill, or maybe just a strong back and arms to offer in exchange for a new life.

A good number of these people had already left England. It seemed to them that their country had moved too far away from what was good and just to ever recover as a nation, to be the kind of place where they would want to live out the rest of their lives, where their children could thrive. They might have wished to remember their nationality and their heritage, but they had given up on the land that had been their birthplace, the country of their families' origins for many past centuries. They were weary of following the battles between the different political factions, and for now, England's rulers and their coteries counted as their greatest achievements the blocking and thwarting of the aims of their enemies. Petty victories from the in-country warfare that pitted one group against another were used to gather all the spoils they could corral for themselves in the moment, often using the convenient justification of religion and divine selection to murder as many of their opponents as possible.

Gilles had learned of this from his worldly friend Jean, who seemed to know all about these things. Jean had explained to him that these escaping Englishmen were of two varieties, one always reigniting the fire and flame of religious purity and the second in search of whatever it was they searched for, perhaps unknown even to themselves, but something different, something better. Both the Puritans and the Pilgrims flocked to freedom as one, like an autumn migration of ducks and geese together, one great outflux of birds flying away from the cold winter of political and religious madness that had torn the fabric of their kingdom into ragged threads of warring factions.

For decades before, many of the English had not dared to voice their opinions, not even in their own homes or to their own family members, for fear that someone, an innocent child or ale-besotted spouse, might let something slip, accidentally or sometimes even intentionally. Under the wrong circumstances they would have to pay dearly for it, possibly with their lives. This English upheaval and misery had been going on now for more than one hundred years, ever since the reign of King Henry VIII. Henry had decided that adhering to the one church, the Catholic Church, was less important than his quest to garner as much personal power as he could and to bed as many women as possible, not just for pleasure, but also to secure a male heir born within the confines of a marriage. Naming himself the head of the official church, on a par with God himself or at least with the Pope, Henry married a half dozen women, changing wives more often than he changed his undergarments. Persecution of the crown's enemies didn't stop with his death. The troubles continued as each of his children in turn reversed the laws of the previous monarchy, wrenching citizens' required loyalties from Henry's Church of England to Mary's Catholic Church and then back again to Elizabeth's Church of England, all within a dozen years. When the fires didn't consume the enemies of the crown fast enough, other executioners were brought in, only pausing in their work long enough to take a rest and resharpen their axes.

While it was fortunate that there had been a long respite without a change in direction during Queen Elizabeth's unusually long rule of forty-five years, she died without surrendering to marriage or naming an heir. The monarchy and the power over life and death of England's subjects then passed to Elizabeth's Scottish kinsman, James. He ordered a translation of the Bible from Latin into English, unthinkable sacrilege to Gilles' way of thinking, and spent his time with distractions and amusements that were certainly not sanctioned in any part of the Bible. James' son Charles, now the King of England, was having no better luck in crushing his subjects into submission. The rebellions that had started in Scotland and Ireland were now spreading across all of the islands, occasionally erupting into open warfare.

This constant upheaval and the severity of the response by those in power had initially kept all of England's people heeling like very well-trained dogs, at least on the surface of it, to whatever command came next from the government, whichever government they woke to each morning. Neither the citizenry nor the judges could make any sense of the frequently contradictory laws. The penalty for religious non-conformism was sometimes banishment, being forced to leave the country, and the penalty for trying to leave the country without permission was death. Staying in the country meant daily surveillance and prison for those who did not comply, and it was not just the continuing prison of their lives, but a real one with walls, bars and all the miseries that were contained within those dank stone walls.

The disenfranchised had tried to leave in secret, sometimes successfully, but not always. One planned escape was discovered by the authorities while it was still in progress. Fearing for their lives, the men sailed off alone, leaving their stranded wives and children to be incarcerated for months while the authorities puzzled over what to do with them. It would have been unseemly to execute a load of women and children, even if they were a financial burden on the jailers and an embarrassment to the officials. Miraculously, these dependents somehow just disappeared from the prison one day and reappeared in the Netherlands to join up with their husbands and fathers without anyone knowing how they managed to do this. It might not have had anything at all to do with witchcraft as some asserted, but no matter how it happened, there were many in England who were greatly relieved to be rid of these irritants.

When the Pure Ones decided to leave the Netherlands for the new world, other English citizens, strangers to these purists, seized the opportunity to leave with them, blending in with the crowd of religious exiles as they took their departure. Originally there had been only one English colony near New Netherland, but their numbers continued to grow, from immigration and procreation. With over forty thousand people living in Massachusetts Bay colony alone, these pioneers had spread out, looking for more farm land and starting many new settlements across the land they called New England. The English territory was vast, much larger than the area of their home country and should have offered plenty of land for all of them, but it didn't contain the spread of the English contagion. Sprinkled like handfuls of grain before the stormy winds of the reformation, these wandering malcontents were not only turning up in the Dutch towns and territories in ones and twos, they were establishing more and more of their own settlements in nearby places that were under Dutch control, eschewing the New England territory completely.

The Catholic faith of Gilles' childhood had a rigorous set of requirements for his soul's salvation, but he had heard that these English Puritans were fanatics in the extreme. They continued to pray within their homes, even when it was no longer necessary to avoid the king's spies, and they refused to celebrate holidays that they considered to be pagan or Catholic, holidays like Christmas or the festivals of the saints. Gilles' friend Jean had warned him that there were two types of Englishmen, and Gilles needed to understand the differences if he was going to go live in New Netherland. He hadn't paid much attention to his friend's words at the time, but now Gilles realized that he should try to remember what Jean had told him. An alarming number of these English refugees were living in New Amsterdam now, as much as forty or fifty percent of the settlement by some estimates. Their allegiance and loyalty to the Netherlands was a concern, even though some of them had taken Dutch wives they had acquired along the way. Gilles would not only be seeing many of these undesirables, he was going to have to perform clerical tasks for some of them. If only the WIC didn't take them on and pay them, there might not be so many of them there. They were an inferior race, the English, full of criminals, with their bastard religion and strange language. Gilles was not as proficient in English as he was in Dutch, French, Latin, or Greek, but if he had any say in the matter at all, he would just make it easy on himself and insist that everyone only speak Nederlands.

Gilles linguistic talents had been discovered by his childhood tutor when he was quite young. Father Isaac Jogues, the French Jesuit priest whose services had been retained by Gilles' father, had been gifted in this same way. At the time, Gilles had been impatient to finish his education, but if he had known the direction that his life would later take, he might have had a little more enthusiasm and commitment to his language studies. The West India Company had probably learned of Gilles' abilities in languages and accounting, leading them to offer him the position of company clerk and translator.

Although Gilles would have to work with these foreigners, he didn't have to like it. His life-long distrust and disdain for Englishmen had been nurtured from birth by his father who recounted stories from his own grandfather of the long-ago brutal conquest of France by England. Gilles' father didn't turn down trade or business dealings with anyone, not even the English, but he usually complained bitterly about them, both during and after the transactions. He often reminded young Gilles that all of the English were crude, dishonest and greedy. Gilles wondered if maybe one day, when the company had enough laborers and no longer had any use for them, Les Anglais could be persuaded to leave the colony, especially now that the WIC's increasing importation of some African slaves might alleviate their current labor shortage.

As he stood at the rail on the upper deck of the ship, Gilles was reminded that some of these English people were traveling with them. He must have been peripherally aware of their presence today, precipitating his previous line of thought. He tried not to stare. Their dress was unusual and the language they used among themselves, although slightly more similar to Nederlands than French, was odd. It was a peculiar flattened and drawn-out kind of speech, a guttural growl without any musical pleasantry, fearsome and worrisome too, in that you could never tell if they might be wishing you a good day or threatening some aggression. If there weren't very many people in New Amsterdam who understood their language, it would be impossible to know if they were plotting something until it was too late. The West India officers had already warned Gilles that the English in the colony were not to be trusted, so perhaps he was to be employed as a spy as well, warning the authorities of malevolence afoot, with a role that was much more important to the company than he realized. Maybe Gilles could just listen in on their conversations and pretend that he was a lowly clerk who did not understand any of their language at all.

There had occasionally been a few of these olive, gray, and lavender–clad people in Amsterdam, but Gilles did not know why some of them might be here on the ship. It was possible that they were going all the way to New Amsterdam, but it was more likely that they would disembark somewhere else before Den Eyckenboom reached her final destination. Gilles wondered if they were the peaceful type or the fanatical type, why the master had allowed them on board at all and if they had paid the full fare. He also wondered if anyone would object very much to their being thrown overboard in the interest of saving space and conserving food supplies. Their presence irritated him, reminding him of the religious upheaval that had deprived him of his former life. If only everyone had just kept their rebellious thoughts to themselves, he might still be living his life of privilege back in France.

But then Gilles remembered that he had done just that, and his life had taken this wrong turn anyway. It was ironic that now Gilles had a Dutch protestant wife, and by extension, a protestant family, so perhaps that made him a protestant too, a Jansenist, a Brownist, a Huguenot. Why were there so many different names for them? They could all just call themselves "heretic" and be done with it. Gilles supposed he was still a Catholic, although he no longer attended a Catholic church or kept any of the sacraments. Someday, when he was very old, he might have to seriously think about where he would be spending eternity. For now, he was still young, and his faith was almost entirely in his own abilities and perhaps a little in luck and in the stars. He only had this one life that he was living now, with the limited choices that were before him, so he would just have to live it out as best he could and worry about eternal damnation later.

As Gilles stood there, alone with his thoughts for the moment, he looked out over the undulating sea. It was a fair day today but very humid, with gently rolling waves topped with just a little froth, convincing him to take off his doublet, stripping down to his shirt and letting it flap freely in the warm breeze like a common sailor's. He retreated again into the solitude of his thoughts, surrounded by travelers who chatted among themselves, a backdrop for him as he wondered how he was going to deal with such an overwhelming variety of people when they reached the new land and he started his new position with the company.

"Gilles! Gilles, turn around and say 'Goedemorgen!'"

Elsje made a rare appearance on the upper deck, joining him while he was far away, lost in these thoughts. As if to bring his anxiety and fears to full fruition, she had at her side one of those women, one of the English, the Pure Ones, the Godly Ones, who professed to be so plain. If this was so, why did the woman have such an elaborate collar on her lavender-colored dress? They were not going to church or meeting with anyone important today. The woman had on real leather shoes too, not the clumsy wooden schoenen the Dutch called appropriately, klompen. Gilles had not noticed this woman down below where he certainly would have seen her. Maybe she had a private cabin near the shipmaster's on the upper deck. He was afraid that there would be nothing but trouble to come from this conversation because he knew his opinionated wife only too well.

Elsje could definitely be contentious and argumentative if the mood took her in that direction, so he hoped she would not start an argument here: If she did, he would be stuck on the ship with yet another person he had to avoid. His brief, initial hope that the woman couldn't speak their language vanished quickly when he realized that the other woman must be able to speak Nederlands or Elsje would not have been able to communicate with her at all. She was probably one of those who had been living in the university city of Leiden, learning the language of the Netherlands there. Because the two women seemed to be having an amicable exchange so far, Gilles took a deep breath to recover from this unexpected encounter and decided to try his rarely-used English on her.

"Good day, how are you?" he practiced on the woman's husband who had just come up behind her with a young girl in tow. "I am Yellas Jansen. This is my wife, Elsje Hendricks."

Gilles took off his hat and bowed.

"How should I be on this cursed ship? We make no progress at all. It is a filthy pit and we have been stuck for days in the middle of the ocean!"

The bad-tempered man had a large mouth situated in the middle of an enormous head that emerged from a great collar, one that was even more ostentatious than his wife's. His face was red, either with anger or from exposure to the sun. As he spoke, his large pockmarked nose gradually turned even redder than the rest of him. Wisps of reddish-gray hair stuck out from under the brim of his peculiar hat. He did not bow to Gilles in return.

Gilles wasn't surprised that they were rude, but he was amazed that they seemed so ungodly. He wasn't sure what he had expected their behavior to be, but it was not this. If the man really wanted to see filthy, he might venture down below, where most of the passengers were living in much less sumptuous circumstances, where their faces rarely had the opportunity to be reddened by the sun. But then again, the man was so portly that he probably would not be able to fit through the hatch. Gilles decided that he might have better luck with the man's wife.

"Ah, I see. How are you, Madame, ah, Goodwife?" he asked the woman, wondering if that was the correct way to address her.

"You may address me as 'Mistress Bugg,'" she replied icily.

The sides of Elsje's mouth twitched, but she said nothing. Although the conversational exchange with Gilles had been in English, she definitely understood the tenor of the conversation, if not the words. Elsje's conversation with the woman had surely been going much better before the woman's husband joined them. Gilles noted that his wife's eyes had suddenly become a stormy gray color. He wondered what he should do next. Maybe the English woman mocked him, offering Gilles this name that could not be her own.

He decided that he would try once again to win them over with pleasantries since Gilles could usually charm both men and women if given any opportunity to do so. Besides, he needed the practice with the language. He just hoped he was getting it mostly right. They probably weren't even going to New Amsterdam. They would probably disembark at one of the English colonies they would pass along the way, so Gilles was never going to see them again.

"What a nice daughter you have! My wife has a young sister, Corretje. She travels with us and is about her same age."

The young girl, who looked to be no more than ten or twelve, replied in Nederlands, in a much friendlier manner than her parents.

"Can she come up and talk with me? I'd like that. I have a weak heart you see, so I can't really do anything besides talk. My mother and father just wait for me to die."

The girl's father frowned. "That's enough, Charity!" he said in English.

Gilles assumed this was the girl's name, although he was fairly certain the name was a word that meant the same in French as in English. They had strange names too, these English. They were not named for family, saints, or even anyone in the Bible, in spite of their professing to be so godly. They named their children after virtues they believed were biblical.

"Winter takes every flower, no matter how long it has been blooming," Elsje said, "and the last one to flower in the autumn, we appreciate it most of all."

This contribution of hers did not seem to placate the child's father who glared at Elsje. For the sake of practice and to calm Elsje, who seemed to be on the verge of starting what would probably be a very unfriendly exchange with the father, Gilles made one last effort and smiled down at the girl.

"I am pleased to make your acquaintance, Charity. I am certain that Corretje would like to make your acquaintance too."

The child smiled back. She looked healthy enough to him, though perhaps a little pale and on the small side for her eloquent manner of speech. The parents just stood there, staring at Gilles with blank expressions, saying nothing further for long moments.

It suddenly occurred to Gilles that they were standing in judgement of him. They had already decided that Gilles and his wife were lower creatures, not deserving of their civility or worth engaging in respectful discourse, even if they were fellow travelers. Once, and not so very long ago, it would have been just the opposite, with Gilles looking down on them. If their minds were really so limited, he could think of nothing further to say that would change their already-formed opinions. Gilles gave up on diplomacy, managed to pull the sides of his mouth up into a perfunctory parting smile, excused himself and moved away to the other side of the ship where he pretended to go talk to a man who stood there. He didn't bother to remove his hat or bow this time. It wasn't worth the effort to try and get along with people that he would never see again after the journey. The exchange had confirmed his belief that the English were all inferior.

Not more than two minutes later, Gilles saw Elsje turn angrily away from the English people and storm back down the stairs. She didn't stop to speak with him on her way below, and Gilles just let her go. He was definitely not going back down there when she was in this mental state. He didn't even know why Elsje had ventured up the steps in the first place, but she would surely let him know if it was anything important.

Gilles remembered now, that in addition to the English, he would also have to deal with Gaelic–speaking Scots and Irishmen, Germans, Italians, Flemands and Walloons, although the latter at least spoke a bastard form of French. In fact, there were dozens of different languages spoken by residents in the colony, even Spanish. The Spaniards were hated by the Dutch for their domination and military occupation of the Netherlands over the last three generations, but there probably would not be very many of them living where they were not welcomed. Any Spaniards that were there would probably be able to speak Nederlands quite well though, having learned it from the prostitutes they had frequented.

Gilles needed to think of something happier now, so he turned his thoughts back to his friend Jean, to the long list of questions he had to ask him, and the good things they would do together when the ship finally arrived. Survival, shelter and food were foremost in his mind, but he also had questions about procurement of ale, wine, and livestock. There were other, more general questions that he wanted to ask when they were alone and away from the rest of the family, questions mainly about their safety. The unbidden thought came once again to Gilles that Jean's ship may not have made it safely to New Amsterdam. This was an even more frightening thought than all of the others, man-eating savages and ferocious wild beasts included.

Gilles looked to the skies now to search for happier thoughts. The journey couldn't be very much longer. He had tried to mark the days but had lost count of them, in spite of his starting the journey by naming each day aloud and numbering it, just to try and fix it in his mind. With no markers in the week, the days and weeks just bled into each other. There was no church to attend on Sunday. There were no market days, no baking days or any laundry days. Not knowing the day of the week was more or less inconsequential because their daily activities were all the same now, but naming each day had been a hopeful marker of time passing and progress made.

Gilles knew that the journey could have been worse. The trip had been shortened by taking a more direct route instead of following the longer, established trade route that was more often traveled. Knowing that the latitude of their destination was the same as the northernmost portions of Portugal and Spain, Den Eyckenboom's navigator only had to find the latitude and then run a perfectly westing course all the way in to New Amsterdam. If the weather cooperated, they would be able to cut off almost two thirds of their sailing time.

It seemed simple enough, but when one thought about this for a moment, it was frightening to go this radical way, traveling directly across the deep, open water with no islands or land in sight along the way. It was like walking blindly ahead in a thick fog and trusting that solid land would always be within a footfall. Most of the passengers, and maybe some of the crew as well, understood this and were as fearful as rabbits crossing open fields under the ever-present possibility of a hawk's shadow. Trade ships almost always used the familiar old route, traveling south along the coastlines of Europe to Africa, then heading west to the stepping stones of the West Indies, crossing the ocean from harbor to harbor, from trade to trade before connecting with the southernmost reaches of the new continent and then proceeding north. Hugging that wild new land's coastline, they would travel past the Spanish colonies, past the southern English Virginia colonies and past New Sweden before reaching New Amsterdam. If they were to continue traveling north, they would eventually reach the colonies in New France. Trading along the way ensured the profitability of the lengthy voyage if there was a sharp master who could increase the value of his cargo with every transaction along the way. Cargos varied with the size of the vessels and the origin of the ships; the English sent their iron, coal, wool and textiles to see what might be gained in exchange for these items. The French exported silk fabric, fustian, canvas and wine, and the Portuguese traded in slaves, sugar, molasses and rum.

Slavery was not permitted in the Netherlands, but there were those who acquired these dark men somehow and brought their favorite "servants" back with them from their military and trade ventures abroad. Before he left Amsterdam, Gilles learned that the company had obtained some of these slaves and there would be more of them coming to New Amsterdam due to the continuing need for cheap labor. A recently signed treaty with Portugal secured this workforce, expanded trade between the two countries and further united the Dutch and Portuguese against their common enemy, Spain. Gilles had been told that these Africans were often very fine craftsmen and were usually put to work in carpentry or masonry. Their labors were not wasted working in the fields or the orchards: The crops were so vital to survival of the colony that these activities were only entrusted to those who had some experience and success in dealing with the alien soil, weather, and growing seasons.

At first, before he had started to lose patience with the long journey, Gilles was disappointed that the ship would be taking this direct route because he wouldn't be able to get even a glimpse of the other colonies along the way. Tales of these places had been circulating around France and the Netherlands for decades. He couldn't quite believe they were all true, but he would have liked to have seen these places for himself, if only from the deck of the ship. Most of them were so far away from New Amsterdam that Gilles would probably never have the chance to see them, but other experiments might be close enough to visit one day. The ten-year old Catholic Maryland colony of Lord Baltimore and the newly–established colony that the Swedes called, of course, New Sweden sounded interesting. Maybe the company would send him there as a translator one day if there was trade between other colonies and New Netherland.

New Sweden had been started by none other than New Amsterdam's own former governor, Peter Minuit, who had originally negotiated the "purchase" of Mannahatta Island from the savages. The wild men who sold it to him weren't highly educated in European law and may not have properly understood what the transaction was about, only that they received some wonderful gifts just for making a dark mark on the stranger's piece of paper. When the West India Company felt that he no longer served the best interests of the investors and dismissed him as governor, Minuit responded by going to another country's monarch to obtain a commission and financing to start a different colony. After all, he was experienced in starting new settlements, and there were plenty of other countries in the world with a desire for colonial expansion.

Gilles had heard the WIC's version of Minuit's story, but the details and intricacies of the man's life were probably too nuanced for the West India Company's leadership to grasp. He was a man who knew how to take responsibility and get things done, and Minuit was not afraid of great challenges. With family roots in the French Catholic part of the Netherlands occupied by Spain, Minuit's family had taken refuge with the French protestants in the German Palatinate as Gilles and Elsje had done for a time. After his father's death and while still only in his twenties, Minuit took over the family business and was responsible enough and respected enough to be appointed guardian for several orphans. In addition to his proven business acumen, Minuit might also have been recruited by the Westindische Company to serve as a vital liaison between the company and his fellow countrymen, the Walloons. Gilles worried that the WIC would put him in the same category as their discredited former governor because they might not see much of a distinction between a true Frenchman and a French-speaking Walloon. Who could say whether Minuit's failures were mismanagement, corruption, or just taking on an impossible task? Perhaps his surname had been a harbinger of his fate in life, his family taking the word for midnight, the darkest of hours or the very beginning of a new day.

New Amsterdam did seem to go through a lot of governors, having gone through four of them in quick succession before the present Governor Kieft. Gilles knew next to nothing about Kieft except that the man was having no better luck in organizing the colony, improving the sagging morale, or turning a profit for the company. For now, the governing board was inclined to give Kieft a little more time since they already had so much time and money invested, or time and money wasted, depending on one's view of the situation. It was hoped that the less constricting regulations and new opportunities offered to the colonists would keep the precarious settlement from imminent and total collapse for a little longer.

The competing world powers, Portugal, Spain, Sweden, France and England, hearing rumors of the disarray, all waited to see what would happen next. Some of them had their own privateer ships positioned along the coast and trade routes, lying in wait to seize the Dutch ships and strip them of their goods before pressing the seamen, the ship, and sometimes even the hardiest of the ship's passengers into their service. Gilles had no wish to serve as a sailor on a foreign ship, although as a healthy adult man, this made him a likely candidate. If this happened, Gilles worried that they would take Elsje's teenage brother Heintje, small as he was, and also Van Amsterdam, Gilles' servant. He had no idea what would become of the girls, Elsje, and his infant children if the ship was taken.

A woman on the deck approached Gilles, and he hoped she wasn't going to ask him how much longer he thought it would be. He thought about turning his back to her, but he decided not to. It would be unkind, uncharitable, rude.

"You're Gilles, right?"

"Ja?"

"I just wanted to say, if you ever feel like you want to come over to talk with me at night, I'm way over in the corner and I'm all alone in my bed."

A smile lingered on her lips as she waited for a reply. Gilles took a moment to consider his words, but luckily, a loud splash distracted them at that moment. It sounded like a very large fish had just jumped out of the water behind the ship, but turning around, Gilles saw no great fish, only the gray woman who was standing there. The sailors were all gathered to the fore of the ship, laughing and drinking one of the day's rations of ale.

Seeing nothing of any danger or interest to him, Gilles turned his attention back to the young woman in front of him. He didn't know what to say to her. For one thing, she had no teeth, and for another, a smell accompanied her that was not good. She was certainly over the age of sixteen so it briefly occurred to him that she could be counted as one of the settlers on his plantation. He had no need of what he presumed to be her chief talents and services. Thinking about Elsje and what her reaction might be to bringing this woman into their midst, he knew this was not one of his better ideas. He just hoped that he wouldn't have to avoid this woman for the remainder of the journey too.

"I have seen the stars and your suffering. Come to me when you want to hear your fortune," she whispered in his ear.

Still smiling at Gilles, her eyes lingering for just a moment at the front of his pants, she turned away and approached a very young sailor who was sitting all alone, finishing his ale.

"I have seen the stars and your suffering," Gilles heard her cooing to him.

Gilles turned back around to look at the sea. All was peaceful and tranquil on this day, including the gray woman, passing serenely by Gilles a few minutes later, engaged in a friendly conversation with herself.

*I*n the morning the sound of sobbing woke Gilles. The old woman across the way was crying as though her heart would break.

"It's just a damned dog and it fell overboard before I could catch it," the daughter snarled at her, shaking her gray hair out of her pustulated face.

The old woman wailed even louder and the daughter pushed a dirty shawl into her face. "Dry your eyes! You're disturbing everyone else!"

She looked over at Gilles as if to say, "What are you looking at?"

Gilles could plainly see that she was a coward as well as a bully, but he had no wish to start anything that he might have to finish on the ship. He also didn't want to worry about his family whenever he slept or left them alone for a few minutes. He averted his eyes, thinking now about the dog he had in France. He wondered if his dog was still alive or what kind of end it might have met. He decided that he was not going to start the day by thinking about past sorrows, possible future problems, or present worries. He needed something else to think about right now, something that would bring him to a happier place.

He went through his list of good thoughts and future plans, but these didn't come fast enough or give him peace quickly enough. All he could hear was the old woman who continued to sob, this time more quietly. The waves of sadness coming from her throat were even more difficult to listen to than her constant, irritating humming. He wished desperately that he could race up the stairs and be outside, away from the sound, but the hatch was not open. For the moment there was no escape. Now it suddenly came into his mind that before he left Amsterdam, a neighbor had asked

Gilles what he would do with all of this wonderful, restful time off from his labors while he was on this voyage.

Gilles laughed out loud and briefly considered writing that neighbor an informative letter, but then he remembered that the man couldn't read, and besides, the less said about the trip, the better. Maybe in the coming years they would forget the miserable details of this journey, only recalling what life had been like before they left and after they arrived, deliberately leaving this chapter out as they told the narratives of their lives.

Still searching for something to distract and amuse himself, he thought about waking Elsje or perhaps not even waking Elsje first, just taking some time with her before everyone else was awake. Gilles knew that others were passing time in the same way; he could hear other couples engaged in the same activity during the night and sometimes even during the day. Before the first week of the voyage was behind them, the realization had struck even the most reticent of passengers that two or three months was too long to wait for any kind of personal privacy. There were also those who took great enjoyment in making it a public spectacle, engaging in it loudly and occasionally in areas that were not solely their own domain. Some passengers just ignored the activity, while others tried to distract their curious young children.

Gilles didn't really care what the others might think. He had been vilified, condemned and damned by much better people than the disheveled bunch of outcasts assembled on this ship. He was healthy, young, and legally married. The Netherlanders did seem to have even fewer inhibitions than the French who had even more of a reputation for their strong carnal appetites. Sometimes in the darkness, he heard these familiar noises coming from the few women who traveled alone and from women solely in the company of other women. He was shocked at first, but then he felt sorry for them, knowing how painfully lonely and envious of their married sisters they must be. Gilles supposed that sometimes there might have been men, both sailors and voyagers, moving among the women during the night, finding companionship, perhaps spending some time with the woman who had offered to tell his future. Thinking about the fortune-teller now, he wondered idly if she was looking for payment or if she was just lonely, taken by his charm and good looks, offering herself for free. He would never take her up on it of course, he was just curious about it. It was a little disappointing that he wouldn't get to hear the details of his future.

Gilles could hear many of his neighbors already stirring and coughing, so he knew that soon there would be more daylight coming in through the spaces around the old, poorly-sealed gun ports. The sun was ready to come up if it was not already on the horizon, and he prayed that those who held the power over his freedom would open the hatch to let him escape for at least a little while. Even with counting days, even with having some knowledge of the process of travel across the ocean and its vagaries, even with passing the time with his wife, reviewing his great future plans and finding or inventing as many distractions as he could, Gilles was growing more and more impatient every day. At times his reserves of serenity and peace drained away from him through a continuous slow ebbing, but at other times major breaches occurred in his inner calm.

Frightening dreams occasionally interrupted his sleep, and now he worried that he was losing control of his mind. This, more than anything else, terrified him. It felt like a slow but steady approach to madness, and he feared that it might be a permanent state of things. He had seen the poor creatures on the streets, and he knew of their residency in the prisons. These people who had been taken by insanity wandered the byways dressed in rags, shouting and arguing with themselves and with passersby. Occasionally they found places, cozy niches, where they curled up like dogs, staying there until someone noticed they had not moved and had been in the same position for a few days. New Amsterdam would not be a better place for such as those: The insane were probably just shot like mad dogs, if they could spare the extra gun shot, their carcasses left by the wayside until the crows and ants carried away the very last of their earthly remains. Gilles had always been so determined and strong-willed, even through all of the trauma he had endured in his young life, but perhaps too many hardships and miseries in quick succession had at last brought him to the limits of what his mind could endure. Maybe he really was losing his grip on sanity, sliding down the sharp-sided cliffs to whatever it was that waited for him in the depths below.

Gilles slept as much as he could, both to escape the life he was currently living and to pass the time, even though his dreams were not always his friends. Sometimes he dreamed of his past, mostly of living with Elsje in her father's inn. In those dreams there were many rooms that he had never seen in his waking life, rooms that could certainly never have existed like the ones in his dreams. Occasionally he went all the way back to his childhood in France with his brothers and sisters, but he always woke himself up when he started to dream of his recent troubled sojourn in the Rhine River Valley that had ended so badly. When this happened, Gilles reminded himself that they were safe now, that they were on the ship, sailing away from the past and moving forward to a better future. These nightmares were only catching up to him now because there had been no time to recover from the assault of that past reality, no time to start healing their souls before they were forced to gather up what was left of their lives and set out immediately on the next journey.

In one dream, Gilles sailed on a ship where the master and crew were all savage red men. Gilles was in the hold with a large number of animals. He looked up through the grating over the hatch which turned out to be a great open window to the heavens. Looking up through the blue skies and clouds, he tried to discern what might lie beyond that, but he woke up before he found the answer. Sometimes he dreamed of arriving at the new land and coming upon his house in the colony. At times it was an abandoned castle in the woods, occupied by ghosts of the dead, sometimes a complete ruin and at other times a fine and comfortable refuge. His dreams were a senseless accumulation and mélange of past, present and future. Gilles was just grateful that, unlike some of his fellow travelers, he did not wake up screaming from whatever terror they had survived in the past or feared was lying in wait for them when they rounded this blind corner into the future.

In his waking hours now, as well as in his dreams, sudden flashes of places that he used to frequent appeared to him, just ordinary street scenes and crossroads, as though his mind was constantly casting about for something familiar on which to attach itself, to touch base upon, some familiar sight or landmark. Nothing of any great significance was shown to him in these visions, just a bridge he used to cross, a building he had often passed by, or an intersection that he used to navigate. There were times when people came into his mind, bringing back to Gilles the familiar faces he had known in the past: the rat catcher, Rembrandt van Rijn, Rene Descartes, his old friend Ste Germaine, or the usual beggars in the town square. In his dreams these people sometimes appeared on the ship or spoke to him.

Gilles tried to take control of his thoughts in his waking moments, but his mood vacillated, alternating between the brief euphoria of going to a new place with the promise of new beginnings and the gut-wrenching panic at what he would find there. He was acutely aware that he had left behind everything that was familiar to him. They were all going to a wild and alien place where the people were savage, the weather was cruel and the wild beasts that roamed the countryside were more fearsome than the bears or werewolves of Europe. Gilles' emotions and his moods changed frequently these days, swinging back and forth like the great scales that stood outside the customs weigh house in the Netherlands. There was no turning back though; there were only ashes left of the past, ashes of hopes that had just disintegrated in his hands.

For now, he was stranded here in this confined space, sailing under the unfinished canvas of eternity. He would have liked to share his burden with someone, but Gilles could not share his worries with anyone else here. He was the head of the family now, and his responsibility was to continue in the role of self-assured leader and patriarch, even though he had not yet fully grown into it. He was crammed on the boat with so many others and yet Gilles was alone, isolated with his thoughts, sentenced to speaking only of hope and bright things to come while he wrestled with his doubts alone. He certainly could not divulge so much as a whiff of fear to his father-in-law who doubted and disparaged Gilles' capabilities even in the best of times, and no, not even to Elsje.

He had come to recognize that his wife was different than what he had thought all women were and what he once thought they were supposed to be. She was a strong, practical and worldly woman, a business person at home in a grittier world than the one Gilles had been raised in. She was a little older than Gilles, accustomed to running her father's tavern business and quite capable of single-handedly turning most trouble-makers out into the street. It wasn't only his pride that wouldn't allow him to reveal this weakness of his to Elsje though.

He had expected that his wife might change after the early days of their marriage, with the arrival of children and more responsibilities in their lives. Gilles knew that she had her own worries about their future and how she was going to manage daily tasks that had been routine, easy enough for her back in their old home city, but Gilles believed there was more to it, something else that was troubling her. There was something different about her now, something that had changed. He could not say how or why, not even exactly when this change had occurred, only that he had first noticed it just before they had left Amsterdam. She had closed a part of herself off, not just to him, but also to everyone else.

They could not both go insane. Who would care for their children and the others? The entire Hendricks family had been through far too much for Gilles to burden her now with any of his own worries and fears. Their past troubles had shaken Gilles' faith, but he was determined to bring them through their future challenges. Surely it was Elsje's job to provide the encouragement and support, the glue that bound them all together and feeling secure, while Gilles had the actual task of keeping them safe and well-fed. Had not Elsje herself always said that the man is the head, but the woman is the neck?

If Elsje had changed, Gilles was a different person now too. He was the same man, and yet not the same. He hadn't really changed his name, only his nationality, the better to slip through the snares of the bounty hunters. Born a Frenchman, Gilles Montroville, the son of Jean Montroville, now he was Yellas Jansen Van Amsterdam, a Netherlander. He had only dropped the French last name and convention, adopting the place he purported to be from. With some satisfaction, he thought that this was a common enough name in more ways than one. It was common in frequency, and it had no hint of gentlemanly status that might call attention to a man whose only wish was to blend in with the other emigres, to travel away from the past and live the rest of his life out in peace. There would probably be plenty of other Jansens in New Amsterdam and probably a good number of Jans who had named their sons Yellas.

Gilles looked through the gate, over to where the single men were, traveling alone on the voyage, unfettered by familial responsibilities. While this might have been an enviable freedom on the surface of it, most of the men over there had only the company of strangers. Having this large a family did offer Gilles a certain measure of safety: Anyone from his dangerous past would be looking for a young Frenchman on his own in the Netherlands, not the head of a Dutch household across the ocean in

New Netherland. Gilles counted himself as one of the lucky ones now, too, because it was his good fortune to have a family, a community to travel with him through whatever was ahead. They would all work together to bring in sustenance for each other, whether it was in the form of fish from the bay, crops from their garden, or gathering wild food in the forest if it came to that. There was indeed Strength in Unity, Eendracht Maakt Macht, as the Dutch would say. Gilles found good comfort in this thought. Starting from this small beginning and with everyone working together, they would find a way to transmute what little they started with into something bigger.

As if in answer to his prayers, a last-minute reprieve when he thought he might be sliding back toward the edges of insanity this morning, the hatch opened and once again a few of the passengers were allowed up on deck.

"You always push ahead! Let someone else go up!" a red-faced man shouted at Gilles, shaking his finger at him.

Gilles ignored the man. He needed this time up on the deck and he needed it desperately. He had to have it, no matter what he had to do to get it. The man pushed ahead of him, but Gilles let him go. Gilles was younger and taller and probably could have bested him in a fight, but maybe the man needed the time as badly as he did. The crew would probably let Gilles go up with the others. If not, Gilles certainly understood how murder could be committed for much less than what would be usual back in their old lives, back on civilized land. They had opened the far hatch for the single men too, so Gilles wasted no time in getting up there behind the red-faced man.

"They shouldn't let any of them come up! They only get in the way of our work! Leave them down there! It won't kill them to be down there for a few months," one sailor shouted over to another.

"We wouldn't want them all to die. Then we'd have to haul their stinking corpses out," the other sailor answered his shipmate with a laugh.

"They won't die. The slavers pack them into the holds and most of them make it through with very little to eat."

Gilles ignored these remarks and tried to suppress his rage, but inside he seethed with anger. He had to remember his mission today though, and that was to find a way to ease his mental turbulence. He made his way over to the railing which happened to be where the ship's navigator, the route master, was standing at the moment.

"Goedemorgen!" Gilles greeted him, hoping to learn something about the man's science and perhaps their arrival time.

The navigator ignored Gilles for the most part, but he did grunt in reply, which Gilles took to be a good sign. Lining up his own vision with the direction of the man's field of study, Gilles saw nothing at all on the horizon.

"Can you really tell where we are and when we might arrive?"

The man of science stopped long enough to fix a glare at Gilles and then silently put his eye back to the instrument he cradled in his hand.

"If we travel due west, away from the rising sun and into the setting sun, we should be taking the right path, ja?" Gilles tried again.

Perhaps the man was not Dutch at all and his apparent unfriendliness was due to his not understanding the language. He looked like a Netherlander though, and he was dressed like a Netherlander. Gilles wondered if he might try some other languages, but he didn't know which one he might start with. The man did not seem to be warming up to him but neither had he moved away.

Unfortunately, Gilles did not know that the navigator, even though he was one of the best on the seas, had no way of knowing how much longer it would be or how much farther they had to go. The man had learned long ago not to discuss his knowledge with ordinary men who were ignorant in the extreme about science. The route master had spent his early years answering questions and explaining his profession over and over, but at some point in his career he had stopped wasting his breath on anyone, especially the ignorant young seamen who never tired of mocking him. The crew members pranced and postured for each other, all bragging of their strength and adventures on the sea, although it was obvious to everyone, and especially to the navigator, that they were valued only as long as they possessed strong backs, fast feet, and agile hands with most of their fingers. Still, the route master had to travel along with them, spending his days scrutinizing the sun and his nights tracking the stars. When neither were seen due to cloud cover, he relied on the compass to keep them on course, hoping it would not vacillate or fall into a bewitched vortex that would make it spin wildly as it did on occasion. He told no one this, but he also kept a Norse Crystal hidden away in his pocket. It was an ancient thing, but it still worked when nothing else did. It also served as his good luck piece, so if he needed it for either purpose during a voyage, it was always there.

The sun was shining brightly today and there was no difficulty in finding the heading, but there was scarcely enough wind to take them forward. There was nothing to be done on this day except to curse the weather, the beautiful, hot, humid, sticky, fair weather. They might die a slow death on the sea, running out of food and water, dying there in the beauty of it all.

Even among the sailors, the subject of progress was becoming a contentious one. The small crew was made up of barely over a dozen hardy young men. They were not particularly intelligent, nor were they interested in learning anything from the navigator. They did understand the dangers and challenges of the voyage, having learned these lessons mostly through hard personal experience. To a man they disdained and disregarded the route master, this overly-educated fool who strolled around the deck in his fur-trimmed doublet and lace jabot, protecting his peculiar-looking pieces of brass, glass and polished wood, constantly preening his graying beard and squinting at the sky. If the navigator spoke little to the crew, he did not speak at all with the passengers. When approached as he was now, he knew what all the questions were and had trained himself to ignore any occasional attempted pleasantries because they only led to further conversation. All they ever wanted to know was, "How much longer?".

The route master was an important man to have on board, particularly on this voyage. The rough crew knew it was so, keeping their sharp tongues mostly in check, although there were many comments and more than a few rude and suggestive gestures made behind his back. There was no doubt that the navigator was accustomed to seeing and overhearing these remarks, but the solitary man took refuge in his silence and solace in his superiority. He refused to answer or speak to anyone except the master of the vessel and then only when he was addressed directly. It was a thankless and lonely position for a man of science, particularly if he hated the miseries that accompanied every trip or was fearful of the dangers that came along with his occupation. The compensation had to be adequate to secure a learned man like this one, but even so, he spent a good portion of every voyage considering some other line of work in the future.

His science had come a long way from the use of only a sunstone, the stars, and the span of a man's hand to navigate. With the latest version of the Davis Quadrant, the latitude could now be known with near-certainty under the right conditions, but the determination of longitude still proved to be an impossible problem to solve. Great wealth and high honors had been offered by kings across the world for anyone who could step forward and accurately determine the east-west position of a ship without visual sight of land. As helpful as it would be for determining when a ship might reach its destination, especially across open water, knowing the location was even more important for safety concerns. Mistaking the ship's position could have some very serious and even deadly consequences. The longitudinal position might be known when they set out, but storms and variable winds easily confounded their perceived progress. It was impossible to know with any certainty whether a ship was just off the coast of the Virginia colonies or in closer proximity to Spain or Morocco, a blunder that could well prove to be fatal. It was not just about the limited supply of food and water on board; it was also the danger from the pirates and corsairs who prowled the African coast looking for victims when ships unknowingly moved into the wrong waters.

"You up there! Come down and give some others a chance to get some air!"

Gilles ignored the other man calling out to him from below, but at the same time and not even ten feet away, he saw the gray woman who had suddenly stopped in her tracks and was looking directly at him. Caught in her icy stare, Gilles had the distinct impression that she was going to come over to him now and make trouble. Gilles moved to the other side of the ship, but the man in the hatchway observed Gilles' actions and called out to him once more.

"You! Do I have to speak to the master?"

Gilles took a last deep breath of fresh air, as far as his lungs would expand. His time on the open deck was up, and in truth, he didn't want to be near some of the undesirables that were up there with him now. Other passengers only wanted a little of their own time in daylight before the sun went down, before they were locked away for the night once more. Gilles took his hat off and bowed low, gesturing for the man to come up. Deciding that he would try to go back to sleep to pass some time, Gilles hoped they were one day closer to the end of their journey, one day closer to his new life. He would attack his fears again later and attempt to rid himself of them once and for all, peeling them off though they clung to him like ticks or other parasites, not on the surface of him, but living under his skin.

*T*he next morning Elsje started questioning Gilles before he even opened his eyes.

"Did you find out anything? Do you think it will be much longer? How many days? Is it still weeks? You fell asleep before I could ask you again and then, when I woke up to feed Jacomina, you were still asleep."

"Elsje! Stop! I'm not even awake yet," Gilles protested, pulling the blanket up over his head as he squeezed his eyes shut.

"It looked like your eyes were open, so I thought you were awake. Can you take Bruinje with you for a time? He's been trying to get down for the past hour, and I just can't manage him today. My head hurts and I really don't feel well."

Gilles gave up, pushing the blanket back as he sat up and ran one hand through his hair, tossing something he found in it on to the floor.

"Give him to me. We will walk around and have another adventure before they bring our food down."

"Take him to the chamber pots first!"

"I will, I will."

He didn't know why his wife got to sleep longer this morning and he didn't, but if it gave him some peace while she slept, he would not start an argument with her this early in the day. The thought crossed his mind that maybe she really was sick, more so than he realized. Elsje could even be dying, and this concern sent a fast flood of panic over him. How would he manage without her?

That was an unreasonable worry, though. She was only sick from the sea. She certainly could not be pregnant because she still nursed Jacomina. Gilles pushed these thoughts away and focused his attention on his son. He was relieved to see that Bruinje had not soiled himself. At least today he would be spared the chore of changing the child's clothes and Elsje wouldn't have to wash them later. She had already washed Bruinje's clothes out so much that they were as stiff as a ship's canvas sail, giving the child a perpetual rash and making him as fussy as his infant sister.

Gilles wondered if changing their clothes mattered at all anymore when the inside of the ship smelled so much like the inside of a privy. Every day a very young cabin boy and two other sailors were sent down to gather up the waste. Afterwards they brought the voyagers buckets of salt water for them to bathe, but unfortunately, these actions didn't make Gilles feel any cleaner than he was before washing, and it didn't mitigate the smell very much either.

When it was Gilles' turn to watch Bruinje, they played a game that amused them both, as well as the passengers who watched them. Gilles took the boy around the bunks and passengers, taking him on different imaginary journeys. One tour was of a French seaport.

"See the men unloading the ships? They have wheat and furs coming from the far north, from Russia! Your mother will take those and make us delicious hot bread with butter and warm winter coats. We will trade our cider, calvados, cloth and faience, filling their ships up again before we send them back across the sea."

Another ship was from the orient, bringing a few things that Gilles had seen in the Amsterdam market and others that he had only heard about.

"They bring us fantastic animals such as you have never seen! The dragons are friendly and some of them have two heads. They have warm tea for us to drink and beautiful porcelain dishes to trade. See the pretty bright silks? Your mother will like that! She will make a beautiful dress that she can wear to church on Sunday. Do you smell that wonderful smell? Those are special spices for cooking. Your mother will make us a special dinner with those spices, serving it to us on the pretty dishes, and then we will all have tea."

Gilles thought up new countries for them to visit, but he had not been to very many himself, so he had to use his imagination as to what he thought they might be like. He always included France and the Netherlands, knowing that Bruinje would probably have very little knowledge of either country and few memories of his own. If the child ever did return to the Netherlands, it would be a completely alien land to him, with only the language of his mother and her cooking connecting him to the old country.

"This is the great city of Amsterdam! See the Dam? In the marketplace you can buy anything, anything you can think of in all the world. What will we buy today?"

"Cheval!" Bruinje replied.

"A horse? What will you do with a horse?"

"Ride! Ride far away!"

"We like horses, don't we? I will buy us both fine riding horses in the new land and you will become a great horseman."

Although he mostly spoke Nederlands to his son, sometimes, especially when Gilles had no one else to talk to, he told his son his secrets, speaking to the boy in French. This had started when Bruinje was just days old. Gilles told his son that he would grow up to be an important man one day and that someday they would have a great plantation with fine vineyards. At the time it had not mattered that the child couldn't understand what was being said, so Gilles felt completely at ease in sharing his most unlikely dreams and voicing all of his complaints; after all, no one else would ever hear the details of the conversation. Now that Bruinje did have an understanding of what was being said to him, Gilles was a little more cautious in what he told his son, at least when he thought that it should not be repeated. Bruinje seemed to have inherited Gilles' ability to understand and speak several languages, and he had the same restless curiosity as his father. Gilles smiled to himself with satisfaction: The boy would make a good businessman and heir. Before that time though, Gilles was certain that they would have many adventures together, real adventures when they reached the new world.

Seeing this bit of himself in his son, Gilles was not only accommodating in giving his time and attention to the boy, he was amused, but it was this very adventurousness in Bruinje that drove Elsje to distraction and panic whenever Bruinje decided to wander off on his own. In the first weeks on board the ship she had retrieved him from under the bunks, from other families, from the toilet area and from the stairs. Once she had been unable to find him at all, running up the stairs to see if he had somehow escaped to the upper deck and fallen overboard. Now this task had become a group effort with everyone in the family and even some of their fellow travelers trying to keep an eye on Bruinje.

Gilles transported this seed, his two small children, across the sea to be planted there. He didn't know what the future held for them, but he hoped their young lives would not be wasted, their blood carelessly spilled out on the ground as so much had been in the old homelands by uncaring and warring monarchs. Hopefully their new home would offer them long, peaceful, healthy and prosperous lives so they would one day join their bloodlines to the bloodlines of others, the line continuing far into the future as the generations passed. Because Gilles was still so young himself, it was a peculiar feeling he had as he looked at this small child, this unfinished being, and thought about Bruinje's children, grandchildren, and beyond. This journey had the unexpected effect of making him examine the past and the future, taking him to places beyond his own lifespan.

Bruinje sometimes looked up at his father in wide-eyed wonder, as if he, too, could see the things his father pointed out, both sets of eyes adjusted far beyond what others could see, beyond the berths Gilles pointed to, beyond the deck of the ship and out past a mere ocean. The other passengers frequently smiled and joined in the game, acquiring and sharing with each other a little more patience and goodwill as they watched the father and son exploring the world solely from the confines and darkness of the hold.

The women no longer had their fires to tend, the laundry or the cooking, but they still had many of their regular duties to keep them occupied. They cared for their families and had their usual pastimes of gossiping, knitting and worrying over whatever they most enjoyed worrying about. The men had none of their usual activities, no jobs to go to, no toiling in the fields, no shop keeping or crafting items of wood, metal, or leather, not even any tavern-visiting. They had nothing to do except join in the women's chatter or play a few games of chance that were frequently frowned upon by their wives, even if no money was being exchanged. The English ships forbid gambling due to the fights it often engendered, but the Dutch were less concerned, and besides, who was going to be around all day to enforce it? The shipmaster kept the small crew busy day and night. Even with easy sailing there were constant repairs being made on a ship that was this old. On the other side of the grating the single men were as bored as the others, so occasionally they moved up closer, peering through the lattice and looking over the young girls in the family section. This put Elsje on her guard, keeping a close eye on her young sister and Aafje, although Elsje was also an object of salacious interest.

Besides Elsje's consistently asking "How much longer?" there was something else that Gilles had not anticipated to be almost as annoying, and that was the dearth of anything new in their lives. Under these conditions, everyone experienced everything at the same time. Anything that was novel in a day was observed instantly by everyone else unless they happened to be distracted or sleeping at the time. All that was left was to add commentary on the event or relate it to something in the past or anticipated future. A few of the passengers enjoyed recounting their past memories, but Gilles was not one of them. His fugitive status aside, the past was too painful. Gilles made the commitment to speak aloud only of the good things to come. Every day he beat back his fears, one by one, trying to hold his hard-fought-for ground in a place of optimism. This was enough of a challenge when he was alone, but when he was with the rest of the family, Elsje was always trying to initiate conversation with him. These efforts disrupted his thoughts and usually left Elsje frustrated in the process.

"It's cloudy today. Do you think it will be cloudy all the time over there?"

"It's hard to say."

"The old man coughs. I hope he doesn't infect our children."

"Ja, I heard. Old people cough for no reason."

When he didn't talk with her though, she seemed to have a compulsion to talk with someone else, and this concerned him. The Amsterdammers on board this ship were mostly like his wife, natives of a city that regularly produced talkative, contentious and scrappy individuals of both the male and female variety. Elsje could definitely be difficult, even tough when the occasion warranted it. He certainly didn't need her help in making any more enemies: He already had plenty of those. Gilles had learned through painful first-hand experience that his wife was as capable of starting an argument as anyone, and this could extend to a physical fight if the circumstances warranted it, sometimes even taking sides and joining in on one that was getting off to a good start on its own. Elsje fought her own battles and often the battles of others. Although he had grudgingly come to admire this ability of hers to defend herself and stand up for others that she thought needed her help, Gilles just wanted to make it to their destination without any trouble. If Elsje made a mortal enemy or two along the way, there would be no escaping them, not on the ship and probably not even after they reached New Amsterdam, being surrounded as they would be by wilderness, water or savage beasts on all sides. When Elsje met Gilles, she had taken up his cause too, defending him and taking him under her protective wing at a time when he needed it the most. The thought had never occurred to him before, perhaps because he had never wanted to entertain it, but this was probably another reason why he had married her.

Thinking about his wife now and worrying anew about Elsje's health, Gilles took Bruinje back to their assigned space, only to find Elsje, not languishing and headed toward death, but wide awake and engaged in conversation with another one of the English women on board the ship, one of those who called themselves "Pilgrim", or maybe it was "Puritan". It made no difference to him which name they used. Both were varieties of the always-peculiar Anglais, like the difference between two varieties of apples, one over the other better for making cider or pies, but both still apples. Why couldn't Elsje stay in their own space and just talk with her own family? Why was she always talking to the other travelers? It probably had something to do with growing up in her father's tavern; she had no lack of curiosity about the experiences of others who had seen more of the world than she had so far.

"Gilles, come here and tell this woman what you know about New Amsterdam," Elsje called over to him, dragging him into the conversation.

"*Everything* I know? Maybe she isn't interested in learning *all* that I know," he replied with a sardonic smile.

"She wants to know what it's like over there. Her husband will be working for the company too." Elsje gestured to a man sitting on a berth a slight distance across the way.

The woman and Elsje continued to speak while Gilles took a fast moment to look the man over, determining quickly that this was a man of some substance, maybe even a university graduate. What caught Gilles' eye was the book in the man's hands. The man had positioned himself and the book next to a small crevice in the ship's outer wall, holding it up to the light so he could make out the words. Intrigued, Gilles wondered what the man was reading and if he had any other books. The man appeared to have skills beyond those of a laborer or craftsman, presumably in a profession that the WIC believed would be of particular use to them. The man might be the only person on board this ship that Gilles would want to converse with.

Gilles could read and write, not only to keep accounts and document basic business transactions, but enough to actually read books. He had brought about a dozen of them along with him, no great library, but enough to keep him contented for a time until he could procure some more. Written in French, Latin and Nederlands, Gilles justified this use of their allotted space by telling Elsje that they would be needed to teach everyone how to read. He had only recently discovered that his wife could not read or write, so he had started to teach her about letters. Like this variety of the English people, but unlike most of the rest of the world, the Dutch often educated their daughters when the opportunity presented itself. Back in France, Gilles' sisters had a superior education, having been taught enough so they could read poetry when they weren't perfecting their lace-making skills. Gilles hoped that Elsje might someday be able to write letters to her family in the Netherlands so he would not have to perform that tiresome task for her. Elsje couldn't tell that Gilles's books were not all in the same language, and she would only be using the books in her native tongue, but Gilles just couldn't bring himself to leave the other books behind. He didn't know if there would be any books at all besides the accounting ledgers in New Amsterdam. Gilles particularly cherished one book in Latin and two others in French, having read them over and over until the pages were stained with the oils of his hands, the prints of his fingers visible and darkening over time on some of the pages. Unfortunately, he had packed them all up and had not kept any of the books out to read during the journey. Knowing that the hold would be dark and his family would keep him occupied, Gilles didn't believe he would have any opportunity to read at all. Now he wished that he had one in hand, and it pained him to know that they were locked away down below, unreachable until their arrival. There was nothing he could do about it for now. He could only wait, hoping they had survived the journey and had not succumbed to the dampness.

Gilles thought he heard the woman say the word "physician", and if this was so, her husband was of much greater status than any man trained in the job of chiurgeon or mere blood-letter. What was he doing on this ship, down here in the darkness and headed to New Amsterdam?

"Good day, Mistress," Gilles addressed the woman in her own language before continuing in Nederlands. He did this for Elsje's benefit, demonstrating for her the manners that she should try to emulate if she was going to survive in the West India Company's social milieu. Elsje might know how to get along with a variety of people from working long days and nights in her father's tavern, but she had no life experience in higher society, no knowledge of protocol in the upper classes. This was an opportunity that presented itself for her to learn and to practice.

"Allow me to introduce myself: I am Yellas Jansen and I see that you have met my wife, Elsje Hendricks."

Gilles believed that this Englishwoman would have had enough experience with the Netherlanders to know about the Dutch naming customs so he wouldn't have to go through the entire explanation of how women from the Netherlands were always and forever known by the names they were given at birth, not at marriage. This had become as tiresome to Gilles as it was to the Netherlanders, but if this woman had been living in the Netherlands for a time, she would surely be familiar with their ways by now.

Gilles was careful to accompany his introduction with a bow and not shake her hand as the Netherlanders greeted each other, nor to touch her at all, especially not by kissing her hand in the French fashion, as it was not the way of the English.

"It's a pleasure to meet you, Heer Jansen. I'm Frances Marbury. My husband is over there and my four children travel with us."

Gilles looked the woman over quickly, hoping not to be too obvious about it. From the way she said it, he knew that some or all of the children might be from a previous marriage or perhaps were orphaned relations that had been taken in by them, but she had run her hand over her stomach, quickly, unconsciously, and so he assumed she was with child now too, possibly her husband's first, although he did not look to be a very young man. Gilles worried that it wouldn't be too hard for Elsje to offend these English people if they were all so narrow-minded and rigid, but then a happy thought occurred to him: Elsje's blunt and direct manner might quickly offend them all and Gilles wouldn't have to talk with any of them. He might make an exception for the man with the book, though.

"So you're going to live in Nieuw Amsterdam then? Have you no family or friends there at all?" Gilles asked.

"My husband has some family living in Nieuw Nederlandt, but they are not living in the village, in Nieuw Amsterdam, where we are going."

"Did you hear that, Gilles? They are going to settle there too!"

"I heard it," Gilles replied.

He had to wonder why this woman and her husband, probably in their late thirties or maybe even forties, well on in years, traveled to such a remote place, but seemed to have no plans to join up with the family that was already on the other side of the ocean. Gilles had been a stranger in a strange land himself and remembered only too well his early days in Amsterdam where he was so alone. Unlike Gilles though, at least they had the advantage of understanding the language where they were going. This English woman seemed friendly enough and was not like the others he had met on the upper deck. Now he was curious as well. Perhaps not all of the English were unpleasant. Gilles ventured to speak with her a little more.

"I have not been over there myself, but I understand that it is a good place or I would not be taking my wife and children there. I know there are many Engelse mensen who already live there; they need me to translate for those who do not speak our language."

"Gilles can speak English," Elsje proudly informed her new friend.

"Is that so?" the woman looked at Gilles with some curiosity of her own.

"Gilles is a *Patroon*, what you English call a *Gentleman*, so if you have no other place to live, you can come and live on our lands."

Elsje, even with no formal education, was a consummate politician, always supporting her husband's business ventures. She was constantly on the lookout for people to fulfill the conditions of Gilles' land grant contract, but Gilles colored a little at Elsje's offer. In this setting of shared misery, his wife surely did not recognize the woman's higher social status. Elsje was probably insulting this fine lady by offering her settlement on wild lands and the opportunity to work as a laborer in Gilles' fields. These people, like Gilles, might have been bereft of some former wealth, but Gilles could see that they had passed into this one from a very different world.

"*Gentleman* may be a bit of an exaggeration, Elsje," Gilles demurred.

Maybe when he had been born, the term "gentleman" might have aptly been applied to his circumstances, but he hardly could be called that now, except by virtue of his education and the few assets he had. Aside from his land and a few coins in his pocket, their only other wealth was invested in Gilles' plumed hat and Elsje's pearls, the outline of the strand just barely visible now under the sweat-stained neckline of her dress. Gilles might arrive in the new world only to discover that his glorious patroonship was actually useless swampland, in spite of the drawings around the margins of the deed indicating the presence of hills, great trees and small structures of some sort, perhaps a small town.

"Gilles' family was in the shipping business," Elsje interjected.

"Do you know much about the route then? My husband is a little concerned. He tells me the ships don't usually travel straight across the ocean and that it is a bad omen when you see the new moon holding the old moon in her arm."

Noting the expression of concern on Elsje's face regarding this remark, Gilles tried to reassure both women.

"I'm sure we'll have no bad luck on our journey. We'll be there soon."

His heart leapt just then, as his attuned ears heard the one sound that he wanted to hear more than any other besides a cry of sighted land, the sound of the hatch opening up. Gilles pushed Bruinje into Elsje's hands, made his hasty excuses, poor ones admittedly, tossing them over his shoulder as he raced forward to the stairway and the open hatch. Others moved forward too, but they were not as fast as Gilles was today.

Arriving up on the open deck and stepping over the small boy who was on his knees scrubbing the planking, Gilles took his usual place at the rail just as he was overtaken and passed by the gray woman, leading her elderly mother along to the stern of the ship.

"Come along mother, you need the fresh air!" the daughter cajoled.

The old woman whimpered and dragged her feet.

"Out of our way!" the madwoman growled, a lightning-fast change in her demeanor taking place before Gilles' eyes. She lunged at Gilles with claws at the ready. Fortunately, she missed him and didn't stop walking. She continued on her way, pushing and dragging the old lady.

On this day the navigator had come out of his den too, but he was not standing still. He was a caged fox, pacing impatiently, looking up to the skies and out to the horizon. Gilles wouldn't bother to try and make conversation with him now, while he was in this state. Gilles wondered if he should have brought his family over on a different ship, maybe the Wapen Van Rensselaerswijck that had sailed just before their own ship left port. It was a larger ship, and it could have arrived already in New Amsterdam. It might also have granted Gilles a little more room to escape all of the other passengers that he did not want to see. There had been good reasons not to take the Wapen though: For one thing, it was Van Rensselaer's private ship and not a WIC ship. The other shipmaster might not be as good, and besides, the West India Company would not have paid for their passage over. With the kind of weather they had been having since they left the Netherlands, the Wapen was probably not making any better sailing time than the Eyckenboom.

A large school of fish passed by, eliciting exclamations from the passengers on the deck. The shiny silver missiles were leaping out of the water with what looked like great joy, splashing back down into the ocean again, leaving Gilles and others soaked in the frolic. He welcomed the cool water, even though he knew he might be damp for days to come if the sun couldn't dry his clothing out completely today. He would worry about that later; for the moment it felt wonderful. The school of fish was so large that it seemed to cover all of the ocean in every direction. He didn't know what kind of fish they might be, but some of them were quite large, all of them gleaming a blinding light in the sun. Passengers pointed to the frothing waves created by the migration, and the deafening noise enveloped them as the water displaced from their wake nearly washed over the sides of the ship. Gilles thought he heard laughter coming from the creatures, joy in their playfulness. The passengers on the open deck stood pressed together, watching as the fish passed, and then, just as suddenly as they came, the fish were gone and the ocean was tranquil once more.

Looking into the water that was calm enough now to mimic a mirror, Gilles saw the reflection of faces lined up alongside him at the ship's rail. He realized with a start and some degree of panic that he couldn't identify his own face in the crowd. Turning to his left, he observed a very tall man with a large plumed hat standing at his side. Looking back and locating the man's reflection in the water, Gilles knew that the man standing next to the hat had to be him. It had been a long time since he had seen his own reflection, and now he gazed at it in disbelief. The unkempt beard, the disheveled collar and the weathered red face stared back at him from under wild and tangled hair.

He could not be this man.

The sight disturbed him so greatly that he turned his back on it, facing into the center of the ship, looking up at the sky and the limp sails that were starved for any moving air that could propel the ship forward. Gilles breathed in deeply. He tried to summon peace back into his mind and reach communion with the great power that he could feel beneath the surface of the waters. The quiet was only disturbed by some slight noises from the sails as the rhythm of the waves provided a hypnotic background, in tune with his own heartbeat.

He decided that the reflection in the water was not his. He would clean himself up and return to the person he knew himself to be. He was not going to accept as reality the terrible vision he had just seen. Even worse, he remembered that he had just recently been talking to the Englishwoman who had seen him looking like this. It had been difficult enough to escape his own harsh thoughts and stay connected to the good ones, but now it seemed that his increasing malaise was coming at him from all different directions. This day was not finished with him though; it produced yet another disquieting event.

He had been peripherally aware of a man he saw on the upper deck once before, a man who had looked at him strangely and seemed to be watching him. The thought crossed his mind now that this might be more than just mere curiosity. Knowing that there were still spies looking to bring him back to France, to collect the reward for his capture and deliver him to the death sentence that waited for him there, Gilles tried to shake the feeling and rationalize his way out of this new fear.

He reminded himself that if he was safe anywhere in the world, it was on board this ship, in the middle of the ocean, headed for a lawless land where the authorities had too many other problems and concerns, survival being chief among them, to help any French bounty hunters.

The New Amsterdam authorities hadn't put forth any effort at all in bringing to justice the bold and arrogant pirates who had just moved in and settled among them, fighting, intimidating their neighbors, and selling illegal commodities right under their noses. They certainly wouldn't bother returning Gilles to France, especially if he was needed in New Amsterdam as their company clerk and translator.

Gilles trusted his inner voice which had generally served him well in the past. Although it was an uneasy feeling, it was not a sense of dread that he had from this stranger, it was something else. He reasoned that of course the man would look familiar: Most of the people on board the ship had resided in Amsterdam, anywhere from a few days prior to their departure to having lived in the city for their entire lives. Gilles would certainly have seen most of them around town, in the streets, and especially in the Dam during the days and weeks just before their departure.

There was more that nagged at his memory though, the conviction that he had conversed face to face with the man before. Suddenly the realization came to him that the man had not previously had a beard. Now Gilles recognized him as Alain Gagner, a Frenchman who had been their neighbor when they had been living in the German Palatinate. This man might once have been a friend of Gilles' if it had been under other circumstances. In that past place, their neighbors, all members of the same religious sect, had continually derided and verbally assaulted Gilles and his family for a variety of deviations from the community's religious expectations, which were to Gilles' way of thinking, overly rigorous.

When Gilles came to this realization, he put his back to the ghost, turning around to look back out to sea. He could feel the man continuing to watch him and was peripherally aware that Alain had repositioned himself between Gilles and the open hatch. Gilles could wait. He wasn't ready to return below anyway. Maybe Alain would just go away if Gilles continued to ignore him. Maybe he was unable to recall how he knew Gilles, especially with the appearance of both men having changed so much. Alain did not go away though, and now he approached Gilles directly, cutting off any hope of escape.

"Vous souvenez-vous de moi? Do you remember me, Gilles?" he asked.

"Ah, Msr. Gagner, I thought you looked familiar! You have a new beard," Gilles replied.

"We are a long way from the Palatinate, that is certain," Alain said, "and no one speaks French here besides you. I heard you down below, speaking to your son."

"You speak no Nederlands at all?" Gilles asked.

"Non. I try to learn a few words. I am a stranger here, but there is nowhere left to go on our home shores, nowhere that they speak our language where I am safe. We are a generation of refugees."

"C'est vrai," Gilles replied as he looked out over the rail to the open sea, "I certainly never thought my life would be like this."

"All I have ever wanted was peace and the security of my home, to practice my trade, to have a family, and yet, they will not leave me alone."

"Life may not be easy in New Amsterdam, either," Gilles warned him.

"But I see that you are taking the chance, too," Alain replied.

"Do we have a choice?" Gilles asked. He was surprised at his reply and the edge he heard in his own voice.

"Non, I suppose not, but at least you have much to live for. My first wife and children died during the siege at La Rochelle, but I escaped. My second wife and children all died at Nouvelle Rochelle in the Palatinate. I'm getting too old to bury many more wives and children, yet as you say, we have few alternatives."

"Have you always farmed?" Gilles asked, changing the subject and remembering the hundred more settlers he would need for his patroonship.

"I'm really a silversmith. I learned from my father and my uncle and I'm very good at it. I do fine work, but I haven't been able to practice my trade for some time now, especially in the wilderness areas where I have been living lately."

Gilles knew that many of the expatriate French had been unable to carry on their trades outside of their homeland. France had lost most of her middle class, retaining mainly the very rich and the very poor. Gilles had changed professions himself after he had left France, doing what he could to just stay alive. He shoveled out stables, managed an eating establishment and worked as a poor farmer after he had been unable to find any work in keeping accounts. He had moved from one profession to another, making bargains here and there to keep himself fed.

"Maybe you need to live in a city, a prosperous one," Gilles suggested.

"The Netherlands had guilds and regulations keeping outlanders from working in certain professions there. I'm hoping that New Amsterdam will be more open to letting me work in my trade."

"That's not a bad plan," Gilles said, remembering the West India Company's recently rescinded restrictions.

He couldn't imagine that the trades were that busy now though, especially in luxury items like silver, and where would Alain get the raw materials? Gilles seized the opportunity and wondered if this was providence. It had been difficult to find anyone in Amsterdam willing to settle on his patroonship, even with the overcrowded conditions in the old city. Most of the residents were either too comfortable or too fearful to go to the wild new lands. He presented his proposal to Alain.

"Maybe you could work in iron, copper or brass. There is always a need for horse harnesses and cooking pots. Ecoute, Alain: I have some land that you could live on. For the moment I have no need of a silversmith, but if you want to help me work the land, I can see about setting you up as a silver smith once again, sometime in the future."

"Life has treated you well my friend, spared your family, and given you a second chance, but helas, I am unable to accept your kind offer."

"Mais pourquoi pas? But why not?" Gilles asked.

"I have had to indenture myself out. I am bonded to Msr. Marbury, an English physician who is on board. I am hoping that he is a kind man, because I will be his servant for the next eight years. At the end of that time, if I have not died by then, I will have my freedom. Perhaps then, when I am allowed, I can find a wife who will have me. I will be old and poor by then, but maybe I will not have to live my last days out completely alone. If the truth be told though, I have no need of a wife right now, not to mother my children as they have all been murdered, and not to share in my life's misery."

Gilles didn't know what to say to this or how to respond. He had known of such agreements and knew they were commonplace among great numbers of the poor, but he had never before known anyone who had entered into such an arrangement. Silversmiths almost always came from good families with a higher social position than the rest of the masses, the trade and skills being passed down in families for generations, from father to son. It was not a trade like blacksmithing where anyone might have his apprenticeship by virtue of only brute strength and a modicum of skill, working in the cruder metals.

"Maybe our luck will change in the new country," Gilles suggested.

"New country, old country, will it ever be any different? Is there a place on this earth that is any better? When I was a child, I thought that my home in Bordeaux was the best place in the world. I could never have imagined leaving it. I thought that was where I would always be, until they came and took my father away. I don't think I ever asked you Gilles, what town are you from? Are you from near Bordeaux?"

"I'm a citizen of the world now, I suppose."

Gilles avoided the question. He wanted to give away nothing that might identify his French family or the circumstances of his exile, although Alain and Gilles shared this very personal experience, of the king's soldiers coming and taking away family members. Alain might be a good man, a man of principles, but the reward for turning Gilles in to the authorities would buy both Alain's freedom and his future, all eight years of his life back and more. It would also attract a fine wife for him in the new country. In short, it was too great a temptation for most men, even if Alain might be able to keep Gilles' secret without a slip of the tongue for a lifetime. Now Gilles searched his memory, wondering if he had ever told Alain his true name or mentioned where exactly in France he was from. He could not remember. If he had divulged personal details of his life, he hoped that Alain would not remember them either.

"Our generation has suffered as no other. We are like the trees, having no choice but to try and survive where we have been planted, even if that happens to be on the side of a rock-faced cliff. Our king took everything we had managed to accumulate in a lifetime, in many lifetimes. He convinced us that to hope for anything more than life is futile and this despair keeps us living on in misery," Alain opined.

"Unlike the trees, we *do* have choices," Gilles said. "The choices may be hard, but we have to insist on growing and flourishing if we can, no matter where we find ourselves. It is, in the end, our best revenge."

Gilles still had plenty of fight left in him, unlike the older man who seemed to be completely broken in spirit.

"You are a young man, Gilles, but for me it's difficult. I have lost my family over and over, and each time it has been at the hands of my own countrymen, at the direction of our own king. Dying or living a miserable life, both give my enemies their victories. I grow so very weary of burying wives and children though."

Alain shook his balding head, then pushed back long wisps of graying hair. He looked over the side of the ship, gazing into the deep waters. Both men were silent for a few moments, and it looked to Gilles as if he was contemplating something, trying to come to a decision on an unknown question. Gilles was struck by the sudden thought that Alain might be planning an escape from his life by jumping over the railing, but then Alain spoke again.

"Each time I think I cannot recover and go on, but maybe I am just too much of a coward to die."

"We survived, even when the king's soldiers attacked," Gilles reminded him. "We have to go on."

"I pretended to be dead and they did not run me through with their swords as they did the rest of my family. I lay there silently, listening to my family and friends as they were murdered, as they were dying. And you, Gilles? How did your family survive?

"My children were not there that day. My wife hid under a stoop."

"Ce n'est pas possible!" Alain replied. "She was working alongside us and you remember the poor homes we had. There were no stoops."

Gilles tried to remember what Elsje had told him. He was certain that was what she said, that she hid under a stoop. He had been separated from her during the attack and it was only later that they talked about the events of that terrible day.

Gilles did not want to talk with Alain any longer: It only made him feel old and more troubled than he was already.

"Alain, it does no good to complain about the voyage we are on. We are here now and must believe that it will take us on to better shores."

Gilles wasn't entirely sure if he believed this himself, but it was all he could think of to say to the man. He wished Alain a good day, telling him that he was going to get out of the hot sun and go below where it might be a little cooler. It was true that there was very little shade on the deck now, and the faint hot breeze did nothing to cool him off or to move the ship along at a faster pace. Gilles went back down the stairs, yielding his position on the deck to a woman who went up to take his place.

The list of people that Gilles was avoiding on the ship was growing, with no place to go and get away from them. This ship was just too small. He might pretend to sleep all the time, for the next days, weeks or months ahead, but then Elsje would certainly inquire constantly about his health. Gilles only hoped that the voyage and his time on the ship would soon come to a merciful end.

The heat on the upper deck was too much for many passengers and Gilles observed that the gray woman had already returned below and was sitting next to her sister, shouting something loud and incomprehensible at her. He didn't see the old woman who was probably relieving herself over in the corner at the chamber pots. Gilles put his head down on the berth, pretending to be tired, covering his ears with his hands and the blanket, trying to shut out the sound of the woman shrieking and his infant daughter. Jacomina was crying incessantly today, and it seemed as though every other infant on the ship was howling too, adding to his misery.

After the meals had been served and the family settled down for the night, Gilles at last started to fall asleep in spite of the continuing noise, heat and unbearable humidity. Thinking about his earlier encounter with his old neighbor, Gilles was somewhat disappointed that Alain could not be taken on as a settler to fulfill the WIC's patroonship contract, but maybe it was for the best. Gilles might not want to have Alain around him at all, for several reasons. What Alain had said to Gilles earlier came back to him as he was falling asleep:

"There were no stoops."

This was true, but at the moment he was very tired, completely overcome with fatigue. He would ask Elsje about that in the morning.

That night Gilles dreamed again of the brightest greens of the springtime fields, of trees and plants coming up through the rich earth of the Netherlands. He dreamed of reds and oranges and yellows, the colors of the tulips that bloomed all over Holland in the spring. Maybe it was not the Netherlands at all, but the new land that he was dreaming about. He was in both places at once in his dream. In his sleep Gilles escaped, leaving behind the dull grays, pale greens and washed-out blues that were the limited colors of his present world. The Pilgrims entered into his dreams with their dark colors of plum, somber blue, and forest green. They disappeared into the distance, and then he dreamed that he saw red and yellow eyes staring at him, stalking him in the darkness, eyes belonging to a creature that was crouched on one of the berths across the way. He woke in fear, waiting for this heart-pounding nightmare to fade so he could regain his composure and go back to sleep, to dream again of the green crops that he hoped were his, of abundance just waiting to be harvested by him somewhere in his future.

he fair weather continued into the next day. When Gilles went back up on the deck, the ship was passed by a school of whales. The whales came up on them fast, moving in a great dark wave all around them, some off the bow of the ship and some astern, for a brief and terrifying time completely surrounding it. Some of the huge creatures came in very close, but they seemed more curious than aggressive, perhaps impatient at encountering a large floating obstacle on their planned route. They passed by for some time, long minutes, with the seamen staying on alert, being too preoccupied with the closeness of the large creatures to bother with ordering passengers below. It was a different world on the open ocean, with nature in control, and those who were uncomfortable with this arrangement were unable to do anything to change it.

The only creatures aboard the ship, other than the human passengers, were the dogs. Except for when they relieved themselves, they were mostly well behaved. This might not have been the case if this ship carried any of the cattle, sheep or horses that were sometimes transported to the colony along with the passengers. Gilles didn't especially like having the dogs around: They were hunting dogs and somewhat of a concern to him. His young son probably presented himself as a type of small game, prey to be hunted, especially if the dogs were now suffering as much boredom from their confinement as the humans. When Gilles thought about one of the dogs, his great teeth showing in the middle of a furry mass of black and brown, he thought about Cardinal Richelieu and the slaughter of so many innocents back in Europe, particularly in the Palatinate and at La Rochelle.

Because Gilles had never seen any representations of the man, this was what he imagined Richelieu to look like, an animal with teeth bared, only distinguished from lower beasts by the red skullcap and red robes he wore. The man's vestments could well have attained this hue from being soaked in the blood of the many whose executions he had ordered.

Animals of any kind, except for the dogs, were far from Gilles' thoughts now. There were many things from his past life on land that were receding from his memory, becoming strange and alien to him with more and more time away from the rest of the world. The endless weeks of isolation on the vessel had nearly erased some of these experiences from his conscious mind, but his dreams sometimes brought them back vividly to him. There were fields of fragrant grass, forests of oak and pine-smelling trees, horse hooves clattering on cobblestones, singing birds and roaring fires on the hearth in wintertime that first warmed, then roasted icy-cold hands and feet. There were the smells of wood smoke, baking bread, freshly plowed dirt and sweet apple blossom petals that drizzled a soft fragrance down on the warm spring earth, the taste of roasted meat and fresh berries with cream. These sights, sounds, smells and tastes were as alive as ever, being experienced by someone somewhere else in the world right now, but the travelers on Den Eyckenboom only experienced these as distant memories or in their dreams. These places had been pushed aside, neglected due to the travelers' barren present reality which was either a long-term residence or a prison sentence, depending upon how they perceived it. Patience was a hard thing to maintain, never Gilles' strong suite, and he wondered if he would ever know these wonderful things again, even as he thought longingly of them and realized that his mouth was watering. Gilles did tell Elsje about his dreams because they were the only new events that happened only to him and had been observed exclusively by him.

That night he dreamed that he heard the thundering hooves of horses in his sleep, a long race that thrilled him as he gripped his saddle atop a great gray beast of a horse. Bets were being made all around them by a number of spectators, and there was a large fortune riding on the outcome. As he rode on through his dream, he was jostled by his fellow riders who seemed to be men, women and children, along with another rider that appeared to be a dog. The track was long and never-ending, but the beast beneath him seemed to know Gilles' thoughts, pouring his heart into the race as they strove together to get to the finish line first.

Before the outcome of the race, Gilles woke to the same noise, but it turned out to be the pounding noise of a rainstorm, the deluge hitting the deck above them. Den Eyckenboom was rolling from side to side, but the motion was not the most notable part of the storm. Lightning flashes could be seen through the small crevasses in the decking over their heads and the small cracks in the sides of the ship, briefly illuminating their quarters before the thunder reverberated through the hold. The lightning was bright enough for Gilles to momentarily see the frightened faces of other passengers who were not sleeping through the storm. Gilles' family slept heavily and peacefully on, nestled under their damp woolen blankets, deep sleep through any commotion being a family trait of this tribe into which Gilles had married. He hoped that the coming day would be sunny and warm enough for them to dry the blankets out on the upper deck so they would not be miserably damp for the next few days or longer. The hours of daylight were already getting noticeably shorter, and soon autumn's sun would not be as strong, but for now it seemed as though this year's summer was going to last forever.

A flash and crack of thunder at nearly the same instant brought with it a downpour of loud curses from the seamen above their heads, along with whimpers and voices raised in prayer from some of those below. The Hendricks family continued to sleep on, old Hendrick's snores echoing through the passenger deck, but Gilles could see his maidservant, Aafje Vander Cloot, sitting up on her bunk, wide awake and as terrified as any of the others.

"It's all right," Gilles said to her. "I have been through storms on ships before, and you are as safe here as you are on land."

Gilles wasn't sure if this was true or not, but her terror would not serve any useful purpose. The winds from the storm whistled through the fissures in the body of the ship and water dripped down from the spaces between the planks over their heads. Gilles heard angry voices of the crew above him, even louder than the noise of the storm as they exchanged shouts.

"How the hell am I supposed to do that?!"

"Do it now! And do it quickly before they rip to pieces or pull us over! You there! You go up too! You just need to keep the ship upright and follow my orders! If we didn't need the extra ballast, I'd throw you overboard myself!"

Apparently one of the sails had come loose and was catching the wind. One sailor had been ordered to climb up to the top of the mast to secure it. The crew moved away from their position near the hatch, to a more remote part of the ship. Gilles could still hear their distant shouts but could make out no further words above the noise of the wind and the pelting rain. The storm passed, taking with it the fear of those who had been awake, allowing them to finally fall back asleep.

When morning came, it was unexpectedly sunny and hot. This only made the hold even more steamy and sticky, with no relief at all from the continuing humidity. This weather was unlike anything Gilles had ever experienced. It was very much like being shut inside a very small kitchen filled with many bubbling cooking pots. He had heard of the extremes of weather and wondered if the summers and autumns in New Amsterdam would all be like this one. If this was so, then raising their food, grapes and tobacco would be easy, just as long as the heavy rains didn't damage or destroy the crops. Perhaps the new world really was like Africa. Gilles had heard that it was as hot as a bake oven in summer, but what about the stories he had heard regarding the winters, that they were colder than a Norseman's grave with the snow covering dwellings up to the rooftops? Maybe the tales about the winter were just that, and it was always hot there, all year long.

While Gilles was taking his allotted time on the deck a few hours later, Elsje joined him, bringing up the blankets for him to dry out. Gilles was telling his wife about the storm that she and the rest of the family had slept through when another great migration of whales approached. As they stood watching the creatures' determined progress, Elsje clung to Gilles, the tension in her body transmitted in waves of fear to him. He smiled, having seen the same spectacle the day before, sure in the knowledge that it would be resolved in the same way, with the giant creatures continuing on their way without incident, leaving the passengers awestruck but safe. This was exactly what did happen, but as Gilles looked out beyond them, it was then that he first saw the unusual clouds and pointed them out to Elsje.

"Do those clouds look different to you?" he asked.

"Different than what? They are just clouds. The sky here is a beautiful color! I'd like a dress in that color blue."

"It looks somehow to be between gold and lavender."

"I think your eyes deceive you! It *is* pretty though."

They both watched the clouds for a few moments in silence, each alone in their thoughts, with the weather very calm now, a great contrast to the winds and rain of the night before. With very little wind once again, the seamen now cursed the calm instead of the rain. It seemed they were always cursing the weather, no matter what it was. Gilles decided that just for today, because they were not going to be arriving anywhere before nightfall, he would try to be patient and appreciate a beautiful day on board a great ship. For now, he would enjoy the luxury of the time he had left on the ocean, to daydream and be away from the hard labor that was sure to be his future when they reached land. There would be years of toil ahead of him, in the fields and in the West India office. Who knew if this might be the last sea voyage of his lifetime? He needed to try and enjoy all of his remaining days on the sea and tamp down his simmering impatience.

"You there! Your time is up! Go below so someone else can have a turn!" a man shouted up at Gilles from the open hatch.

"I'll go below," Elsje volunteered. "I don't care for it much up here, seeing the wide ocean and always having to keep watch for the sea monsters."

"You! Come below!" the man shouted again, pointing his finger at Gilles.

"I am going below now and you can go in my place, but first you need to get out of my way and let me pass!" Elsje shouted back at him.

Gilles shook his head and smiled as the man hastily retreated from Gilles' fearsome wife.

Gilles spread the wet wool blankets out as best he could where they would not be in the way of the crew. As he watched, the line of clouds, looking like a row of freshly raked hay on an open field, was moved across the sky by a slight breeze. Puzzling over the strange clouds in the sky, he wondered what omen it portended. The wind only lasted for about fifteen minutes before it died down again, just as suddenly as it had come up, but a short time later the strange clouds returned and changed again. What at first looked like a straight line across the sky in the distance became a great thin curved line, stretching nearly from horizon to horizon. There were definitely some wonders in the world that he had not seen before, and he hoped it was an augury of a good harvest, that he was seeing long rows of hay in the fields to feed the animals he would someday house in his future barn.

Gilles only went below when the first meal was served, taking the blankets back with him so no one would steal them, and eating as quickly as possible so he would be able to return to the upper deck afterwards. It was then that he saw a second thin band of clouds appear behind the first. A circling, wheeling effect of the most recent clouds on the horizon made some of the passengers on the deck point at it. They speculated among themselves as to what kind of a sign it was that reminded them of the windmills back in the Netherlands. Surely it was a good sign, that they were heading into peace and prosperity, the windmills portending ground grain aplenty. The feathery clouds up high reminded Gilles of the wings of young birds, all fluff and delicacy, not very good for flying, but with the promise of great heights to soar to later in their lives, when the birds were mature and their wings were fully developed.

Although it had been humid when Gilles was up on the deck earlier, there had been some relief up in the fresh air. Now it was suddenly much warmer, uncomfortable there, even with the slight breeze. The seamen exchanged quiet comments among themselves as they gestured toward the clouds, and Gilles wondered what could have suddenly taken their interest. Certainly they had neither the leisure time nor the intellectual refinement for admiring the beauty of nature. Among the travelers on the open deck there was renewed debate as to how much warmer or cooler it was likely to be in New Amsterdam as compared to the old Amsterdam, but especially so at this time of year with the winter months approaching. They all wondered whether the new land would be good for growing the crops that each man hoped to grow. Which crops could be grown at all depended not just upon the weather, but also the soil, the duration of the winters and when farmers would be able to first work the ground in the spring.

Andries Claesen only talked about wheat, both winter wheat and spring wheat. He cornered other men on the upper deck, always starting the conversation by saying he had heard that winter wheat grew very well in New Amsterdam, with ideal weather and soil, and then he would ask if his fellow travelers had heard the same. Tyler Tunisen and Samuel Luyster, two single men, had lived for a time in the southernmost English colonies. As Gilles listened in on their conversation, he learned that they were very knowledgeable about tropical crops including indigo, rice and sugar. They mainly talked about getting some land so they could grow a cash crop of tobacco. The two men spoke alternately in Dutch, English, and another language that had echoes of English, but was completely unlike anything Gilles had ever heard before. When the words suited the conversation, the two men switched languages, changing direction together as easily as playful colts running in a wide-open field. Gilles listened intently to their conversation, but the two swarthy men seemed to have a language of their own. For the moment Gilles was content to just listen in, but he decided he would seek the men out later, either during the rest of the voyage or after they arrived at their destination, to learn all that he could from them. He might even be able to talk them into working his patroonship for a time, helping Gilles to meet his quota.

Behind the chatter of the passengers though, Gilles couldn't help noticing that the crew was engaged in a very private discussion among themselves. He worried about mutiny at first, but then he remembered that they had started talking in whispers just after the appearance of the second set of clouds. Maybe they were wondering where the winds were that should be accompanying those clouds and how much longer it was going to take them to get there.

Gilles slept that night, but it was a hot, sweaty, fitful sleep, his clothes drenched in stale sweat and his hair matting at the nape of his neck. When he dreamed, it was of cool waters to wade in and a full bath he had once, an unknown thing in most of the world unless one counted the children swimming in the canals of old Amsterdam on rare hot days. Thinking back on this, it had been a pleasant sensation to immerse himself totally in the water and no serious illness or imbalance of humors had come of it afterwards.

The next day brought change, but it was not a change that Gilles welcomed. It was one of the most difficult days of the voyage with the dogs howling, the babies all crying and Bruinje tearfully complaining about his ears hurting. Anxious to escape the din, Gilles had the further bad luck of having to wait impatiently for others to go to the upper deck and a few of them to come back down before he could escape the noise. When he finally made it up to his sanctuary in the afternoon, there was little relief from the heat, but at least he had the distraction of watching as two great arms of cloud spiraled overhead, moving too slowly for him to see any movement at first, but then changing visibly as he continued watching the sky. When the sunset came, it was glorious, like those on hot summer evenings in France, with a gentle warm breeze coming across the ocean.

Gilles couldn't go to sleep that night at all, and discovering that the hatch had been left unsecured, he crept up onto the open deck, even though he knew that passengers were not permitted up there except during certain specified times during the day. The seamen had become familiar with Gilles though, had learned that he understood a little something about the sea and knew enough about what their jobs entailed to stay out of their way. Possibly because the shipmaster was already in his quarters and they wanted no disturbance to bring him out again, the crew didn't bother to send Gilles back down below.

Gilles looked up at the sails that seemed to glow in the dark, although they were only catching the reflected light from the heavens along with the evening breeze. Different layers of clouds raced across the sky, past the fixed backdrop of the stars and a waxing moon. The clouds appeared to move in opposite directions, depending upon their rank and position in the sky. He couldn't really tell, but he hoped that the ship was moving as quickly as the clouds and in the right direction.

"Big storm coming!" one sailor remarked to him.

"Ja? Enough to get us there faster?" Gilles asked.

The man did not answer but moved off to join the rest of the crew, all of them now busily trying to take advantage of the new and stronger tailwinds. Gilles worried now that they might be blown off course, landing where he didn't want to be, far to the north of New Netherland, on the very shores of New France where he could be recognized, arrested, and executed on the spot. He put that thought out of his mind quickly, telling himself that this was a ridiculous thought: The men who hunted him would have no idea of what he looked like, even if they knew who they might be looking for. A few years ago, he had been a boy, living very far away from his present location on the face of the earth. Now he was a family man, fuller of body and with a beard he had never grown in France, couldn't have grown at that age.

At last his mind slowed down and stepped into pace with his weary body as the desire to sleep came over him. He took a last look around and bid the world above a good evening before he made his way back down to his berth. Descending into the darkness below, he was a blind man gripping the railing on the side of the steps until his feet finally found firm footing on the solid planking of the deck below. Even then he had to stop for a few moments, letting his eyes adjust a little more so he could make his way back to his bunk without walking directly into any solid objects.

Gilles woke briefly during the night, hearing the sound of rain, and went back to sleep knowing that the passengers would probably not be allowed outside at all the next day. The seamen who brought them their first meal of the day brought it a little earlier than usual, admonishing the passengers to finish quickly and make ready for a storm that was coming. No one below had taken much heed to the warning. They had just grumbled about the dampness, the food, and having to stay down below.

Peering out though a crack in the side of the ship that appeared to get a little larger every day, Gilles observed that some of the clouds in the distance looked like gray spider webs now, wisping down to the surface of the water. In the sky beyond these were rolling gray rows of clouds that moved and changed, building up higher and higher into stacks of dark and moldy-looking mountains in the sky. Gilles returned to his family, settling in wearily for a dull rainy day below deck with his fellow passengers. He hoped that the storm might cool and freshen the air. Maybe it would even move them along at a faster pace now that the wind was picking up. The travelers took up their respective pastimes, told stories, compared notes on their children, and did what they usually did to pass another day.

As the rainy day wore on, Gilles' attention was drawn more and more from thoughts of his grand future plans to the storm outside, and he was finally given to understand that this thunderstorm was no ordinary tempest. He even thought that he heard the wind suddenly change direction, but that couldn't be right. When the heavy rains started, they lasted for about a half hour, splattering on the deck above their heads and then ceasing for a time, only to start up again with more intensity. Gilles could hear the power of the wind increasing with each new round of dousing rain as it hit the boards over their heads and the sides of the vessel, increasing in strength until it hammered the ship, the sound like a hundred carpenters working across the hull and upper deck all at once. Gilles could also sense a struggle playing out above them. He knew that the crew was trying to work with the power of the storm instead of fighting the great energy that was being directed against them, turning the ship first one way and then another in an attempt to safely ride it out. He could hear some of the wooden beams of the ship creaking from the force of the wind and the water. Gilles couldn't imagine being one of the seamen now, perhaps having to climb the masts and walk the footropes that were far, far above the deck of the ship below them. Even worse, a sailor might climb up there only to have a line of sight looking straight down into the roiling sea as the vessel pitched and tossed back and forth.

Unfortunately, it was daytime now, or it would have been if the skies weren't so dark. None of the passengers were sleeping; they were all wide awake. Gilles looked over at his family who sat immobilized with fear, Hendrick with his mouth set grimly, clutching the side of his bunk, Aafje Vander Cloot holding Bruinje, but looking as though she was just barely suppressing a scream, and the two teenagers, Heintje and Corretje, huddled together next to her, shivering, even in the heat. Elsje sat quietly, rocking the baby, but her eyes were big and round, with a fear in them that Gilles had never seen before. Her eyes met Gilles', as if to ask if everything was going to be all right. He gave her a nod and a small smile of reassurance, the best he could muster. He wished he had some way to ease his own fear, to understand what was going on and to make sense out of what he heard happening outside. He wiped the sweat from his face on his sleeve and felt trickles of it running down his chest and his back.

A brief period of calm outside started to convince Gilles that maybe he had overreacted. It was embarrassing really, silly of him to have been worried. He had been acting like a small child without any good reason for his fear. The storm was certainly abating if it was not passing over completely. The other passengers started murmuring among themselves, commenting that it had been quite a storm, and those who could see it were telling the others about the blue sky they could see through the cracks in the side walls.

Unfortunately, this brief peace did not last. It disappeared quickly as a new wave of rain and wind assaulted the ship, and many of the voyagers exclaimed aloud at the renewed ferocity of it. The storm leveled off again, but once more this was only for a short time. The storm's power rose and died several more times, and any temporary hope that it was finished was soon lost in fresh attacks on the ship. Each new wave of wind and rain was more punishing than the last and stayed longer. After several hours of this heavy rain, Gilles decided that he had never heard so much rain fall out of the sky in one storm. He thought of the great biblical flood and wondered if this enormous amount of rain was being dropped on the land now, as well as on the sea. Perhaps it would wash away the entire settlement before they arrived.

The winds continued to shift and change with mercurial speed. Gilles knew that the master would have long before ordered all of the sails in as the crew struggled to keep the ship upright. The sailors were using only the rudder to steer the ship, and they might have already secured themselves to the masts to avoid being swept overboard by great waves that were taller than most buildings. Occasionally Gilles could hear objects that had broken loose sliding or rolling across the upper deck over their heads.

Then Gilles heard an odd thing: The wind seemed to surround them, encircling the ship completely. The only thing his mind could fix upon was the biblical story of a pillar of fire, a whirlwind of flame. If there was such a force out there, it was one of water, not one of fire. It puzzled him and terrified him at the same time, and now Gilles was convinced that there was something supernatural about this storm. He hoped it was a divine presence that was protecting them and not an attacking demon that was encompassing the ship. There was no longer any lull in the storm at all. The wind grew stronger, howling louder than any noise Gilles had ever heard before. Annatje Pieterse cried out that it was the roar of the sea monsters they were hearing, coming up from the bottom of the sea to eat them.

Den Eyckenboom climbed high atop mountainous waves, one peak at a time, and then dropped off the cliff edge of each one, slamming down onto the hard water below as the passengers tried not to be beaten black and blue inside the wooden crate of their ship. With each wave the ship pitched over, nearly to her beam ends, as the ocean surged beneath one side of the ship and then the other, not pausing for any period of time beneath the true flooring of the vessel. Den Eyckenboom groaned and creaked, protesting that the strain was too much for a solid object to bear and threatened to come apart at the seams. The force of the waves, the shearing of the winds and the hammering of the rainwater hit the ship with a relentless assault. The ship's rocking motion continued to wind up as she listed hard to one side before wrenching back to the other, each time promising to go over completely while the passengers inside clung to the posts at the corners of the berths and to anything else that seemed to be a permanent part of the vessel. Water from the stormy seas invaded every crack in the ship. With each wave, sea water also gushed down from the hatchway in spite of the solid cover that had been secured earlier, before the storm had reached the apex of its strength.

Now it was obvious that there would be no time for anyone to escape up the narrow stairs if the ship went over, even if the hatch had not been battened down from the outside. They would all be drowned, and every last one of them would be trapped under the deck. They had little choice now except to join fates with that of the ship, to pray, and ultimately to just accept whatever it was that was coming. From the dark recesses of the ship, Gilles could almost see the ocean throwing sharp needles of salt water at the crew, inflicting pain on even the most weather-hardened faces and calloused hands of the seamen who were working so hard to save the ship and their own lives. He knew there must be a very large quantity of water washing across the open deck above, too much for it to drain out through the scuppers where the flooring of the upper deck met the low side walls. He could hear the unimpeded wash of great waves over the upper deck of the ship, right over his head, with each roll of the ship. A flash of green light outside invaded their chamber, and Gilles could make no sense at all of what that might be.

The storm was one continuous fury now. Those passengers that did not openly cry or whimper sat ashen-faced, clinging to the insides of the ship and to their families, many in prayer, each certainly contemplating the heaven or hell they expected to be entering very soon and just hoping that the end would be swift when it came. One man, a few berths over from Gilles, suddenly cried out as if in great pain, ran to the stairs, and climbing to the hatch, held on to the railing with one hand while he pounded on the hatch with the other, crying out for the crew to open it up, to let them out so they might survive by clinging to the ship's wreckage after it went down. The noise of the storm was too loud for anyone up there to hear him, and his only reply was the roaring wind and the driving rain.

"They have all been killed up there, washed overboard, and we are here, forgotten and trapped!" he screamed, beating even harder on the hatch until his hand was bloodied.

There was still no response from up above, and no one from below joined him because they were all too busy holding on. Gilles hoped the man was mistaken in his assessment, that the crew had not all been washed overboard, leaving the travelers alone, helpless and trapped inside the ship. A loud rumbling noise came from overhead, and Gilles knew that one of the hogsheads had broken loose and was rolling across the deck. If it was empty, it was dangerous enough, but if it was still full of anything, it was a terrible weapon, capable of easily killing a man or two in its path or seriously damaging the ship.

Though the darkness still surrounded him, his eyes had become accustomed to it, and now Gilles could see that there were some significant injuries among his fellow passengers. Cuts and bruises were already in evidence and he knew there were almost certainly some broken bones. They could not tend to any injuries though, not yet, because they could not safely release their grips on the individual moorings they clung to. There were howls and cries of fear and pain that were coming from human throats, but they were more animal-like in their tone. As the ship wrenched over to the opposite side once more, the man who had been pounding on the hatch lost his grip on the railing and was thrown down the stairs by the force of it. He was left lying at the foot of the steps, not moving.

Gilles sat with one hand securing himself to one of their bunk's posts and the other wrapped around his wife and infant daughter. Elsje held baby Jacomina tightly to her with one arm and clung to another post with her free hand. The family had now gathered together on two berths instead of three. Hendrick, Heintje, Corretje and Aafje were on the berth closest to Gilles and Elsje, holding tightly to the corner posts and each other, encircling a sobbing Bruinje. Gilles tried to seem protective but not fearful, as if he might have experienced something like this before, as if he possessed the sure and certain knowledge that it was absolutely going to be all right for every one of them. He knew that Elsje could feel his fear, and could probably feel him shaking, but she followed his lead of bravery for the sake of her family. She just pressed her lips together in silence, suppressing everything, questions, cries, or any other utterances.

The ship was still on her beam-ends, almost completely on her side with each roll of the waves, and Gilles waited for it to capsize, for them to be done with this mental agony and their imminent death to be over. Time was lost to him as the storm continued for too long while the unconscious man's body at the foot of the stairs slid back and forth along the flooring with each new wave. Possibly in answer to their prayers though, the winds suddenly subsided and Gilles could see light outside. The clouds had parted, as if some heavenly force had forcefully drawn back a great black curtain. At last, they could hear the reassuring sound of shouts and footsteps above their heads. To their astonishment, those passengers closest to the cracks in the side of the ship called out to the others that they saw a miraculous circle of clear blue sky and calm above them. A few passengers ran over to see for themselves and confirm that they were indeed inside a heavenly ring of protection. Cautiously, Gilles let go of the post and hastily looked over his family as Elsje did the same, even as her crying baby continued to flail in her arms. Several passengers went to relieve themselves after the long ordeal, but it was too late for some, including Bruinje, who had quickly extricated himself from his caretakers to join his infant sister on his mother's lap.

The ship continued to rock back and forth while her momentum from the storm began to unwind. Water that had seeped in from every opening had joined forces with loose debris inside the ship. This inner flood continued to surge at their feet, traveling from one side of the vessel to the other, like some great running and searching animal, while the ship gradually slowed its motion. The mucky water was seeping down through the cracks from the middle passenger deck into the cargo hold below, and it was quite possible that the food, supplies bound for New Amsterdam and their personal belongings were all ruined.

"God has delivered us!" Barent Van Gelder cried, tears of gratitude running down his face. The travelers started to tend to their wounds, many of them falling to their knees to give thanks first. Elsje put Jacomina to her breast, soothed Bruinje by stroking his hair briefly and then handed him back to Corretje. With her baby still cradled in her arm, she went over to check on the man who was lying at the foot of the steps.

"Gilles! Help me get him to his bed!"

Before Gilles could get to her, two other men jumped up in response to Elsje's plea for help, carrying the man to his berth where his two young sons sat crying inconsolably.

The English physician, Marbury, with his wife accompanying him, went over to the injured man.

"Can you help him?" Elsje asked.

Mr. Marbury gave no immediate answer but examined the man from his toes to his head, feeling the bones and prodding the man's stomach and chest. Marbury's wife watched silently, familiar with this procedure it seemed, waiting, and Elsje followed her lead. Gilles did not want to be involved in any way with this; he had nothing to contribute, no skills or knowledge when it came to healing, so he was happy to stand back while others did what they could for the man. The examination seemed routine until the physician reached the man's neck and head. Marbury shifted his position, feeling behind the man's neck, then across his skull, finally pulling up one of the injured man's limp eyelids. The man was not making any sounds, nor were his children, who watched in silent terror with tears still streaming down their cheeks.

"Let him sleep, as much as he can," Marbury said to the man's sons.

"We can get the master and see if he has any aqua vitae," Elsje offered.

"Nee, best to let him sleep. I will check on him later."

"Do you want to come over with us, to let your father sleep?" Elsje asked the man's children.

Still crying though, the boys clung to each other, the older one shaking his head in rejection of her offer. Gilles and Elsje started to return to their own family, but as soon as Elsje had turned her back, Gilles observed the unmistakable private look Marbury gave to his wife along with the small shake of his head.

Marbury looked over some of the others, although it was not really his responsibility, and Gilles was impressed by his concern for his fellow passengers. Some refused his care, perhaps being well enough that a bandage and some time would suffice to heal them, and others possibly because he was an Englishman, their medical science known to be greatly inferior to that of the Netherlands.

Unfortunately, the physician did not have enough time to complete his examinations. The short-lived thanksgiving was abruptly ended by the storm turning around and coming back to finish them off, a murderous predator that refused to leave its prey just wounded, not leaving them alone until it was certain they were all dead. Some unsuspecting passengers were caught off guard by the sudden return of the storm. They were thrown to the floor, acquiring new bruises and cuts. Children that had just started to quiet were now screaming and crying at the top of their lungs again. The sound of this hysteria was soon drowned out in the renewed roaring of the wind and pouring rain.

In the suddenly returned darkness, with the hatch still tightly shut, Gilles heard the terrifying sound of water as it continued to pour in with each new wave that covered the ship. The water inside the ship still sloshed from side to side, the air hot and sticky, as well as putrid from the spilled contents of the chamber pots. The dogs had stopped whimpering or howling and just cowered in fear, standing in the filthy waters at the feet of their masters.

Gilles could feel that the ship was riding lower in the water. He wasn't sure how much more water the ship could take on before they would ride low enough for the ocean to reach the less seaworthy portions of the vessel, the old gun ports or maybe even the overhead hatch. He had heard it said that these great storms occasionally lasted for as long as several days, and now he knew that he had started to rejoice a little too prematurely. He had to acknowledge that death was still very much a possibility, and he wondered again if this was what all of the rain storms were like in the new land.

His mind flashed back to a time in the German Palatinate when his cowardice had nearly cost his wife and his children their lives, when he had run away from danger to save himself. This was not going to happen again, and it was not just because he was locked inside the ship with no escape. Surviving that past experience had forced Gilles to examine his soul. He had decided that he would stay and protect his family if he was ever faced with such a situation again, even if it meant losing his own life. His vow had been made in the peaceful aftermath of that past crisis, but

Gilles didn't believe his oath would be put to this great a test so soon. If they were all going to die anyway, he hoped they would die quickly and without the fearful expectation of what was coming. He tried not to think about water slowly filling the compartment, all the way up to the ceiling.

He silently said some Hail Marys so his family and the other passengers, protestants to a man Gilles believed, would not hear him. It was the supplication of his childhood, an appeal to the magic of an all-powerful and protective Father that he had been told could accomplish anything. Unfortunately, his experiences in life had left him uncertain as to which power was stronger, good or evil. He had seen the powerlessness of his own father who had ruled over his own petty kingdom but had come up against an even greater power, the power of evil that was personified in the French king and in Cardinal Richelieu. It was ironic that both despots, king and cardinal, purported to represent the benevolence of God on earth. Gilles knew that his wife must be praying now. He had never discussed his religious convictions with his wife, because he believed that women were just inclined that way naturally, his mother having a deep belief in her Catholic faith and his wife an unshakable trust in her protestant god. He wondered now if they were one in the same or different gods. He wondered which one of them was the god of storms.

A loud cracking noise preceded a thunderous blast, like a cannon ball hitting the upper deck or perhaps a large tree shaking the ground as it was felled, sending the shock through the ship and interrupting Gilles' ecclesiastical thoughts. The explosion of noise was immediately followed by loud shrieks and screams from the passengers.

"Gilles! What is happening?" Elsje cried out to him, unable to keep silent any longer.

"I don't know, but the sides of the ship hold fast! That is all we need to get us through," Gilles shouted back to her, although he was fairly certain they had just been dismasted.

If they had lost the main mast, they could be in serious navigational trouble, even if they somehow survived the storm. Drifting in the ocean for weeks or months could mean death from thirst or starvation. Instead of decreasing, now the possibilities of terrible fates and painful endings to their lives only seemed to be increasing.

"I have heard the Spaniards in our tavern at home tell of such storms!

They called them *oricans*, but I thought it was just a tale!" Elsje shouted above the din.

"The crew will know how to ride it out and bring us through. The sailors lived to tell their stories, and so will we," Gilles replied.

"How long will it last? I've heard they can last for weeks!"

"Now that is surely an exaggeration," Gilles called back to her, wishing she had not heard the same tales he had heard. "How are the children?"

"They seem all right. Jacomina holds on for dear life, hasn't stopped crying and wants to nurse, but this is not the time! She still pulls at her ears and so does Bruinje. The noise hurts them."

Bruinje still whimpered, even with his thumb in his mouth. He kept his face buried in Corretje's lap while Aafje held fast to the child, perhaps as much to comfort herself as to protect the little boy. Gilles attempted to keep up his outward show of bravery, taking several deep breaths, trying to slow the rate of his pounding heart. His family did appear to draw strength from his resolve and from Elsje's brave attempts as well, but many of the other passengers continued to wail and pray out loud for God to save them. Looking around, Gilles' eyes fell on the old gun ports. They were not keeping very much water out. It occurred to him now that he might be able to smash through one of them to escape if the ship started to go down. He looked around to see if there were any tools besides his feet that might help him to accomplish this and which men might be enlisted in the endeavor.

As Gilles was contemplating this and other options, he wondered if he was becoming accustomed to the rages of the storm or if it really was calmer in some way, with less violence outside. He could faintly hear frantic movements and cries of the seamen above them, but now there seemed to be more repetitive movements and fewer panicked shouts. Did he imagine that there was also somewhat less of a drop of the ship after each new hilly wave was climbed, crested, and then fell suddenly away beneath them?

Before very much longer though, it was apparent that the storm was dying down. The cyclical waves of wind and water continued, but they were ebbing. Some passengers were now able to feel the sickness of motion instead of the sickness of fear, and a few tried to maintain their footing while slowly creeping over toward the large earthenware containers that were able to serve their purpose once more. The containers had been secured but still had given up most of their contents in the storm. The smell was carried throughout the ship, in the air and on the sloshing waters. The passengers dry heaved into them, their emptied stomachs having little to offer because no food had come down to them during the day. There would probably be fights that would break out later between passengers who wanted to go up or stay up on the open deck while the crew attempted to drain, clean and air out the lower compartments. Few travelers would want to stay below, but the crew wouldn't be able to get their regular work done or complete the many repairs that they were certain to need.

Marytje DeWitt, ever polite and considerate of her fellow passengers, waited almost until the end of the storm to inform her husband that she could wait no longer, the child she carried was on the way. He called out to the other women on the ship, seeking their help for the delivery. Peeling Bruinje from her leg and remanding him over to her husband's care this time, Elsje was then able to hand the baby to Corretje and go over to see how she might help Marytje. Gilles wondered why their servant girl wasn't asked to go with her or to hold Jacomina, but when he looked closer at the girl's face, he saw that she was incapable of helping. She was still in shock from the fearful storm and was still struggling to bring her attention back to the present reality that the storm was at last, finally ending.

"It's all right now," he whispered over to the girl, but judging from her lack of response, he doubted that she believed him.

Even after several years of marriage, Gilles still couldn't get used to his wife's jumping right in whenever there was anything to be done, any injured person, any hungry wanderer, any lost child, or any soul in need of direction. He also couldn't get used to the Dutch men being expected to care for children. It was not that way in the rest of the world and certainly not in France. Gilles remembered hearing that it was a public event in France whenever the nation's queen gave birth. In France, the doors of the palace were opened and everyone came, bringing their lunch with them as they watched, elbowing their way up to the front of the crowd in the royal bedroom to get a better view.

The passengers were still taking stock of their injuries when there was a pounding noise on the hatch cover that capped the frame at the top of the ladder. The crewmen were trying to open the hatch but were having some difficulty due to the sodden and swollen wood. After a few more minutes of effort, the cover was finally pried open. Two of the ship's crew provided the passengers with biscuits, cold salt beef, herring and ale. It was the first food they had since their hasty meal early that morning.

"What news have you?" one of the men asked the sailors. "Will we sink?"

"We won't sink. We are busy making repairs."

"Where are we now? Are we closer or lost?" another man demanded.

"Why is the food cold?" another woman wanted to know.

"The fire is out so there won't be any warm food for now."

"When can we go up again?"

"My son is bleeding, we need help!"

"We have no physician. You'll have to do the best you can."

"We will manage," Marbury interjected.

"You down there! Enough talking! We need you up here! Do your job, get them fed and hurry back!" the master called down to his men. He was definitely not in the mood to allow any leisurely conversations his crew might have with the passengers.

Marbury first examined the boy who had a deep gash across his forehead. He smiled at the child and his parents.

"It's not so bad. There is much blood, but once the bleeding stops, he will be fine. He'll have a nice scar though, something to tell his grandchildren about. We'll need some bandages for it."

The boy's mother quickly tore a long strip from her dress and handed it to Marbury who wrapped it around the child's head. While the two crew members finished passing out the food and Marbury was making his rounds, the ship's carpenter came down the steps and looked around, examining quickly, but thoroughly, every inch of the ship. Gilles knew that he was checking for any serious damage, and he was relieved to see what he thought was a miniscule look of relief on the man's face. The carpenter then opened the hatch by the foot of the stairs and proceeded to the lowest deck, continuing on to check the condition of the vessel down there. Gilles prayed for the same results, knowing that they really had no option besides keeping the vessel afloat. It was now almost entirely up to the ship's carpenter to get them through the rest of the journey. There were no ports that could make repairs in the middle of the great ocean, and it was doubtful that there would be any other ships nearby that were capable of rendering aid. Drained from their exhausting experience, the travelers all eventually found sleep after the day's terror that followed most of them into their dreams that night.

The next morning another cold meal was served, along with buckets of water so they could bathe.

"Has the navigator determined where we are yet?" Gilles asked the sailor.

"Not yet," the man replied.

Gilles just hoped they had not been blown back to the Netherlands or somewhere even worse, like the African coast or New France.

"When can we go up?"

"We'll let you know."

They did not see the deck that day though, and the only interruption to the day's routine was when two sailors came down to remove the body of the man who had finally died after his attempt to escape the ship during the storm. His two children were allowed on the upper deck while the master said a prayer over the body. Gilles heard the splash as he was thrown overboard, then thought he heard the corpse bumping into the ship all day long, but perhaps it was only his imagination. Elsje went over to the man's children and put her arms around them, urging them to join the family whenever they wanted to, but the boys stayed where they were, clinging to each other. Even at this young age, they knew what their future held: As orphans, they would be indentured out and might well be separated from each other for the rest of their lives.

All day long there had been noisy banging, hammering, sawing, and the sound of objects being dragged across the upper deck. There was also the sound of some great labor ending with a splash that was so loud and so forceful that it rocked the ship. The activity above their heads had only paused for the fast funeral and then continued into the evening with the air still hanging damp and heavy around them, still thickly saturated with heat and moisture. With night upon them once again, the great storm was already receding into memory as something that perhaps could not really have been as bad as they recalled, although there was physical proof to the contrary. There were many injuries among the passengers, including a few broken bones. Gilles and his family fared better than most, although old

Hendrick had a large red and purple bruise on his cheek from connecting with a post, Bruinje had some bruises on one leg and Aafje Vander Cloot had a long wooden splinter embedded in her hand.

At the end of the day, the passengers were mostly able to sleep, even in the suffocating heat. They were still very tired from their long and nerve-wracking ordeal the day before. It wasn't until the following evening, in the last hour of daylight, when darkness was coming upon them once again, that the master of the ship ordered the hatch opened. He went down below, looking around at all the passengers and taking note of their conditions. Marytje DeWitt slept, the child she bore having been stillborn and already buried at sea, but others were still awake. The master inquired quietly as to their conditions, an unusual and uncommonly kind gesture for the master of a vessel. He urged the travelers to get some sleep and told them that there would be better food the next day when they found more of what could be salvaged.

Gilles watched as the master went back up the steps through the hatch, probably heading to his tiny cabin to complete his log entries regarding the day's activities, the ship's progress, passenger injuries and completed repairs. Not one to miss an opportunity though, Gilles quickly and quietly followed him up into the fresh air. The crew, perhaps thinking that Gilles accompanied the master or being too tired to care about his being there, said nothing to him.

Now Gilles observed a few new wooden patches and other changes around the deck, the most striking being a great open space where one of the masts had been, with only a great stump where it had once stood like a tall and sheltering tree. Gilles stayed there for a few minutes, taking in the fresh air and marveling at the peace, calm, and reassurance of an ages-old phenomenon, the moon rising up out of the water into the night sky. The navigator was there with his compass and sunstone out, but now the evening sky had darkened enough for him to locate the first stars. Under the guidance of the heavens, he was now able to direct the crew back onto the watery path that was invisible to men who did not possess his type of clairvoyance. Gilles didn't approach him tonight, but listened in on the mates' subdued conversations, learning that Den Eyckenboom was to make her first stop in the English Massachusetts Bay Colony. They had probably planned to stop there anyway, to resupply before the final leg of the journey, but it was all the more urgent now due to the ravages of the storm. It was hoped that they would get a friendly and charitable reception there and not be turned away, or worse, seized by enemy privateers in the service of the English king.

Gilles knew that most of the WIC's shipmasters didn't want to admit, much less make it known, that they were dealing with the English people of Massachusetts Bay at all, but now there was definitely a good reason. Trade was going on between them, no matter what the official positions of both governments had been. There was puffery and posturing, declarations of no trade allowed, promises of no trade being done, all meaning nothing. The merchants and the shipmasters would do as they wished, just as long as it was safe and profitable. The nineteen gentlemen on the board of the WIC could pass as many laws and rules as they pleased when they were back home in the comfort of their opulent offices, but when a commodity was needed and someone on this side of the ocean had it, who was to say what deals could or could not be made?

The relationship between this English colony and the Dutch had been rocky over the past few years. The belligerent English had enough disagreements among themselves, leading to many of their own colonists relocating to other places, either by choice or after expulsion. The church-affiliated authorities ran their settlement with a severity that they took great pride in. Sometimes these runaways only went as far as the English Plymouth Bay or Rhode Island colonies, taking their rebellious non-conformity with them, but at other times they removed themselves all the way to the greater freedoms of Dutch-claimed territory. On rare occasions these wanderers even ventured as far as the wilderness, trusting in the benevolence of the Indians and the wild animals more than in that of their own kind. Although the local English authorities were often quite happy to be rid of these troublemakers, they certainly perceived these actions as affronts, a rejection of their authority, their ideals, and often, of God.

Massachusetts Bay and the growing settlement of Boston were not in any danger of disappearing from the map; in fact, they were thriving. With over 1,200 people living there, they had a good supply of provisions available for consumption and some excess for trade. This abundance might have been due in part to the good relations they had with the church and financial backers in their home country, especially with those whose misty eyes were filled with the vision of a shining city of Christianity on a hill. The colony worked to keep this illusion alive, staying in dutiful contact with the clinging mother country that had given birth to it. The English colonists did their part, spreading the gospel as far as they could across the new continent, their main doctrine being that their way to salvation was the only way. As long as the Dutch shipmaster had something to trade other than English Bibles, hard cash preferred, Den Eyckenboom would probably be able to successfully negotiate for fresh supplies.

Many of the other colonies up and down the coast, filled with settlers who were the angry, disinherited bastard children of their mother countries, were having a difficult time feeding their own and might be unable or unwilling to trade. If Den Eyckenboom had been blown too far off course by the storm, the master would have to make a decision as to whether they should chance putting in to a port where the reception might be uncertain. It was always possible that the ship, cargo, and passengers could be seized and claimed for any purpose at all, and the captors would do as they wished with Den Eyckenboom. The master would have to decide ahead of time whether the need for food and repairs warranted any contact at all with those barbarians. At least in Massachusetts Bay, he could always make an appeal based upon Christian charity. Just as long as it was safe, Gilles wouldn't mind another stop. This might be his last chance to see more of the new continent before family obligations tied him forever to the land, keeping him from going back to sea. He was not as eager to travel across this savaging ocean as he had once been, not after his recent experience with the great storm.

The night air was still very warm, but Gilles breathed in deeply, taking the salt freshness into his lungs as far as possible before he had to return to the putrid air below. He knew he should be going down to get some sleep, but his legs were not taking him there, not yet. He wouldn't consider the possibility that the ship might have lost all of the distance it had gained and been blown back to where the journey started. It was painful to think they might have to do this voyage all over again from the first day out. He quickly pushed that thought out of his mind, feeling a weariness creeping into his bones that surprised him. He wondered if this was what growing old felt like. He had escaped death three times in his life and he wondered if he was granted any limited number of chances at survival before his luck ran out.

Now the sky was awash in milky starlight, presided over by a half moon. The ocean flashed white light on the surface of the waves, reflecting the moonlight and starlight back in pulsations to the sky. Beneath the ship the waters were black, veiled, and unfathomable, as was Gilles' future. He lingered for a few moments longer, thinking ahead to what New Amsterdam might be like. It was a place of adventure too, the land of *les sauvages,* as the French referred to them, the savages, or the *Wilden*, the Wild Men, as the Netherlanders called them. The aborigines of that land mass controlled and traded the beaver skins, more valued at this moment in time than the nutmeg, mace and clove spices of Malaysia, the sugar from Brazil, the tar from Sweden, or the diamonds from India, almost singly driving the wealth and economy of world trade. The need for warm clothing, especially animal fur, had become greater in the recently colder European winters. There was also an eager market for the felt from the beaver skins that made the much-coveted and stylish hats.

Gilles remembered very well his meeting with one of the copper-colored men and the fur trade agreement he had made with him. Francois Pelletier was a young man, only half a red man, and his sire, a Frenchman, traveled with him to Amsterdam. They were lower creatures than Gilles and yet he was envious, jealous of their freedom and the lives they lived, exploring the mountains and valleys of the new world's wilderness. The vagabond father and his half-breed son had traveled across the ocean to see the world and the father's birthplace. They had spent some time in Hendrick's tavern in Amsterdam, telling Gilles about the beaver, "Brother Tamakwa", as they called the furry creatures in the language of the savages. They called themselves "The People", the "Sokoki Abenaki", and explained that they were the people of the dawn-land, of the east, the people of the sunrise, and they told tales all day long and through most of the night about the land, their people, and their legends.

It was a different kind of wealth that they possessed. Most of the people in the world that Gilles knew tied themselves to the bondage of making a living, finding food, and getting enough money together to pay the tithes and taxes required by the church, the landowners and the king. Gilles knew this: His father had been one of those wealthy landholders and that extra wealth had only served to bind his father more tightly to his way of life and to the belief that he was superior to other men. Privilege and wealth were the gods his father had worshiped, holding this reverence above anyone and anything else, including love of his homeland and maybe even his family.

Fathers and sons.

It was strange to think now about the vast differences between the two French families, his own family in France and the Pelletiers in New France. Meeting the Pelletiers had turned his beliefs upside down, but at the same time it struck a chord that resonated deeply inside of him. It had changed his life, although now it seemed like a dream that had not happened at all. Gilles wondered if the Pelletiers, in all of their travels, had ever experienced anything like the orican they had just passed through. They had not mentioned it, so he supposed they had not, but maybe they were just accustomed to such storms.

A hopeful thought presented itself to Gilles now: It was just possible that the storm had blown them even closer to their destination, making up some of the time that had been lost to them in the many becalmed days of the journey. He would take that thought to sleep with him. He would try to hold fast to it through the night and through the days to come, for as long as he could manage to keep his mind attached to it. Gilles was tired. He was finally ready for sleep.

The open hatch belched up a hot, steaming, sewer stench, boiling up from below and assailing him, but there was nothing to be done about it except to pull part of his shirt up over his nose and go down into it. He just hoped the poison did not upset his bodily humors to make him ill, or worse, kill him. He was not going to entertain that thought at all though: His family needed him. He felt his way through the total darkness, making slow progress along the row of bunks. He thought he heard footsteps behind him and someone clinging to his shirt, but it was probably just his shirt sticking to him with his own sweat. He moved forward step by step, his eyes continuing to adjust until he found his place among his other family members.

"Listen!" Elsje hissed at him in the darkness.

Oh, what now? Gilles wondered, making certain that he kept his mouth closed and this thought to himself.

113

At first, he heard nothing more than a few snores and coughs, but then he heard it, a small sound, a quiet hiccupping sound.

"I'll be back soon," Elsje said, sliding off the bunk, Jacomina cradled in one arm as she felt her way along with her other hand.

He was not sure what she was up to, but he wasn't going to call out or interfere. He assumed Elsje was going to comfort Marytje DeWitt as she had helped the young woman give birth two days before.

Gilles listened in the darkness and only heard a murmuring, like the sound of a gurgling brook. He knew it was his wife's voice, soothing and comforting their neighbor. After a short time Elsje returned, but Gilles noticed with alarm that she traveled back unencumbered, her arms empty.

"Elsje, where is our daughter?" Gilles demanded in a panicked whisper.

"She'll be fine. Marytje cares for her for a time."

"What?! She could drop her! She could kill her!" Gilles sputtered.

"Hush! She'll hear you! Do you know what pain she is in?" Elsje asked.

"It's a hard thing to lose a child and it happens every day, but it was only an infant. She never knew this child or spent any time with it."

Gilles remembered the older brother he had lost, the eighteen short years he had on the earth, not nearly enough time for Gilles to spend with him. If he had known his brother would not always be there, he would have spent more time with him, appreciated him more, and told him so. Gilles clung to every memory he had of his older brother, but now these thoughts were always tinged with the sadness of knowing that he would never see him again.

Elsje snorted in reply. "Men! Her breasts are hard as rocks, swollen with the milk ready for the child, burning in pain, and the child was not an 'it'! She mourns for her daughter and the dreams she had for her little girl in the new land."

"Does that happen? I mean to the breasts?"

Elsje made a sound that was somewhere between exasperated and disgusted.

Gilles thought for a moment about this bit of physiology that he did not know about. He was taken aback that a part of women that he found so pleasurable could be so inhospitable to a woman's lover. The milk was bad enough.

"Elsje, what if she never wants to give our baby back? Maybe she has gone mad with the loss! Why would you do this?"

"It will relieve the discomfort of her body, and I hope it will relieve the pain in her soul a little. I told her that she will have a dozen children and will have to herd them all around like a flock of geese. When this settles into her, she and her husband will get to work on it and our Jacomina will be returned to us. I'm quite sure we'll have our baby back before it's time for you to find her a husband."

Gilles heard the smile in her voice even in the dark. It was his turn to smile and he had another question for his wife.

"So do you think it will be very soon? I mean when she will bring Jacomina back?"

"Do you miss having her here? She has done nothing lately but cry, even before the storm, and you haven't taken care of her once since we left Amsterdam! We will have our little one back soon enough, but in the meantime, I will be relieved to have a wet nurse for a while. She's a big baby who needs a lot of feeding, and I don't always have enough milk for her."

"Maybe she can keep Jacomina for a little longer then," Gilles said as he pulled his wife over to him on the bunk and kissed her. "Until then, you and I can spend some time alone together."

*A*s the days slowly ground past again, one by one, for the time being Gilles was grateful that they were boring days once more, glad they were not going through any more storms like the demonic one they had experienced. At times he thought he remembered seeing red eyes glowing, looking back at him through the darkness from one corner of the ship's hold just before the storm, but perhaps it had only been part of a dream he had one night. Residents of this sailing settlement had been living on the ocean now for more time than Gilles believed it would take and still there was no land in sight. He had long since passed disappointment and boredom. He was also beyond frustration at the almost daily servings of dried and salted cod, the edges sometimes showing green mold, and the plentiful supply of dried peas which, unfortunately, never seemed to run out and had not been lost in the storm. Gilles swore he would not plant this particular crop when he started his planting in the spring since he never wanted to see peas again. Without a cooking fire, the peas could not be cooked, so they were served cold after having been soaked in water or ale, a terrible waste of decent ale to Gilles' way of thinking.

Other food that had not been ruined in the storm was running low as Gilles could see the portions of the herring getting smaller on the few occasions when they had it. They had cold, uncooked food for over a week until the fuel dried out sufficiently for the fire to be restarted with the cook's iron and flint. Warm pea soup with bits of dried ham never tasted so good to him. Gilles didn't want to know where the water might have come from to make the soup, but it was very salty.

The salted pork, fatty stuff that the Dutch people seemed to love, turned Gilles' stomach. It had been offered to them before the fire was restarted, but few wanted to eat it cold, at least not in the beginning, until hunger for something different drove them to try and struggle it down. Gilles swore he could taste the mold on it, even though they tore the discolored parts off their portions. Gilles had never particularly cared for pork of any kind, although he gladly made an exception to this rule if it was cooked with minced apples, Calvados and heavy cream.

He wondered if he would ever taste lamb, chicken or real beef again. Maybe these were luxury foods that might not be available in the colony at any price. He remembered the Pelletiers mentioning other wild animals that were unknown on the civilized side of the ocean and wondered if that meat would taste like anything that was familiar to him. He thought about how much he would enjoy some venison, quail or rabbit that might be found there. He even thought longingly about fresh vegetables, just as long as they were not peas.

Although the rations had been very precisely planned and portioned out for each person before they left, the days of calm and their being blown off course during the storm had extended the duration of the trip and damaged some of those supplies. When the ale started to run low, there were strict rations and they were given rain water to drink that had been collected in barrels up on the deck. This was a dangerous practice. Gilles could see the bugs and bits of wood from the collection buckets floating in it, but the master ordered them all to drink a cup of the rain water every day. A little extra water was given to Hans Cornelissen when he complained of great pain in his nether parts that only water would ease and for Katrina Van Hoorne when she suddenly developed a fever.

Cornelissen survived, but Van Hoorne died of her illness, whatever it was, and over her family's tearful objections, her body was dropped into the ocean. The crew completely supported the master's decision on this matter: They knew that keeping a dead body on board for any amount of time was bad luck and would lead to more trouble. It was also feared that whatever fever killed the woman would infect others with the contagion. This concern seemed to be born out when others aboard the ship developed fevers a few days after the storm had passed. Even Marbury, the physician, did not know what he could do to treat them because he had not brought any leeches with him.

As others got sick, including Hendrick and Aafje Vander Cloot, Corretje joined Gilles and Elsje on their bunk as the girl tried to keep her distance from Aafje. Not satisfied with the situation, Elsje got a determined look in her eyes that Gilles had seen before, and he knew that his wife was going to do something about it. He didn't know what that might be, but he wasn't going to ask. Elsje handed Jacomina to Corretje and ordered Gilles to watch Bruinje. She marched over to the steps, hiked up her skirts and ascended them with a stomp that meant business, although the hatch had not been opened up for them today.

A stronger man, or a man who didn't know Elsje as well as Gilles did, might have gone after her, but Gilles knew better. He wondered if he should just pretend to be asleep or distracted so he could disavow any knowledge of whatever his wife was about to do. Elsje banged on the hatch with her wooden shoe until Gilles heard the shouts of sailors above, yelling at her to stop and then swearing at her when she didn't. Elsje continued, unperturbed, until the hatch was finally opened. Gilles heard her berating them, pushing her way past them, shouting in angry Nederlands, and then storming across the deck toward the forecastle where the master was probably standing, overseeing the crew's work and the ship's progress.

The annoyed oaths of the men died away, but now Gilles' keen hearing picked out his wife's voice, still loud enough to be heard above the noise of the waves and the slight whoosh of the wind passing over the sails. As he listened, straining his ears to hear Elsje's voice up above, he realized that it was difficult to hear her. The winds had picked up and Gilles was heartened to think that now they might finally be traveling at a faster rate of speed. The vigorous breeze was probably the reason why the travelers had not been allowed up on the open deck today and if this was so, Gilles would gladly stay below until they arrived on the shores of their new home, just as long as it would not be very much longer.

Maybe he only imagined what he was hearing his wife shouting, but it seemed to have something to do with sauerkraut. Long minutes passed, and for a time it was quiet up above. Gilles hoped that whatever was transpiring was amicable, that the master hadn't thrown his wife overboard and that Elsje hadn't done anything to the master. Finally, her familiar footfalls crossed the upper deck and descended the steep steps. With a self-satisfied smile on her face, she settled herself back down on the bunk like a contented cat before a fire, straightened her skirts, and took Jacomina back into her arms. She said not a word to her husband and this, more than anything else that she could have done, aggravated and annoyed Gilles, but he was still hesitant to ask her what had taken place on the deck above.

A short time later a crew of seamen came down to the passenger deck with swabbing mops, a cup and a crowbar. Opening the hatch to the supply and cargo hold, they brought up a heavy cask and set to work. As they pried the top off the cask, the aroma of sauerkraut filled the air. It permeated the compartment, overpowering everything, even the suffocating stench. The crewmen passed out bowls of the stuff to the passengers, but this was only after they had meticulously strained out the juice.

Gilles was not in the mood for a plate full of sauerkraut and had no idea what was going on. When the shreds of cabbage were gone with only the juice left in the keg, the crew took the liquid out by the cupful, pouring it over the floorboards, over the emptied chamber pots, and over everything else around them before the last drop ran out. The liquid seeped into the worn wooden flooring, soaking down through the cracks between the boards, back into the cargo area from whence it came, leaving very little at all for them to mop up.

At last Elsje spoke to Gilles, a smile of satisfaction on her face.

"Vinegar! It cures the plague and fevers too."

For whatever reason, whether it was Elsje's vinegar cure, the prayers of the worried passengers, or because it was a malady that did not travel to everyone, the outbreak of illness started to subside soon afterwards, and there was no great contagion on the ship. Aafje was the only one who was no better. Her fever continued, and after feeling the girl's forehead, Elsje went over to seek help from the English physician. Gilles knew that Elsje had to be very worried about Aafje since she had so little faith in the men who practiced medicine in the Netherlands and certainly much less, if any at all, in the English.

Marbury looked at the girl's feverish face and examined her neck. As he took up her hand, Aafje cried out in pain. He gently held it up to examine it more closely.

"What is this?" he asked, seeing the long splinter still embedded there.

Gilles could see that the hand was swollen and red, all the way to her wrist.

"It has to come out," Marbury said to them.

Aafje's eyes grew large with fright. "It's not so bad!" she protested.

"It could kill you, or you could lose the hand if it doesn't," the physician admonished the girl. "We need to do it now."

He left them and went up the stairs to speak with the master. Soon he returned with a large jug.

"Start drinking this," he ordered, filling her cup and handing it to her.

"This is ...strong drink!" Aafje protested. "It's not ale or cider! I don't..."

"That's right, and you are going to drink it all," the physician replied.

She sipped it at first, but at Marbury's urging, she struggled it down, the strong stuff making her eyes water and burning her throat.

"I finished," she gasped triumphantly, smiling at him as she waived the cup in the air. "I feel a little dizzy..."

"You need to drink all of it," Marbury said, pointing to the jug. He poured another cupful and pushed it back at her.

"Nee, I can't do that," she smiled at him. "I never drank this before."

"Go ahead, have another, drink it all down."

When she finished the second cup, Aafje wobbled around on her seat, looked at the physician for a few moments and said, "You are a very nice man."

She smiled a coquettish smile at him and Gilles turned away, hiding his amusement at her clumsy attempt at flirtation. She could certainly take some lessons from Elsje's sister Tryntje who had mastered that womanly art. Marbury took no notice, or at least did not acknowledge the comment as he filled her cup again. She made no move to drink more so he held it to her lips, tipping it up until she started to cough and the liquid ran down her chin. When she had finished that cup, Aafje leaned slowly over to one side as her head continued all the way down to the berth. In astonishingly quick succession, she closed her eyes and then started to snore.

"Now, then. You two hold her down and I will go get my knives to remove it," the physician told Elsje and Gilles.

Marbury returned with a rolled-up piece of leather. Untying the cord that bound the bundle, he spread out his implements. Each one had its own place in the pockets sewn into it, but he already knew exactly which one he wanted. He poured a little of the spirits over the area where the splinter was lodged. Aafje giggled in her sleep at the cool sensation and pulled her hand back.

"What are you doing that for?!" Elsje exclaimed.

"I have discovered that aqua vitae has magical healing properties, both inside and outside," he explained.

"Like sauerkraut. We could have used sauerkraut," Elsje offered.

"I suppose," he said. "Maybe I'll try that next time."

Gilles knew the man was humoring his wife, and he was grateful that Marbury was also accomplished in the area of diplomacy, in short, astute enough to know how to avoid long discussions or getting into an argument with Elsje.

They positioned Aafje so Gilles could put his full weight on Aafje's arm and Elsje held the rest of the girl down while the physician quickly sliced a long opening across her hand. Aafje jumped, screaming in pain, her eyes flying open momentarily as she yanked on her arm. Being unable to move it though, she collapsed once again, whimpering in her sleep.

"Give her a minute to settle down again," Marbury advised, "but not too long."

Elsje pulled up her skirt, ripped off a length of her petticoat and dabbed at Aafje's hand. Pus was draining out of the wound along with the blood that ran down the side of her hand. The other passengers and family members watched in horror from their nearby bunks.

"If only I had my leeches," Marbury said wistfully. "We will have to watch this carefully and see how it heals."

Gilles worried that the infection might cost the girl her hand and she would have to have it amputated. She wouldn't be much use to him with one hand. He had no time to worry about this at the moment though: Aafje settled into her stupor again and Marbury moved quickly to finish the procedure.

"One more time, hold her still so I can do it in one pass if I can."

The physician was ready, using some pincers to grab the end of the splinter. Grasping his instrument firmly, with one long pull he brought the piece out completely. Aafje yelped again. Wrenching her arm free from Gilles, she managed to sit up for a few moments, but because she was still under the effects of the aqua vitae, her head soon went back down again. Gilles knew that she was in the hands of a master. The removal had been fast, even though the splinter was gruesome, several inches long and covered with blood and tissue.

"Let me look one more time," Marbury said as he carefully took up the hand and turned it to get a better look. "I wish I had more light to see, but I think I got it all. There are yellow humors collecting there that need to drain. I will come by to look at it every day."

Once again he poured a little of the alcohol into the wound and once again Aafje screamed in pain. With no further restraint from Elsje and Gilles, the girl sat upright with her eyes wide open. Elsje was ready for her, putting one arm around her shoulders and the cup to the girl's lips once more. Aafje accepted it at first, then pushed it away as she started to cough again. Elsje spoke soothingly to her as she coaxed the girl back down onto her berth, stroking her hair and telling her that she would be fine in just a few days. Marbury gave Giles and Elsje some final orders for his patient before he returned to his own space.

"Let her sleep and give her more to drink when she wakes, at least until the pain is under control."

Gilles could see in Elsje's eyes that Marbury performed better than she had expected. In doing so, he had managed to earn her respect, even if she still refused to abandon entirely her uniformly low opinion of physicians and chiurgeons in general.

"Gilles, pay the man!" Elsje said.

"Nee, no money. I hope I have saved the girl's hand," Marbury replied.

He wiped his knife and pincers off on a piece of cloth that he had in his kit and put them away again, inside their respective pockets. As he did this, Gilles noticed that he had there, in addition to his surgical implements, his eating utensils. His knife and trencher were no surprise, but he also had an eating fork. Now Gilles was more curious than ever, wanting to learn more about this man and why he traveled with such a thing.

Elsje plied Aafje with the drink when she woke and urged her to eat too, offering to help with anything the girl needed, eating or bathing included. During the next few days her fever came down, and Aafje gradually began improving. The heat in the hold had eased a little too, and when the passengers were finally allowed back up on the deck, there was even some relief there with a nice breeze filling the sails. Gilles looked out impatiently to the western horizon. His vision was as good as any man's, serving him well enough on land before this journey had begun, but now he wished that his eyesight was better so he could see what lay ahead of them. He found himself growing frustrated and angry once again as he searched in vain for some sign of hope that land might be near.

Realizing that this did nothing except leave him in a state of agitation, he reminded himself that they were all well enough, had food enough, and should be getting closer to land every day. Had he been looking for a dove with an olive branch, a rainbow, or some other celestial or divine manifestation? He wasn't sure if he believed in omens at all, but he would have been quite satisfied to see a clump of clouds gathered over some distant land, a sea gull, or anything else that might presage the journey's approaching end.

Perhaps he really was going mad, going up there every minute of every day that he could, barely talking to anyone else anymore, just staring out to the west, searching until his eyes believed they were seeing things that were just not there, whole cities and towns on some land far in the distance. He withdrew from everyone, believing that he simply couldn't let his family know how he felt and how deep was his despair. They were all tired, discouraged, and worried about the future. Gilles knew they would arrive there eventually, but their patience and their faith had been sorely tested during these past months. He felt the weight of his thoughts, but he had to keep believing that all would be well when they got there. He counted his blessings and nursed his hopes as one would nurse a frail newborn or fever-surviving relative, regularly and with determination, until it seemed to be an ingrained ritual that he practiced with more regularity than Catholic Mass, the Hours starting the day and Nocturne ending it before he went to sleep.

One morning a few days later, when he had just about given up hope of ever reaching their journey's end, Gilles stood on the deck, lost in thought, when he came to the joyful realization that he was looking out at birds flying in the distance. His eyes had rested on them, following their movements without his even realizing it. He felt a rush of excitement, and his first thought was to run down the stairs and tell Elsje. He quickly decided though, that he didn't dare say anything to his wife about this hopeful sign, not just yet, in case they were not real, only existing in his desperate and eager imagination. It was as if he had come to believe and accept that they would never reach their destination, but would continue journeying forever. If they died here, maybe they would continue this journey into eternity. Maybe they had already died, possibly during the storm, and had just not realized it yet.

Elsje had been sitting patiently, knitting throughout the trip when she felt well enough, having brought plenty of yarn to pass the time, or so she thought. She had been knitting since she was a small child and could easily do it in the dark while nursing Jacomina and carrying on a full conversation. Now she started pulling the yarn out of old worn-through stockings, unraveling the old ones to reknit the yarn into new ones after her supply of virgin wool ran out. There had been no need to wear any of the new stockings yet due to the warm weather on the journey, so the woolens were all in pristine condition, ready and waiting for the winter weather that was supposed to come. Gilles found it extraordinary that Elsje could be so calm and patient, just as long as her family was healthy and they had enough food.

It did seem to Gilles that there had been a shift in the moods of the sailors and it had been for the better. They no longer seemed like grim warriors waking each day to fight relentlessly ongoing battles, but were more like enthusiastic bridegrooms or expectant fathers who had been waiting for an event that had been a long time in coming. Slightly cooler air and stronger breezes settled in around them, keeping the ship moving forward at the right latitude on their charted course.

It was only a day or so after sighting the birds when Gilles saw his first land in the distance. It really was going to happen: They would be landing soon on the other side of the world. He was about to run laughing back down the steps to Elsje who still slept in the early morning hours, but he was glad that he thought better of it when they got closer. The land that he saw turned out to be only a rocky outcropping above the surface of the water with very little vegetation on it, only some bushes growing up through the cracks in the rocks. A few seagulls were basking in the sun there, but that was the only evidence of life he could see on the tiny barren island. The ship quickly passed by this isolated dry patch and there were no other signs of land for a long time afterwards. This realization gave him a quick pang of disappointment, but then he reminded himself that he had not seen this much since they had started their journey.

"Are we getting close?" Gilles asked one amiable-looking young seaman that he had exchanged some words with once before.

"It's one of the first landmarks," the sailor replied. "We'll be at Massachusetts Bay soon, but don't get the others excited yet. We still have a long way to go. I'll be happy to see land after this trip."

"I can see why. Once I thought I might become a sailor, but that didn't happen," Gilles confided.

"I thought I would be a farmer, but that didn't happen either," the seaman replied.

"Life will do that sometimes," Gilles said, thinking about the unanticipated turns his own life had taken.

He had expected to live his life out in the comfort of his family estate in France as he watched over fields of grain and vineyards, trading these commodities while his servants toiled in the house and the fields, as his ships brought wealth in to him from foreign ports. It hadn't worked out that way at all; Gilles couldn't have come any further from that life if he had planned, plotted, and maneuvered his way into this reality.

The ship picked up a strong and favorable wind, speeding along now, moving faster over the ocean than it had for many past weeks. Den Eyckenboom had a lighter load now that some provisions had been consumed and others had been lost. There were also fewer passengers and one less crew member who had been washed overboard during the great storm. A lone seagull flew over the ship and was soon joined by other flock members, keeping up with the ship now, floating over the deck, diving down behind them and then soaring out in front of their approach.

"Damned dirty birds! Sometimes the sailors feed them for fun. I can't see wasting the food, and the master will have them whipped if he catches them at it," the young seaman informed Gilles.

"I'm Gil-, uh, Yellas Jansen, going to work for the company in New Amsterdam." Gilles offered his hand, remembering to use the Nederlands form of his name that he had so recently adopted. "You seem to know a lot about this route. How far out are we?"

The youth grinned at Gilles, perhaps being unaccustomed to being treated with any respect at all, especially by the passengers, and heartily shook his hand.

"Willem Zufeldt. I know this route, done it a *few* times," the jan maet said. "If the weather and winds hold, we could be one day out of Massachusetts Bay, but it's not a sure thing."

"Will we see much of the land before we get to New Netherland?"

"A little. We'll run along the south shore of the long island, *Matouwacs* they sometimes call it, but we won't go in too close. There are pirates at Southold, on the east end of the island, and we need no more trouble before we get there, not from the English, the pirates, or the Wilden."

"I thought the Wilden only lived in the woods," Gilles said.

"They do travel on the rivers and the ocean."

"The Wilden have ships? They can't catch us, can they?" Gilles asked, alarmed at this bit of news.

"Their little ships have no sails, 'kan-oos' they call them. They are strong oarsmen and can overtake us if there is no wind to fill our sails, but that's what guns are for!" Zufeldt winked at him. "We only have ten cannons, but that's enough. With the women and children on board, the master doesn't want to use the guns. The powder may be too wet to work anyway, so we need to just keep our distance and outrun whoever is out there."

The sailor talked on and on as if he had found no one to speak to for the past ten years. Gilles was happy to get the information, although the wet powder situation and learning of sea-faring savages concerned him.

"It seems quiet enough now," Gilles noted, hoping he didn't sound too patronizing.

Zufeldt smiled good-naturedly at him. "There aren't usually a lot of pirates here at this time of year. It's mostly the weather and what's in the water that we have to watch for now, otherwise any simple farm boy, like I used to be, could do it."

"How long have you been working on this route?" Gilles reappraised the very young man, certainly no older than he was. The sailor might even be a few years younger than Gilles, although it was hard to tell from his tanned and weathered face that was already showing lines across his forehead and at the corners of his eyes.

"Close to four years now. My first trip I was a cabin boy. My parents died and a couple took me in to work their farm, but I didn't like the daily beatings, so I traded in the cows for a ship. The first three years I was terrified, watching all the mates around me die, and every trip I swore would be my last. I'm still here though. I know the landmarks and the hazards, just as long as they don't change a lot after the big storms. I'm too valuable to the company and they pay me too much now to stay home and farm."

"Four years! Have you done a lot of trips?"

"A few. In hell's heat of summer and cold to freeze a man's fingers, toes and privates off, through whales and the kanoo ships of the savages, good masters and bad, plenty of ale and no ale or food."

Have you ever thought to stay there, with those of us who are going? Maybe to farm? I have a farm you could go live on."

Zufeldt laughed out loud. "I probably won't live long enough to think about it. But nee, it's a savage land. I can't understand you people who leave the Netherlands to go live in that terrible place."

"Sometimes things are so bad that you can't stay," Gilles said, and he heard the bitterness in his own voice as he said it aloud.

"So go somewhere else in Europe!" Zufeldt grinned at him, wondering why these people never did what should have been the most obvious thing to do in the first place.

"We *did*. It didn't work out."

Gilles thought back grimly to the French soldiers who took such pleasure in murdering the innocent and unarmed settlers in the Palatinate, the children, old people and farmers armed only with wooden rakes and hay forks.

Zufeldt shook his head. "I would *never* choose to live over here," he said. "Never. Oh! The wind has shifted again."

The young seaman moved off to work some sails with the rest of the small crew. Gilles watched, speechless and amazed, as the barefoot young man climbed up the ropes as easily as the monkeys climbed up on the shoulders of their keepers during festival days in the old city of Amsterdam. It was so simple really: The young man's life was laid out before him like clothes spread on a bed, made ready for Sunday church services. Zufeldt knew his future, all except for the exact timing and manner of his death.

Gilles' own life had been planned out for him once too, but fate had intervened.

Having no one to talk with now, Gilles looked around at the other passengers. All of them had hope showing on their faces now. After having spent so many weeks together, Gilles' fellow travelers were almost like family now, good family as well as bad. He believed he had come to know the nature of every one of them. After the passengers had boarded the ship, there had been only a few additions and subtractions along the way, the deaths, the birth and death of the infant, and the as-yet unknown conceptions of future children that had taken place on board. There were shysters and liars among the passengers, whiners and complainers and a few who were patient and saintly. There were old people who might just manage to live long enough to set eyes and feet upon the foreign shores before the end of their lives. There were children like Bruinje and Jacomina who were so young that they would probably have no memories at all of the old homeland or the ship's journey. The remembrance of the voyage might be kept alive as the story of the great storm was told by others again and again until they were no longer certain if it was their own memory or memories passed on through the tales of others.

There was the new romance of a very young couple that captured the interest of more than a few other passengers. Both looked to be no older than sixteen and did not seem to know each other very well when they left Amsterdam. At some time during the journey, they had become much better acquainted and decided to join their futures together after they reached their destination. They would have to negotiate the legal and church hurdles to make it official, or failing that, just move in together and bear the opprobrium of their neighbors. Because they were underage and sent over by the orphanage to work for the WIC, they would have to complete their service first. The engagement, if one could call it such, would have to last the five to seven years of servitude. Gilles wondered if either of them had seven years of interest in waiting for their freedom to be with the other one. The girl had taken a small space with a charitable family in return for helping them with their six children on the way over. The boy was over in the single men's quarters on the other side, behind the grating.

The romance had started just after the ship left European shores, with a short conversation on the deck, then talking down below while they rested their hands on the grating that separated them. Their hands moved closer and closer until they were touching, and then one night there was a kiss across the barrier. The couple took every opportunity to go to the upper deck with a few fellow voyagers being sympathetic enough to give up their time for the young couple to be together. When the hatches were secured, they stood talking to each other down below. One morning they were both found asleep on the floor, on either side of the fencing between them. Elsje was of the opinion that they should have been allowed to take the young man in, on the family side, for the couple to be together if only during the great storm.

The shoemaker's son was of marriageable age, but he had run away with his sweetheart to the new world because his father's objections would have ended their relationship. They had the money for the fare and the master never questioned them, seeing the ring on the girl's hand and the swelling in her belly.

Of more interest to Gilles was the young stowaway the sailors had discovered after the first full day out of Texel, too late to turn around and drop him back there, even if the master had been so inclined. There was no place to stop and put him off the ship until they reached land again, so he was put to work. The master had laid claim to him as his own private property, one reason being that the boy's food had to come out of the allotted provisions. Although the child was worked hard, the master's claim and close watch also kept the boy from some of the sailors who might have had more personal uses for him. He was too small to do very much heavy labor aboard the ship and was either unable or unwilling to speak. With a strong and able-bodied crew under his command, the master had no need of another servant, so the child would likely be sold as an indentured servant when they arrived in New Amsterdam. Whenever Gilles saw the boy, hauling a bucket of water with both hands or scrubbing the decks on his knees, the child's dark curly hair, green eyes and bronze skin reminded Gilles of the Mediterranean people he had seen sometimes in Amsterdam's marketplace. What one of them would be doing on his own, so far away and at such a young age, was a mystery. The boy didn't look to be any more than seven or eight years old.

A few of the travelers looked financially comfortable, but most brought little with them besides their hope for a better future. Like Gilles, some had suffered reversals of fortune or had left their homes in fear for their lives. Some had situations that they needed to leave behind and others had nothing to leave behind, only something to be going forward to. They left for reasons that were more important to them than staying on their ancestral homelands or continuing to live among their family, friends and neighbors who had shared their history and their language. These people had decided that they couldn't wait around to see how it all turned out; they were hoping and believing that the new land would offer something better than the old one. If the inclination was there, there had been more than enough time on board the ship to share all of the stories as to how each man and woman came to be here, traveling away from their native shores toward New Amsterdam. Some would not open up, from shame, fear, or simply a desire to forget, but most had become comfortable enough with their fellow voyagers to share their own versions of their life stories.

As they were nearing their destination now, Gilles' thoughts turned to the other servant he had taken on, a dark Spanish Moor. It was only now that Gilles wondered what kind of man would be living under his roof with his family. He had seemed personable enough, but perhaps he was a thief or worse, a murderer, or someone who could not be left alone with his wife or the teenage girls. Back in Amsterdam, with the ship ready to sail, there had only been hours to spare for Gilles to find someone, anyone, to comply with the initial terms of the patroonship agreement. Now that Gilles thought about it a some more, it was maybe a little too easy to convince the man to sign on with him. What was the man running from, and what he was capable of? He was a great big man, two heads taller than Gilles, powerful, and now, for the first time, Gilles gave some thought as to where the man was going to sleep. They would all be living in the little house for the coming winter or longer, so now he added this to his list of concerns and worries.

Gilles was suddenly aware of a wave of energy, coming from underneath his feet, rising up to him from within the ship. Returning his attention quickly to the present, now he could see what had caused this excitement to run through the ship like a wind-whipped firestorm. Outlines in the distance of a coastline had been seen by more than one person, so it could not be an illusion; there was definitely land ahead in the distance.

Excitement overwhelmed them, and even those passengers who had not once climbed to the upper deck during the voyage either forgot or ignored the rules, racing up the steps to have a closer look, causing the master to order them all back down below. The joy at simply seeing land again sparked a new energy in all of the weary travelers, creating an invisible force that jumped from person to person. Gilles felt this energy surging through him, along with the sense that his strength, determination and faith in the future were returning, renewing and revitalizing him, making him feel in a way that he had almost forgotten he could feel over the past few months.

It was absurd, feeling excitement over something as trivial as approaching their destination, the very reason they had boarded the ship in the first place. They were not even there yet, so their arrival was still more in the realm of an unfulfilled promise, but this sign of hope had reinvigorated Gilles and he was not alone. For a brief time in their lives, they had become creatures of the sea. Now that they were about to become land creatures again, they realized just how much they had hungered for this return to their former state of being. As he was being sent below with the others, Gilles looked over his shoulder and thought he could see some distant half-timbered houses with straw-thatched roofs, chimney smoke and stockade fencing to keep the farm animals in and the wild creatures out. He even believed there was the smell of cooking meat on the breeze, but perhaps it was all only in his overly-eager imagination.

Those few voyagers that were going to be disembarking at this first stop in Massachusetts Bay quickly made ready the few belongings they had with them, babbling together excitedly in English. Although it would still be some time before Den Eyckenboom put the anchor down, a few of the English men and women had already gathered their belongings near the bottom of the steps. They were more than ready to arrive at their new home. The Marburys would not be disembarking here, but Gilles noticed that they were curious enough to go peer out through one of the fissures in the side of the ship to see what the English colony looked like while they exchanged a few quiet words with each other.

It did not take a very long time to get there, but the wait was excruciating, exacerbated by everyone's impatience. It was not only trying for those passengers who were disembarking; the others were anxious to see all that they could, the visual evidence coming into view that their time was finally coming and they, too, would soon arrive at their own destination. The sailors on the deck constantly tested the depths of the waters as the ship slowed to a painfully lethargic pace, avoiding the rocks, sand bars and other hazards concealed under the waves.

"Patience!" one of the waiting Englishmen called out to his wife.

Understanding the English word, Gilles thought that an appropriate command, but the man continued, "Patience, hold fast to Theophilus' hand!"

Apparently, it was the woman's name, but Gilles knew the name also had a meaning. He thought once again how peculiar it was that these people named themselves after virtues, after things instead of other people.

Elsje didn't understand their language, but she understood what was being said. She nodded in their direction, smiled, and commented to Gilles, "He doesn't want to lose the little boy."

Gilles' wife did not need to understand any other spoken languages. She spoke the language of humanity and family fluently, better than most. As Gilles watched the little boy, he thought back to his childhood. He had always believed that his family was only concerned with mortaring together financial alliances. Now he saw that it had been more: Having simply shared their food, shelter and knowledge of the world, it was an act of altruism. They might have just separated the wheat from the chaff and discarded any excess children or those not up to their standards, the second or third sons, the sickly ones, any females or illegitimate children. They could have tossed these out of the nest as some other families did, leaving their offspring to fend for themselves as best they could while these newly-orphaned children trudged along life's path and struggled through their trials and tribulations on their own. This thought had never occurred to him before, and now his smoldering anger toward a family that had abandoned him softened just a little. He considered taking the time to write them a letter, just to let them know he was still alive and living across the ocean. He could tell them that he was well and that he had a family now. His friend Jean had frequently urged him to do this, although Gilles had yet to find the time over the past few years. He would give it some thought later, after they reached their destination and after they were settled.

When the anchor was finally released and the ship came to the first full stop of the journey, two crewmen opened the hatch. They didn't allow the disembarking passengers to leave right away, though. They descended the steps and pushed back the small group that had assembled below so they could access the cargo hold at the base of the stairs. The sailors retrieved the belongings of the voyagers who were leaving the ship, and while they were down there, the smell of dampness, mildew and mold wafted up through the opening. Gilles wondered again how his own belongings had fared, but he would have to wait a little while longer to find out. Elsje had packed a little clothing for their future use, but mainly she brought cooking utensils. The iron pots might suffer a little rust, easily removed with some sand, and clothing could surely be replaced with all the weavers of flax, cotton and wool who were already living in the colony. It was mainly his books that Gilles worried about. He doubted there would be any printers or book shops where they were going, and anyone there who had books would probably not want to part with any of them.

The ship had come to rest like a great floating bird, tucking her wings in and riding the gentle waves where she had anchored just off the alien shores. In a very short time Gilles heard the shouts coming from a small skiff that approached their vessel. They must have seen Den Eyckenboom's sails in the distance, perhaps sounding church bells or firing cannon to announce her approach, although Gilles had not been able to hear these sounds above the excited chatter of his fellow travelers.

Up above his head, Gilles could hear something being hoisted down over the side, into the smaller craft. The master finally allowed the departing passengers up the steps and on to the upper deck. Gilles laughed when he heard one of the English ferrymen ask the crew, "Why does everything smell like sauerkraut?"

The sailors didn't reply, possibly due to a lack of understanding their language, disinterest in making the effort, or the belief that it was some kind of slander directed at the Dutch people. It was left to the departing English passengers to provide any explanations while they traveled across the harbor by ferryboat to their new home.

The passengers who remained on board crowded around the cracks in the side of the vessel, elbowing each other to try to get a good look, to see what the landscape and town looked like, but Gilles didn't bother to join them. He would wait to see his own promised land, and besides, there would be some more time here before they continued the journey to their own destination. Because repairs and re-supply were necessary, there would be at least one lay day or two. The travelers were not allowed to go up on the open deck at all, but both hatches were opened up to try and air the passenger deck out a little more. A cool breeze came in, not drying things out very much, but mitigating slightly the smell that had started to return after the sauerkraut saturation. Gilles climbed the steps to the opening so he could listen in on the conversation that was taking place on the deck above him. He hoped he would hear news of when they might set sail again.

He was surprised to hear voices rising in anger as he crept closer to the upper deck. The master and several crew members were having a loud discussion that appeared to be about the broken mast, the one that Gilles heard as it came crashing down during the great storm. Gilles was careful not to be seen listening in, but he was able to look over and see the exchange that was taking place between the master and his crew members.

There were calmer statements from the sailors that Gilles could not distinguish, but louder, harsh words were exchanged between Tiedeman Pels and the master. Tiedeman was an experienced sailor who had survived several great adventures at sea and many more in the brothels on land. His was not the first name that came to mind when the shipmasters looked to recruit disciplined, orderly and sober crew members; in fact, it was rumored that he had survived challenges at sea more than once by sacrificing the lives of his fellow crewmen.

"If that's what you think, just give me my pay now! I'll sign on to the next ship that comes by and you can save your own hide the next time you run into a storm," Tiedeman growled.

"You are the reason we are in such a mess!" the master thundered. "You've damaged my ship!"

"It's not my fault you hired inferior carpenters who left rotting masts on this leaking old barge," Tiedeman sneered.

Gilles judged that Tiedeman was well over six feet tall as he saw the man take one threatening step toward the shorter master. What would happen if there was a fight and Tiedeman took over as master of the vessel?

Would he pirate the ship with everyone on board, taking it somewhere besides New Amsterdam? What would become of his family?

Four sailors who had been standing behind the shipmaster uncrossed their arms and took one step closer to him, taking a defensive stance. Obviously, these four were not going to go with Tiedeman without a fight. Gilles looked around to see if he could find something that he might use as a weapon to help them, but even if he could find one, he worried that there might not be enough able-bodied men in the family quarters to defend against a challenge. Over in the single men's quarters they were strong, but they might also be capable of switching allegiances for the right incentives. When the crew rested at night, many of them slept in hammocks there, possibly building friendships with the single men over the past months. Which side would the rest of the sailors choose? Which side would Gilles' servant, Van Amsterdam, choose?

Gilles had not come this far to be pressed into service with a bunch of mutineers. The master had not yet finished his conversation with Tiedeman, so Gilles tried to still his pounding heart and hear what the master was saying.

"You were seen here just before we sailed, with no business being on my ship at the time, and I'm not paying you anything. The agreement was full pay on arrival, to bring my ship into New Netherland, not to sail halfway there."

"You're almost there now, but you won't make it in safely without me. You'll be lucky if any of you make it in alive!" Tiedeman retorted.

"Gilles, what's going on?" Elsje called over to him.

He motioned for her to be quiet so he could keep listening.

The master kept his eyes fixed on the accused man but gave orders to another sailor.

"Westervelt, escort this man from the ship. The authorities can do what they will with him, but because we have no time to deal with their courts or privileges regarding their jails, we are well rid of him. I'm tired of his insubordination and tired of his mouth." To Tiedeman the master added, "I'll give you a tenth of your pay and you won't be on my ship again."

Gilles braced himself for the upcoming fight he expected, but to his surprise, Tiedeman, known to be a braggart, troublemaker, heavy drinker and fighter in the taverns back in Amsterdam, didn't argue with this arrangement. It was a generous offer because the master did have other options. Tiedeman should have just been thrown off the ship with no pay, and Gilles didn't know why the master would pay him at all, except perhaps to demonstrate to the rest of his crew that he was tough but fair in the extreme, a very good man to continue to crew with.

Gilles could hear Tiedeman, angered by being put off the ship, continue his rantings as he climbed over the side, down the ladder and into the waiting skiff.

"You know the worst part of the journey lies ahead! You will all die before this leaking bucket makes it in, and the savages will make sausage of you after your bodies float up on the shore!"

His voice continued on, trailing off in the distance for a few more minutes, travelling back to them across the water, continuing on with threats and with insults regarding his shipmate's sexual preferences and the master's parentage. Gilles wasn't interested in the man's creative invectives, but he was interested in what had caused the dispute. He tried to listen in to more of the conversation regarding what had happened to the mast. He couldn't make all of it out exactly, being confined as he was at a distance away and below the level of the upper deck. The discussion up above had continued without Tiedeman, but at a lower volume.

He tried to shrug off the threats he had just heard, but Gilles wondered if what Tiedeman said was true, that the most dangerous part of the journey was still in front of them. Fear was assailing Gilles once again, but he was not going to let one man reinstate the fear that he had been working so hard to exorcise over these past weeks. He told himself that this sailor was of no consequence, that he was only a bagatelle and a liar. The voyagers had already reached the other continent, so even if they would be temporarily moving off into deeper waters and out of sight of the shoreline once again, Gilles had to believe they were going to make it in the rest of the way.

Now Gilles wondered if Tiedeman spoke any English at all and if many of the Massachusetts Bay people spoke Dutch. A smile spread slowly across his face as this thought came to him. That might be something to see, the big Dutchman shaking his fist at the departing ship, railing at his shipmates as he watched them sail off while the inhabitants of the colony wondered what kind of madman had just been deposited on their shores, a madman who did not even speak their language.

"Gilles!" Elsje called over again. "What is it? What is going on?"

"Just unloading some more baggage," Gilles replied with a grin.

The little ferry boat from the shore that had already left off Den Eyckenboom's departing passengers now returned with three new passengers to board, two old men and a young woman, bringing only one large bundle with them.

It was a good trade, Gilles thought. *Tiedeman for the three.*

Gilles had to move away from the stairs briefly while the new passengers climbed down to join the others. As soon as he could, Gilles returned to his listening post and heard a little more of the conversation between the master and the crew so he could finally piece together what had happened. He ventured further up the stairs, raising his head above the level of the upper deck, to better see what was going on.

Now that he took a closer look at it, something about the mast stump didn't look right to him. Gilles was no expert, although he had learned a little by watching his father's carpenters as they performed their work. He had seen storm damage to the family ships before, and usually, when a tree or a ship's mast was broken from natural forces during a storm, the wood splintered jaggedly along the lines of the greatest weakness. This mast appeared to have had a neat circular cavity carved into one side, weakening it. This imperfection might have made little difference had it not been for the great storm, but it did look as though someone had purposely hollowed it out. Such a tree with rotten wood, or with an existing cavity made by a bird like *un pivert*, would definitely have been rejected by any competent shipbuilder for use as a ship's mast. This must have been the damage the master accused Tiedeman of doing, but why would he do this? Certainly, Tiedeman would have no wish to endanger his own life during the crossing.

Gilles had heard the thunderous noise when the mast crashed to the upper deck during the storm. He also heard the great splash when it had been maneuvered off the ship the following day, when the waters had calmed enough so it could not threaten the ship by becoming a natural battering ram. It was unfortunate that it could not have been salvaged and repurposed, but the crew would not have had room enough to work around it and perform their duties if it had been kept on the deck. Perhaps some shipwrecked sailor would find it in the middle of the ocean and believe it was God's providence as it saved his life. Another ship's crew might see the mast and wonder if some vessel had been lost, not knowing that they had survived and continued on their way without it.

Maybe it was the time of year, with the weather cooling rapidly and impatient passengers on board, it could have been that all of their supplies were dwindling, that they were only days away from their destination, or maybe the master trusted the craftsmen in New Amsterdam more than he did the English, but whatever the reason, although they were one mast short and progress without it would be slower, the master decided not to replace the missing mast here. He had come to this conclusion after a brief discussion with the ship's carpenter, and with the decision made to continue on without it, the master was not wasting any more time. He moved forward quickly, meeting with the English and arranging for dry cooking fuel to be brought aboard, along with replacements of some of the provisions that had spoiled along the way. He did have some extra money to buy these items since he still had the rest of Tiedeman's pay and the English seemed to have no objections to accepting Dutch guilders.

That night they were all excited to discover that they had a meal of real chicken to celebrate their safe arrival on the other side of the ocean. The master had made a bargain with the Bostonians and was in a celebratory mood, especially after making it through the great storm. There was even an extra ration of ale, although it was English ale and had a peculiar taste. Expenses be damned this one time, they were going to celebrate. The master used his trading experience to negotiate with the farmers and had the chickens delivered to the ship already killed, gutted, scalded and plucked. You just couldn't do any better than that. Unfortunately, there was still an ample supply of peas to go along with it, but no one complained. They ate it all, chicken bones included if their teeth were good enough to handle them.

They spent one last night there, anchored in the harbor beside the English town. When he woke in the middle of the night, Gilles heard what he hoped were just howling winds outside and not the calls of savages or wolves. He was reassured and fell back asleep quickly when he felt the ship rocking back and forth gently, like a baby's cradle, confirming that the wind had come up after the sun went down. The tide came in very early the next morning and they set out again, before most of the passengers were awake, moving off in an easterly direction to deeper waters. The passengers woke to feel cooler air and some of them even pulled on the wool stockings that the women had been knitting ever since they had left the fatherland. The warm and humid weather so recently past had seemed to ridicule their preparations at the time, to belie the fact that they would ever need such things, but now the weather had suddenly changed.

As they rounded a great hook of land with a small settlement on it, Gilles observed that the countryside must have been covered with wild flowers during the previous summer. Although it was barren now, with only a field of dead stems marking where the plants had been, the mere evidence of flowers that promised to return again in the spring heartened him. The glass-green waves were breaking on the tan sands of the beach, and Gilles hoped that his new home would be as pleasing to his eyes as this place.

Den Eyckenboom continued south for a time before turning southwest, anchoring for the night near a large island. This had been done silently, almost surreptitiously, and Gilles wondered if there was danger there or if the crew had just finally reached the point of quiet exhaustion. He never had an answer to this question as the ship pulled up anchor and set out again very early the next morning. Buoying their already rising spirits, passengers were allowed to go up on the open deck again. When he arrived at his usual post to observe their progress, Gilles was a little disappointed to see that they had once more lost sight of any land and the ocean had deepened again into darker blue-gray waters.

This was disheartening. He had believed that once he had seen the land on the new continent, they would continue to see it and not go back to the view of relentlessly open ocean. It was only after the day was nearly gone that Gilles saw land again. He wasn't sure if it was another small island or the long one that he had been told to watch for, so he waited for the sunset and the stars to give him confirmation. When the heavens darkened enough to reveal the answer, his joy returned to him. Now he knew that their heading was once more almost due west and now they were cruising along the southern coast of the very long island. When they reached the end of this island, they would be at their new home on Mannahatta Island, no more than a few days away.

They anchored next to the great island for the night, and Gilles had to continue his observations from his favorite spot down below. Although he could see nothing besides darkness, Gilles heard the noise of the waves breaking on the shore. He slept a little and then returned to his dark portal when he woke up. He didn't know what time it was, but light on the eastern horizon told him that they were closer to the new day than the old one. Soon the crew made ready the sails, hauled up the anchor, and Gilles was able to watch as the new land passed by. Reluctantly, he took a little time out from his observations when the first meal came down to them. As they traveled along the southern coast, Gilles saw sandy beaches, a few of them boasting houses, barns and fences, the structural evidence of civilized men. In other places he saw the obvious presence of savages, their dark little dwellings huddled together on the shore with smoke escaping from holes in the roofs.

Some of these bronze people, accustomed to the alien ships they had been watching pass by for several generations now, openly went about their business of fishing from long wooden craft with spears and nets, pulling in the wealth of the waters. Great wooden baskets in the vessels held future feasts, either for that evening or for drying and use throughout the winter. Half-naked men and women could be seen on the shore, tending fires for smoking the catch, while others swathed in animal skins carried on other activities around these encampments. Gilles watched all of this with fascination, his eyes still glued to the crack in the side of the ship.

He was elated when the master decided to allow passengers up on the open deck again. When Zufeldt had a little time to talk with him, Gilles peppered him with questions, trying to find out as much as he could about the new land.

"Is it cold in the winter here, Zufeldt?"

"Colder than you can believe, colder than Denmark! Two years ago, I woke with snow as deep as my knees covering me while I slept up on the deck."

"It's not hot in the summer then?"

"It's as hot as it is in Africa!"

"And is the land good for farming?"

"The land is good enough," Zufeldt answered, now with some irritation creeping into his voice after all of Gilles' questions. Zufeldt gave Gilles an uncertain look.

"You *have* heard about the Wilden?"

"I have heard a lot of stories about them. Do you know what the native grapes are like?" Gilles asked, continuing his line of questioning in his main area of interest.

"Grapes?" Zufeldt looked at him in wonderment and shook his head. "I don't know. The vines just get in the way of clearing the land and getting the grain in."

Now they were passing a little closer to the island, and Gilles could see that a grove of large trees partly shaded and concealed a group of Wilden shelters. A long, crudely-fashioned boat, carved out of a log if Gilles had to guess, imitated a felled tree, but it was definitely a boat. It was beached on the shoreline, partially obscured by the marsh grasses and cat tails that were now fluffing out the last of a pale yellow stuffing before winter arrived. Gilles searched the shadows, and to his astonishment, he discerned a pair of dark eyes, eyes that watched him too, fixed in a dark face that didn't move.

"Savages!" Gilles breathed.

Although he knew they would be here, now a sudden jolt of realization went through him. They were not just interesting variations on European men or mythical beings that went about their happy daily activities off in the wilderness somewhere. They were living very close to the settlements and this one looked threatening.

Zufeldt showed no surprise. "Ja, of course the Wilden are here! They are all up and down these islands. We don't bother with the ones here. The English try to make friends with these, but they will kill you for no reason at all. We picked up some shipwrecked Englishmen just beyond here once, and they told us all about them. The wild men are of the devil himself, with their dark faces, their stick and mud huts, their drumming all night, fierce drawings and markings all over their faces and bodies, smelly grease covering them, feathers and shells stuck in their hair and the cruel weapons they have. If they don't kill you, the other devils on these shores will, the snakes and the wild animals they call 'rakkoon' and 'skonk'."

Zufeldt shook his head, the revulsion plainly showing on his face.

"Nee, I would not put a foot off the ship, even if I was allowed to, not in this awful place. The English lay claim to this Lange Eylandt and we should let them have it."

"So you have never even been on any of the land here?" Gilles asked. Now he wondered if any of the information he was getting from the young sailor was true at all.

"Nee. It's safer to stay on the sea. Men go to the land and they always die there, sometimes before they have been there for one whole day."

Gilles knew that this wasn't true. Many of the West India Company men had been there for a decade or more, some even traveling back to the Netherlands for company business. He said nothing to Zufeldt about this inside information he had; he just continued to watch the human-like creature on the shore that watched him. Zufeldt didn't seem to see what Gilles did, or perhaps he simply ignored it.

A new tail wind suddenly came up, pushing the ship quickly and easily over the water, rapidly putting distance between the eyes on the shore and the eyes on the ship, but Gilles couldn't let go of the image he had of the being that watched the ships travel past. There was definite fear settling into Gilles' stomach now, the seed of it planted by the tales he had heard in Amsterdam, made worse by Zufeldt's commentary and by the frightening vision of the dark man with dark shadows on his face. Gilles had known that he was taking his family into dangers that were both known and unknown, but with this new wave of fear gripping him, a part of Gilles wanted to find Elsje now, to admit that he might have made a terrible mistake in bringing them to these dangerous shores, and to tell her that they should just stay on the ship and return to the civility of Europe.

Of course he knew that he could not do this. The greatest danger was behind them now, in the land they had left. They had little choice but keep going to whatever might lie ahead of them. After all, the French King had murdering soldiers too. Did it make so much difference if they were killed by polished silver sword or stone-headed spear? There was no possibility of staying in the old place until total safety appeared somewhere else in front of them. They had to leave one place first before they could get to another, better one.

Gilles watched from the safety of the ship as the wild place receded into the distance, his fear and dread only easing slightly as they traveled on. It was hard to believe that these creatures on the shore were really men too, and that there were so many of them living on this land. When the company had offered him the job, they had assured Gilles that the land was mostly empty and was just waiting to be settled by Dutchmen.

At that moment Elsje joined him, wrapping the blanket she wore around her more tightly as she touched his arm. He managed an uneasy smile for her. It was uncanny how often she seemed to hear his thoughts concerning her before she suddenly turned up at his side. He had not expected that she would come up on the deck though, and now he worried that something might have happened to the family down below.

"Gilles, go ask the master if you can get some of the cook's fire to light father's tobacco pipe. He's been without it for the whole journey, and you know how he gets…"

Gilles' concern was quickly replaced by relief and then amusement at what Elsje considered enough of an emergency to bring her up to where she didn't want to be. He didn't argue with this request of Elsje's: He knew that his father-in-law's temperament was never sweetened by much of anything, especially not by the lack of tobacco burning in his pipe these many weeks. Gilles welcomed the excuse to walk away from her, to have a few moments to regain his composure and resume control over his emotions, but he had to wonder why she didn't just go ask the master herself.

He shrugged. It didn't matter. He did as his wife asked. The shipmaster was mercifully quick with a refusal, as was expected. Fire was too much of a danger on the ship to be entrusted to anyone but the cook. Gilles was only too happy to relay the bad news to Elsje; after all, it was the master of the ship's decision, not his, and he reminded her to tell her father as much. Hendrick would just have to be satisfied with keeping the damp old tobacco in his white clay pipe a little longer, until they landed and the singed golden leaves could be rekindled. With the storms and crowded conditions below, Gilles was surprised that the old man hadn't broken his pipe in half yet, but Hendrick seemed to take better care of the pipe than he did of anything else, his family included.

"Is everything all right?" Elsje put a hand on his arm once again as she looked deeply into her husband's eyes.

"Fine, fine, I was just looking at the land," he told her, summoning the most reassuring smile that he could find inside himself.

"It is pretty. I can see hills in the distance." Elsje looked out over the landscape and seemed to like this part of the journey.

"It won't be much longer now." Gilles pulled her closer to him, mostly to comfort himself.

"I am ready to see it. I have been more than ready for two months," Elsje replied.

"Don't I know that!"

"I'm sorry I have been asking so much..."

"It's all right," Gilles reassured her. "Only a few more days."

"I can't wait to see my sister. I never thought I would miss her so much."

"It will be good to see Jean again too, won't it?" Gilles asked.

"Ja!" she replied. "I don't think you ever told me, how did you two meet each other? Had you always known him, as children? He never mentioned you before you came in with him that day at my father's inn."

Elsje smiled, thinking about the day she had first set eyes on Gilles, thinking him a spoiled and foolish young foreigner, never dreaming that she would one day be his wife, let alone that she would ever leave her father's inn and they would travel across the world together.

"Jean was working for my father in France, and we traveled on business together to the Netherlands. The first time I met you was just after I met Jean. I really don't know how my father met him or how long they had known each other."

At the time of their first meeting, Gilles might have been a very favorable prospect as a husband for Elsje, well beyond what Hendrick could ever hope to secure for his oldest daughter, but this was no longer the case by the time the marriage became a reality. Gilles had left the Netherlands as a wealthy young man but returned a short time later as a refugee and little more than a street beggar. It was extraordinary that Elsje had agreed to marry him at all, very nearly an act of bravery on her part, knowing as she did that he was also a wanted fugitive. She knew that Hendrick's objections were as much about concerns for her safety as anything else, but to his credit, the old man had let his daughter make her own decisions about her life.

The citizens of Amsterdam, Hendrick and Elsje included, already knew that Jean Durie was trustworthy, a man of character, decency, conviction and action, so if Gilles was a friend of Jean's, this was recommendation enough for them. In all probability, Gilles had Jean to thank for his survival and his new family. Stubborn, independent, strong-willed Elsje had followed Gilles through all of his ups and downs and now she followed him to this place at the far end of the world. Elsje was the ballast in the ship that kept everything upright, although there were times when Gilles had seen her more as an anchor. He resolved to treat her with a little more respect now, knowing that she had fully supported his dreams, not out of anyone's expectations of obedience to a husband and master, but out of affection and her belief in him.

Gilles suddenly remembered that he had not told Elsje about Alain Gagner's being on the ship when he saw Alain approaching them.

"Bonjour, Madame Elsje," he greeted her.

The cold look in her eyes told Gilles that she remembered Alain quite well. She had no words at all to spare for the man and was still angry with the way their French-speaking neighbors in the Palatinate had treated her. They had gossiped about her, belittled her Dutch ways and disdained her independent spirit.

"I'll talk to you later, Gilles," she said to her husband in Nederlands, "I need to go deliver the bad news to Father."

She turned on her heel and left the two men to each other without even acknowledging Alain's presence.

"The weather is nice and cool today, isn't it?" Alain asked, obviously trying to change the subject from Elsje's snub and abrupt return below.

Alain was happy to talk with Gilles about anything at all, as long as it was in French, and as they conversed, Gilles wondered if Alain would be able to understand the Walloons at all, given their peculiar French dialect. Gilles gave Alain a little of his time, out of compassion and pity for the man, but he had no interest in seeing Alain again after their arrival, especially with Elsje disliking him so intensely. Gilles carefully guarded all of his words and he could think of very little to say to Alain beyond observations regarding the weather. He was actually relieved when it was time to go below for the second meal of the day.

Gilles knew now that his time on the ship, time for worry but also time for daydreaming all day, was coming to an end. Soon they would be arriving on the shores of reality and any free time to himself would be rare, only when he was walking down the road to his company job or working in his fields. He wondered if it would be a very long walk to the company offices and if their new home would be close to the safety of the fort or closer to a wilderness filled with lurking savages and other stalking wild beasts.

During these last few days of the journey, there was less predictability in the waters and the wind, just as there was in their future, with occasional eddying currents and capricious breezes that were deflected from the land. The wind sometimes shifted and picked up suddenly, causing the master to quickly banish all of the passengers from the upper deck. Gilles was herded up and down the steps like a cow going back and forth from the daily pasture lands to the nightly barn. He wanted to stay on the deck all the time, to see what he could of the new world and to breathe in the fresh air, but this was not possible.

As they traveled west, the weather continued to grow cooler, and now it seemed that no one could stay warm enough. The salty dampness penetrated clothing, skin and even bone. Feeling a little more hopeful though, ready to get back into the fight of living, Gilles took the time again, for the thousandth time, to count his assets, or as some would call them, blessings. Gilles could not have set out with better prospects, yet he couldn't fend off his feelings of uncertainty about the future and worries that clung to him as closely as his own shadow. He tried to dismiss this feeling as the result of too many things gone wrong in the past and too many missteps down the road that he had been born to travel. He rejected the idea that it was a premonition of trouble ahead, and he also refused to believe that a lifetime sentence of bad luck was his fate; he angrily dismissed these thoughts as one would any annoying beggar standing at the door. Hadn't he just proved to himself that a man makes his own luck by looking for opportunity? Hadn't he survived all of the attempts on his life already? Jean had told him this as well, on more than a few occasions, that you make your own good luck by making the best choices that you can after considering all the possibilities, even the unlikely ones, while holding fast to the belief in a good outcome. His friend was the very keeper of his sanity and his soul. A part of Gilles knew that he had been blessed with a strange kind of good fortune, but this didn't stop him from worrying that the good things in his life might all just disappear, and his luck, when it came to survival, may not always hold fast.

Gilles hoped the message he had sent to Jean on the Wapen Van Rensselaerswijck had made it there already and it probably had, due to the Wapen's having left Amsterdam long before the Eyckenboom encountered the great storm. There was a great wide ocean to travel on, with many paths to the new world and no single well-worn wagon track to follow into the wilderness. Jean would surely be waiting for them to arrive, ready to help them start their new lives. Jean being Jean, he would probably have all the details covered and matters well in hand already.

Encouraged and soul-refreshed by seeing the new land and knowing how close they were to their destination, all of the travelers began presenting their wish lists to the heavens and to each other, speaking their heart's desires aloud.

"I want a hot meal with some meat that is fresh and has never been salted."

"I want to change my clothes and wash them with real soap and water."

"I want to sit in front of a roaring fire until I am so warm and so dry that I forget what this ship was like these past months!" said another.

"I want a hot apple pie with cream on it," Elsje said.

"It's a bit early for wishing," one man warned sternly. "I heard it might still be another few weeks before we get there. If we pass through another storm, we may never see the shores we have been longing for."

"Don't tell us about your wish for misery!" one woman admonished him. "My wish is for a turnip. I hope they have turnips there."

Gilles couldn't believe that this was her greatest desire, to have a turnip, but if this was so, who was he to argue with her? Who knew what mundane earthly pleasures, items of no consequence to anyone else, would be most missed from their old home? This would be so when they got to any new home, whether it was on the new continent or at the end of all of life's journeys. Gilles could think of a great many things that he would like, but at this moment, what he wanted more than anything else in the world was to see his friend Jean again. His earlier conversation with Elsje had clarified this for him, and finding Jean would be the first thing he would do, just as soon as he possibly could.

*A*t sunset Den Eyckenboom anchored once more in the shallows off the coast of the long island. Two armed sailors kept watch through all night long for any of the savages' sea-going vessels that might come near to them in the darkness. It was impossible to sail on through the dark of night as they had before: In addition to natural rock and sand hazards, there were the protruding carcasses of half-sunken ships. Some of these dangers were known, some were new since the last mapping, and others had shifted locations with the tides and the storms. There was a little more expectation of security now that they were finally in the waters off Dutch-claimed territory.

When they resumed their journey in the morning, the master and crew still had watchful eyes on the coast and the water, looking for trouble of any kind that might be out there. Zufeldt informed Gilles, through the grating that covered the hatch, that it would be even slower going as they got closer, but these obstacles were exactly what protected the colony so that no pirate ship or attacking armada could just easily sail into New Amsterdam at top speed and make a surprise attack. Gilles tried to keep this reassurance of security foremost in his impatient mind, circling back to it when he felt the frustration rising up in him again. Gilles wanted to know if they were still sailing along the great island.

"This can't still be an island!" Gilles protested to Zufeldt. "We have been sailing next to it for two days."

"It is. I have sailed around the other side, on the northern coast, or I wouldn't have believed it myself. That's why they call it the 'long' island."

Gilles wasn't sure if the sailor had his facts straight or not. It was taking a very long time to get beyond it, but Gilles knew the final destination must be nearly within sight now.

"Do you ever get tired, just sitting there all the time on the steps below the hatchway?" Elsje called over to her husband.

"Never!" Gilles called back to her. How else would he listen in on the activity above to find out where they were and what he might expect next?

A slight scramble up above caught Gilles' attention. The crew had sighted another ship in the distance and the fear that he thought was gone had come back, as strong as it had ever been, as if it had never even left him. What vessel could this be? He thought that it must be one of the WIC ships in the area, but it might just as easily be the English or the French who carried on trade in these waters too. It might even be an outlying Spanish vessel, a pirate ship, or a craft of the savages. For some anxious minutes, he heard the sailors trying to identify the other vessel. Because the ship was still at a great distance away, there was discussion among the crew as to the actual size of it, the fact that there were no colors flying on the mast at all, and whether they should make ready the guns. These worrisome comments sent Gilles from his station on the stairs down to the crack in the side of the ship so he could peer outside for a better look. Unfortunately, it was too far away to see anything at all besides a dark smudge on the distant horizon. One sailor's keen eyes had spotted it well before anyone else could see anything at all out there. Distracted now by his apprehension and this new worry, Gilles went back to listening in at the hatch opening. The sailors could see much more from atop the sails than he could from inside his rabbit hole in the water. After a long period of tense silence, at last he heard a loud laugh and renewed conversation from up above.

"It's Xander! He has a new boat! And what is he doing way over here?"

"Trying out his new boat of course!"

"It will hold a lot more fish than his old one."

"If the English don't get him and take it, ship, fish and all!"

Gilles breathed a sigh of relief, hearing that apparently, it was a fisherman known to the crew, and presumably, friendly.

The travelers were allowed one more day on the deck, a last breath of crisp air and the stunning sight of a brilliant blue sky behind golden leaves on the island's shore. It was good to have the sunshine for this, what Gilles hoped would be their last day on board the ship. Finally, Den Eyckenboom approached the entrance to the harbor, turning north toward their final destination, promising an imminent end to their months-long voyage west. Land was all around them for the first time since they had left the Netherlands, even if it was off in the distance.

Upon learning this news, many of the passengers surged up the stairs, through the open hatch and onto the upper deck, ignoring the orders and shouts to limit their numbers. All of them were trying to get a closer look at the land, the place where they were going to live, and then sometime in the future, the place where they were going to die. It was difficult to call a place home when one had never set eyes upon it before or even heard a very good description of it, but the land looked good to Gilles. More importantly, it felt good to him, like a place he could eventually come to call his home. He just hoped that he was right about this feeling and it was not simply wishful thinking on his part.

"Take a last look and then everyone has to get below!" the master bellowed.

The voyagers craned their necks to look around, but seeing little besides trees, reluctantly they drifted back down the steps for what they all believed would be the last time. Down in the hold, some of the passengers had already started gathering up their children, making ready to leave the ship. They would not be able to retrieve any of the items stored on the lowest of the three decks, but they reminded each other not to forget about them in their excitement. Any belongings left behind would be lost to them forever as claimed property of the WIC, sold off to defray expenses, or simply kept by the master if he had any use for them, this being a bonus that was part of his compensation.

Smelling or sensing that a great change was in the air, the dogs were barking excitedly and wagging their tails furiously until the ringing echoes across the low ceiling hurt everyone's ears. The uproar woke sleeping infants and irritated the adults, one of whom promised to cut the dogs' throats if they were not quieted. Along with the excitement, there was now a definite chill in the air, the heat and humidity having finally passed away, almost as quickly as sunshine behind fast-moving clouds on a breezy day. The ship made a little more progress toward their destination, but then, just as they moved to enter the mouth of the great harbor, just as they were prepared to start their new lives, the sun quickly dropped below the horizon and they had to anchor for one more frustrating night, their new home tantalizingly close, almost within sight.

With his eye pressed to the aperture in the side of the ship, Gilles took in whatever his senses could extract from this view of the promised land. A salty, sulfurous, brimstone breeze that reminded Gilles of the devil came across the water on the cold night air, and he hoped it was not an omen of things to come. He did smell the cook fires though, and being unable to remain patient any longer, he called out to the crew, telling them that he needed to ask the shipmaster about something important pertaining to private West India Company business. Reluctantly, the sailors removed the hatch covering and let Gilles through.

"Do you think it best that I report directly to Governor Kieft?" Gilles asked the master, thinking up no better excuse, as his eyes scanned the horizon, taking in what he could in the gathering shadows.

"Van Tienhoven, Kieft's secretary, is the man to see," the master replied.

It seemed as though he thought to say more, but thinking better of it, he shook his head a little before he clamped his mouth shut.

"Oh, ja," Gilles replied. "Such an important man will certainly have someone to handle these things for him."

Gilles slowly made his way back to the hatch, all the better to have just a little more time to look around and see what he could of the new land.

The master stood watching him, smiling in amusement. No fool was he, but a man of experience, good humor and patience who had seen this so many times before. He knew how desperately these people always wanted any small glimpse into the future, as long as it contained some hope that it would be better than the past, especially after the trials of a voyage like this one. He called out after this young man, this passenger who always seemed so troubled, so hungry to see what might lie ahead for him and his young family.

"Jansen! Take a look there, on the other side, over by the shore. This is a land of many mysteries. See the dancing fairies on the swamplands?"

Gilles tried to focus his eyes on where the master pointed. At first, he saw nothing in the mists, but then he did see it: some blue-green lights moving over the sunken meadows, in places that would be good for finding crab or eels at low tide. There couldn't be anyone out there now, fishing the waters by lanternlight. He puzzled over this and asked what he was looking at, but the master offered nothing more than a smile. The deeper darkness overtook the twilight and quickly enveloped them as it rolled out from the east.

"Time to go below now, Jansen. Sleep well, you have a very big day ahead of you tomorrow."

Few on board the ship slept that night. Almost everyone was pulled into one of the ongoing conversations that lasted until dawn. Their minds were filled with jumbles of racing thoughts, joyful expectation, relief at their arrival and other emotions most could not name. At morning's first light they had to wait for the tide to come up to bring the ship safely into the port. The crew was alert and ready to be on the lookout for any and all hazards in the waters ahead of them. It would be too great a cruelty for them to make foolish mistakes in their eagerness to get there, only to die in the harbor when they were so close to their destination. Spotting his friend Zufeldt passing by the grating over the hatch, Gilles called up to him to see when they would be moving forward.

"Are we going soon? Is the tide in?" Gilles called up to him.

"It's not safe to go yet. We have to wait until the water reaches to the tail of the horse."

"What? A horse?" Gilles puzzled over this remark.

"It's a rock on the shore with a dark shape that looks like a horse," Zufeldt explained. "The tides here are bewitched! In all the world there is nothing like them. Some tides rise at the same time others fall. They go far up past the harbor, many miles up the great river into the wilderness. Some call it 'the river that runs both ways'."

Gilles tried to digest this bit of information, which he doubted in the extreme, but there was much outside now that he could see for himself from the crack in the side of the ship, the window into his future. This morning the great expanse of marshland was alive with noisy cackling and honking birds and other wildlife that covered the water and the land. He could see no signs of the legendary tamakwa, although Gilles looked for them, eagerly seeking the mounds of sticks in the water as the homes of the beaver had been described to him.

"Gilles! When are we going in?" Elsje called over to him.

He went back to her and saw that the rest of the family was slowly waking up. Corretje was up on one elbow, a comic sight with her matted and tangled hair wildly straying off to one side of her head and Heintje pushing his thick mop of hair out of his eyes.

"Very Soon! We're going to be there today!"

He gave Elsje a loud kiss and an embrace that was strong enough to squeeze Jacomina in the process, making the baby cry out in protest.

"Then I can finally see my husband," Elsje said tartly. "You have spent the entire trip up on the deck, listening on the stairs, or with your eyes and ears fastened to that hole in the side of the ship!"

"Did you miss me so much then? We will have to make up for lost time."

Gilles leered at her and squeezed her thigh before he returned to his observation post. Elsje shook her head in dismissal, but she was smiling too. She turned her attention to the rest of the family.

"Corretje! Comb your hair and see to it that your brother does too. We can't look this way when we see your Aunt Tryntje and her wealthy husband!"

The entire ship was awake now, a complete buzz of excitement like a hive or a clover meadow filled with bees on the first warm day of spring. The sound slowly grew in amplitude until it turned into loud chatter. Gilles heard the master's orders to the crew to get aloft on the sails and he heard the crank of the capstan. He felt the movement when the anchor had been lifted and they started to slowly make their way forward, the excited conversation and giddy laughter among the passengers gaining in volume as the ship gained speed. Making his move once again, Gilles climbed the ladder and pushed back the grating. He stuck his head out enough to see what he could in the distance as the ship rolled gently from side to side, alternately obscuring his sight and then revealing again the panorama of the land in front of them

"Don't let the master see you!" Zufeldt warned Gilles.

"I'll tell him I have another question," Gilles replied.

"He'll throw you overboard and let you swim in!" Zufeldt laughed.

Gilles was not concerned with this threat in the least. He continued to take in everything that was available to him: the sights, smells, sounds and Zufeldt's words.

"Is that it? What's that over there?" Gilles gestured to the east, at the land they were leaving, near where they had spent the night before. He saw some structures that looked like houses.

"That's Gravesande. Some English *Lady* has started a new settlement there. There are a few villages over there, on the eastern end of the island. They are putting up houses everywhere, from Achter Kol and Pavonia to Breuckelen and into the wilderness beyond. Ach! The wind is changing again!"

Zufeldt turned and raced away, over to the base of the main mast. He knew the wind had shifted even before it was obvious to others, before the sails suddenly went slack and the ship quickly slowed its forward motion. Gilles was nearly knocked off his feet completely, bumping his head against the side of the hatch opening and slipping down a couple of steps before he caught himself. He could hear the shouts from above and knew the sailors were all over the masts now, frenetically moving like ants in an exposed colony. Returning to his former position, it was incredibly peaceful once again until Gilles heard what he believed to be a peppering of gunshot as it bounced against the port side of the ship, coming at them from the west.

"Bastards!" one sailor shouted. "We should turn and give them a shot back!"

The sailors seemed to know who the shots were from, but they appeared to be more annoyed than concerned. Gilles wasn't as assured of their safety as the crew was, so he made a fast retreat to the family berth. With the excited conversation of the passengers, no one else seemed to have heard the sounds or sensed that anything was amiss. He made the conscious decision not to tell anyone else about what had just happened. Gilles noted that his hands were shaking, but he was not surprised at this reaction his body was having without his consent. He had been rudely reminded once more that this was definitely a wild and untamed place, an outpost town on the far edge of the world.

"Are we there then?" Elsje asked, a bright smile lighting up her face.

"Soon," Gilles replied.

"What's going on out there?" Hendrick called over to his son-in-law suspiciously, taking in Gilles' pale look and sudden retreat.

Gilles shrugged and attempted to look nonchalant, bored. He hoped his true emotions were not completely visible on his face. After a few minutes though, all seemed calm once more and there was no great commotion on the upper deck, so Gilles ventured back to the top of the stairs.

"What was that?" he asked Zufeldt as the sailor returned near to where Gilles was standing.

"Only the Wilden, giving you their own special welcome," Zufeldt chuckled.

If the sailor was unconcerned, perhaps Gilles could be unconcerned as well. He took a few deep breaths and tried to relax. The vessel traveled slowly through a narrower part of the bay now, while the master and his crew steered the ship around obstacles, those known from the constantly updated maps and those newly discovered by their watchful eyes. It was slow going, the ship sometimes moving forward east or west of the deepest part of the channel and then edging back in toward a center path as the depths and hazards demanded.

Den Eyckenboom rocked back and forth, the old lady slowly waddling her way in to her destination. At times it looked as if there was only land ahead of them, their route taking them directly toward a piece of sandy marsh land or a rocky promontory, but then the ship would turn at just such an angle that the bay seemed to open up once more. The ship crept forward on half sails, and Gilles knew that the crew would be checking the depths as they went, first with their eyes and then, when the opportunity afforded it or safety demanded it, with their equipment. Now Gilles spied some buildings on the land lying to the west of the channel.

"We are going past it!" Gilles exclaimed. "We've missed New Amsterdam!"

Zufeldt gave a hearty guffaw in reply.

"So that's not New Amsterdam?" Gilles asked, pointing over to a barely-visible rooftop at the edge of a clearing.

Zufeldt had his eyes fastened on the sails as he answered Gilles' question over his shoulder, "Nee, this is another great island, and one man, well really two, own all of it, nearly as far as the eye can see, from here south. It's a great piece of land, enough for a king, if only it was not in such a wild place. They call it Staaten Island."

"It is like a kingdom," Gilles breathed, awed by this first confirmation he had of local wealth on the new continent.

Zufeldt laughed again. "Cornelis Melyn should stay on his land and just grow his melons or tobacco. The Melon King! Some would like him to be the Governor, but he's Flemish, not one of the company men. I was on the voyage that brought him here myself, on this very ship two years ago. It carried so much livestock then that the crew was afraid to board it."

"So there really are fortunes to be made here?" Gilled asked, having seen the proof of it now with his own eyes.

"Maybe so, but he is the governor's chief enemy, so you should stay away from him if you want to keep your company job, far away from him and Melyn's friend De Vries, the tobacco farmer. He lives north of the colony on Mannahatta Island. Those two men, Melyn and DeVries, make Governor Kieft crazy! It's not just their criticism: De Vries is supplying tobacco to Van der Donck for trade with the Wilden."

"Who is Van der Donck?" Gilles asked, intrigued by the cast of characters and hoping he got them all straight before he accidentally wished someone a good morning and lost his job right away. This highly political place presented great challenges, but Gilles could see that there were also marvelous opportunities for those who could navigate the political morass that was New Netherland.

"Snot-nosed bastard, a university lawyer, hired by Van Rensselaer, lives up the river in Rensselaerswyck. He came over on this ship too, with Melyn. Old Van Rensselaer is probably sorry he ever hired him! They say Van der Donck actually *likes* this place and he *likes* the Wilden. He's a crazy bird. 'Honk, Honk, Van der Donck'!"

So I can't talk to them at all, not even for help with growing a tobacco crop?"

"It's up to you. Some say there is rebellion coming and even the church domine conspires with the rebels. Stay far, far away from DeVries and Melyn if you want to get along with the Governor and Van Tienhoven, the one they call 'the Secretary'. Follow their orders, keep your head down, is my advice."

Gilles was determined to be the ideal company man, so he filed away all of this information as best he could, trying very hard to remember all the names. "DeVries, Melyn, the domine and Van Der Donck, stay away from them all, got it. So I shouldn't go to church?"

Gilles was sure this situation would not sit well with Elsje. She never missed a Sunday church service except for when she was on board this ship. She was certainly going to want to make up for lost time when she found the church in New Amsterdam.

"I can't advise you there!" Zufeldt grinned. "I've never been in a church myself."

Gilles recovered his composure after this unexpected revelation before continuing with his questions. Without baptism or following all the rules of the church, how could Zufeldt expect to enter heaven when he died? But then Gilles reminded himself that he no longer followed the dictates of the Catholic Church, so perhaps both of them would end up together, in some place that was not paradise. Maybe their afterlife was forever sailing a ship on an unending ocean somewhere. That wouldn't be so bad, just as long as there weren't any storms there.

Gilles wondered if perhaps he might switch allegiances if the company was about to abandon the colony and leave the settlers behind. Maybe it would be prudent to join the side that would eventually win, at least financially.

"This man who lives here, this Cornelis Melyn, is he the wealthiest man in the colony?" Gilles asked.

"Nee, he's only the patroon of Staaten Island. The richest man in the colony used to be a ship's cook. Gouvert Loockermans was sixteen years old and only a cook's helper when he came over. He's married to one of those women who seem to run the place, most of them related to Van Rensselaer. You do know who Van Rensselaer is?"

"Ja, the diamond and pearl merchant in Amsterdam, made another fortune from the fur trade and has never set foot on a ship. Sleeps at home in a golden bed they say."

Gilles recited the list of gossip from years of hearing it, all except for the part about the vault full of gold that was here on this side of the ocean, hidden somewhere on his great estate, which Gilles doubted was true. If the man had such treasure, certainly he would want it with him in the Netherlands. Gilles knew that there had been some kind of friction between the West India Company and Van Rensselaer, but if these women were influential in New Amsterdam as well as in Rensselaerswyck, he would have to find a way to get Elsje into their social circle. The marriage prospects for Bruinje were looking good, too.

"The women are the ones keeping the colony going, though Governor Kieft claims he's done it all, cleaning up the mess left by other governors. One of them, Governor Meenwee, died in a storm like the one we just came through, but not before he started the Swede's colony south of here. He built a cabin, called it a colony, and claimed all of the land around the South River. Before that, Meenwee was Governor Kieft's hero and idol. He was one of those Walloons, but he had a nice secretary that got along with everyone, not like Kieft's secretary, Van Tienhoven."

Gilles suppressed a chuckle at the exaggerated way Zufeldt pronounced Governor Minuit's name. He pressed forward on his quest to get as much information as possible from Zufeldt before they landed.

"The master told me Van Tienhoven is the man I should report to. So he is not a good man?"

"Some say Van Tienhoven is the devil, has cloven hoofs he hides in his big boots and horns on his head that he hides under his big hat. He carries a cane that casts evil spells. When he comes around, he is there on business for himself, either to get your money, your wife or your daughter. He bewitches them into bed."

Gilles was about to respond with a loud laugh but then he saw that Zufeldt was not joking; there was genuine fear in his eyes when he spoke of Van Tienhoven. The man's very name merited some more contemplation. Understanding now that he had a great deal more to learn about the colony, Gilles was just fortunate that Zufeldt, a terrible gossip and as bad as any old woman, was willing to talk to him and had been quite informative, his best source of information so far.

"This place seems to have some very interesting people," Gilles commented.

"Hm, well, you'll meet Van Salee soon enough," Zufeldt replied, without further explanation as to who this character might be. "There are all kinds here, Jansen!"

Zufeldt said this with a small chuckle, but it fell from his lips as he looked back around to the southwest, over to the large island they had been passing for the past ten minutes. A frown of puzzlement came over his face.

"What is it? What's wrong?" Gilles asked, seeing the look on his face.

"Something's not right. It's…well, it can't be, but…the settlement is *missing.*"

"What do you mean, missing?"

Gilles thought perhaps there was some peculiar seafaring or Nederlands expression the man was using and Gilles was not comprehending the meaning.

"There were many more houses the last time I was here, but I see only a few now, and I see no animals or people."

"How could that be?" Gilles asked, but the sailor had turned his eyes back up to the sails as he shrugged.

"Abandoned I guess."

"How could the houses just disappear though?"

Zufeldt didn't answer, but at that moment Gilles spied a small group of buildings up ahead. Now a new thrill of excitement ran through him.

"Is that it? Is that New Amsterdam?" Gilles asked, pointing to the northeast.

"Nee, that's only Nut Island, covered with chestnut, walnut and hickory trees. Those are all abandoned buildings. New Amsterdam is just beyond that, hidden away. It's a little bit bigger, but not by much. You'll be glad it has the fort. Director Ver Hulst made the first fort and settlement there on Nut Island, but it was too small and not safe from the Wilden, so everything was moved to Mannahatta."

Gilles was not going to mention that Elsje's sister Tryntje had married a relative of Governor Ver Hulst's and was already living here: Zufeldt did not seem to have a very high opinion of any of the people who governed the colony, past or present.

"Well, I know where to go for my supply of winter nuts," Gilles remarked.

Zufeldt shook his head. "Just be careful of the Wilden. They move fast, across the land and across the water. They can sneak up on you and bash your brains in before you even know they are there."

Gilles tried, with limited success, to put that picture out of his mind. He decided to change the subject and find out what the prospects might be for recruiting new settlers for his patroonship.

"How many people are living in New Amsterdam now?"

"You do ask a lot of questions! I guess there are about five hundred. The company sends some people over now and then, and others have come down from Rensselaerswyck. The patroon sent settlers over from every country in the world to work his lands, but I guess things are even worse up there. The WIC has a fort near to his lands, but they can't get soldiers to stay there either. We are always fighting with Van Rensselaer's people over who controls the river. They would get more men to stay if they sent some women up there. The soldiers spend all of their free time at Rensselaerswyck with the servant girls or getting to know the Wilden women better. You have to take opportunity where you get it, if you know what I mean." Zufeldt winked at Gilles.

The shipmaster called over to the sailor. "You there, Zufeldt! Houd vast! Stop wasting time talking and do your work! The passengers need to stay below now," he gestured impatiently in Gilles' direction.

Gilles was irritated with the master's dismissal of him, but he complied because there was no longer anyone there to talk to. What could the master do to him? Put him off the ship at the next port? The master would not speak to him in this manner if he knew who Gilles was, what family he came from. Still, the time had been well spent. Gilles had learned much from Zufeldt, and even though he could not confirm the veracity of all of it yet, having gossip was better than having no information at all. Zufeldt's estimate of the size of the colony was a concern: In order to meet the conditions of his contract, Gilles would have to convince twenty percent, a fifth of the colony, to leave the safety of New Amsterdam to settle on his lands in the wild place. Maybe his friend Jean would have some ideas as to how this could be accomplished.

Gilles knew that the women on the ship were already in a frenzy of anticipation. He could hear the sounds of them in the background as he conversed with Zufeldt. They were still scurrying around below, like excited mice in a food cellar after harvest. They were collecting children and their few belongings, making lists of things to be done first and chattering to friends they had made along the way about reconnecting later. Elsje would be no exception, and Gilles was not looking forward to being drawn into the melee. He had his own list, probably with a very different set of priorities than Elsje's, but she could be supremely overbearing, even downright demanding, as she marshalled her troops. Gilles sighed. Resistance was usually futile.

Hoping that Elsje had not seen him descend the stairs again, he crept over to a different crack in the wall, on the far end of the ship where he could continue to observe his new homeland. The landscape outside seemed oddly familiar, similar to the Netherlands, and yet it was different from the place they had left. The two cities on the water, old Amsterdam and New Amsterdam, were like children of the same mother but different fathers. The ocean waves on a bare shoreline made a very different sound than that of water contained and tamed by the confines of dykes, canals and levees. There were water inlets and outlets everywhere, but here they were carved by nature, not drawn up and executed by men whose guiding principles were those of planning and precision. The old port city across the ocean always hosted a great many large ships, often hundreds of vessels packed together in the harbor, but here Gilles saw only a few small fishing boats. Along with large sections of marshland, he could see in front of him meadows and timbered backdrops of hills. It was not all flat countryside as far as the eye could see, as it had been back in the Netherlands. In this place, there were not nearly as many buildings to deflect the sound back over the water. The sounds that were out there seemed to keep on going into the forested hills beyond the town where any noise from human activity was just swallowed up in the wilderness. Many morgens away, a few rock faces glistened with wetness in the distance, just barely visible to Gilles on this exceptionally clear and sunny morning.

As he scanned the emerging landscape in the distance, Gilles realized that he had not really been prepared for this. The view took his vision by storm after so many weeks of the bland and watered-down colors of the sea. Of course Gilles had known that it would be different here, but he had not expected the vastness of it, the isolation and the wildness of the frontier. It was overwhelming.

The terrain was strikingly pretty and boasted some enormous trees, many of which had already lost their leaves. There were dark archways of branches, looking like leadwork cathedral window frames set in front of the brilliant blue autumn sky. A few other trees with foliage of yellow, orange, red and brown clung to their leaves for a little while longer, refusing as yet to accept the certainty of a coming winter. Gilles supposed that many of those must be oaks, always the last to lose their leaves, and some of those would be excellent for making barrels and casks to store his future wine in. Not to be overlooked in this vision were the immensely tall pines standing out from the other trees with their contrasting dark green. They would make fine ship masts and some of them might be the right variety to provide tar for making the ships watertight.

He was aware of the scent of the land now too, although the cold air dulled this sense somewhat. The smell of marsh grasses, fish and shellfish came in waves to welcome him, traveling on a breeze that had just now picked up energy, snapping the great sails taut once again and thrusting them forward into the future. In addition to the pungent and salty marsh scents, a sweet smell was in the air, fragrant and spicy, the smell of crushed acorns and more. Gilles was convinced that he smelled apples and grapes, both of these being a little like wine, a little like vinegar and a little like sweet preserves. Here too, was the smell of man, the smell of fire, but it was not like the fires that consumed the unrepentant sinners and terrified human souls across the ocean in France, England and Spain. It was the smell of wood smoke, maybe apple, cherry or some other kind of sweet wood. It was the smell of contented home fires on the hearth, and perhaps he only hungrily imagined it, but Gilles was certain he smelled cooking venison and baking bread. It had been too long since he had anything like that to eat, perpetual salt cod, salt pork and peas on the damned ship. Much of that had been eaten cold too, especially in the days after the great storm when they had been unable to rekindle the cook's fire for a time.

Gilles had not fully appreciated it before, but now he realized that he was looking forward to having Elsje's cooking again, especially her bread. Although she loved to experiment with a mélange of spices she had discovered in the marketplace at home in old Amsterdam, her cooking was not exotic; it was mainly plain and hearty, basic food that filled and warmed the stomachs of sailors and plowboys who were just in town for a day. Gilles would have to see if he could find some spices for her to start her collection once more, but he doubted he would ever be able to find anything as exotic as nutmeg or cinnamon here. It didn't matter though: Warm food of any kind was something he would never take for granted again.

Gilles heard the cries of the gulls and he heard the competing calls of dozens of unfamiliar birds coming across the bay to him, echoing off the sides of the ship. A variety of birds wheeled overhead now, riding high up on the breeze. Some were smaller, but there were some giant birds that Gilles could not identify. One of them, a great dark bird with a white head and tail, came from high up in the sky and dove straight down toward the water, then returned to the skies with a great silver and black striped fish that was almost too large for the giant bird to manage. Gilles hoped these great birds were not inclined to swoop down and carry people away, but he might see for himself by sending his father-in-law out to the fields alone when these birds were on the hunt.

He believed he was entering an enchanted land, the accounts of which had long garnered appreciative audiences inside the taverns of old Amsterdam. These stories made their way into the West India Company offices at the stodgy weekly meetings, particularly when the question of allocating more funds for their overseas ventures came up for an important vote or an opportunity for new investment was presented. Although the stories had been interesting and sometimes even enthralling to hear, Gilles realized now that the narratives had fallen far short of depicting the richness of this land. One had to experience in person the sights, sounds and smells of this place to fully understand its wonders, like making a personal visit to a magnificent bakery or to a legendary winery.

The vessel was at the extreme southern tip of the island now. Spread out in front of Gilles was Mannahatta, the Island of the Hills, and except for having fewer trees and more houses now, was probably much as it must have been some thirty years earlier when it greeted Adriaen Block, one of the first Netherlanders to explore the place. Block had to spend an involuntary winter here, building a new ship after his ship burned. Using the native materials of the wild lands, salvage from the *Tyger* and the basic tools they had on hand, Block and his small crew managed to complete the construction of a sea-worthy vessel that could take them home. He named his new ship *Onrust*.

As Elsje tried to explain the meaning of the Dutch word to him, Gilles translated it as The Unrested, or The Restless, but maybe it was closer to The Troubled. Block would never have built a ship in his own backyard in the Netherlands, but he had little choice in the matter. There was no guarantee that any rescue ship was going to come looking for them in the next year or even the next decade. Block knew that this undertaking was their best hope for returning to their homeland and families before the end of their lives. The recognition of that reality must have been a great incentive, some salve to their hands that surely ached, blistered and burned every night after being punished from the effort of such a great project during the frigid winter. The energy of this new land may have magically coursed through the wooden beams of a ship that had been conceived and birthed in this foreign and savage land. It was apropos in the extreme that Gilles would be coming to this place, as his father had often derisively said this of him, that he had always been a restless and unsatisfied child. This place seemed to welcome his kind of people and not the settled and settling, beaten and afraid-to-take-a-chance kind of people he had left behind, an ocean away.

"Gilles! Gilles, are we there yet?" Elsje called over. She had found him, even at his new lookout post.

He removed his eyes from the landscape and reluctantly rejoined his family.

"We are! They are making ready to take us ashore."

"And at last this misery will be over and we can start another one," Hendrick interjected, glaring over at his son-in-law.

Gilles took a deep breath, clenched his teeth and tried with all his might to ignore him. He wondered if the savages would have any use for an annoying old Dutchman. Maybe they would take him in trade for something useful.

*T*he floating village where they had been living for the previous few months had been somewhat hastily populated, without any prior considerations given to compatibility of personalities, prejudices or viewpoints, but they had managed to live together, more or less peacefully, during the voyage. At last the ship pulled up to the harbor anchorage as the travelers made preparations to disembark. They were weary but more than ready to move into the new day and their new lives. The little village of New Amsterdam, a pinpoint stuck in the middle of the vast tamakwa territory, was halfway across the world from their old homes. The transplants brought their expectations with them of course, but they also had ideas as to which personal strengths and talents might be most useful in shaping their new lives into what they wanted them to be. They brought a few things that they loved about their old lives: recipes, tenets and beliefs, a cherished treasure or two, and some of their family members who had not been left behind.

The settlement was a small one, frighteningly far from the kind of civilization that any of them would find familiar. The future was uncertain; this was a wild land with more variables of chance than they could know, even with the most diligent of research and inquiry, even with the greatest of reassurances from anyone they had asked. Most of them believed that they could make life in this new place better. This belief held, even though they knew that it might not happen in the near future, and maybe not even for them personally, but would come to pass eventually for their children and grandchildren. The flaws, shortcomings and miseries of the old world could be discarded, and it was doubtful that anyone on this ship had purposefully packed the miseries of the past to bring along with them. All of the passengers, even many of the children, were very conscious that it would be a different kind of place, a place of possibilities, rebirth and reinvention. Who could say if these same people would live out the rest of their days next to each other, or if they would continue on to other journeys? The families from this voyage might continue being neighbors far into the generations to come, intermarrying their progeny, whether they remembered how they met or not. They might eventually forget their forever tie of the days they spent together on the ship and their shared experience of survival.

There had been a stampede of humanity over to the base of the ship's stairway that led up to their new lives, but the hatch remained secured for an interminably long time. The passengers listened, waiting in anticipation and frustration as items were dragged across the planking over their heads and shouts were heard from the master and crew, until the men up above were finally ready to release the anxious flock into their new reality. At first there was a little jostling, but mostly it was a constant murmur of talk and some instructions to family members spoken in low tones. Finally, the hatch in the ceiling opened and the excited throngs rushed onto the stairs, pushing up from the hold, disgorging the contents of the ship into the fresh, cold air. It was a birth of sorts for them, as they made their debut into this new and different world from the old one. It could just as well have been a death, a passing over from one life to another, from one state of being to another, but all of them were eager to leave. No one stopped to consider whether it would be a paradise or a hell they would be entering. It was far too early to say which it might be; they had not yet set a single wooden shoe upon the alien shore.

Although many of travelers had lived by the sea all of their lives in the Netherlands, been born there, ate the bounty of it, made their livings mostly because of it and buried their dead next to it, these people were not enamored of journeying any great distance by ship, and certainly were not infatuated with the ocean in the way that Gilles was. Most of them just wanted their feet to be firmly on solid ground once more. The most selfish and able bodied, the most alone and without encumbrance of family or concern for others, led the way. They left their shipmates behind, pushing and plowing through those who were in front by happenstance or those who were not moving fast enough to suit them.

Gilles was well aware that his family couldn't compete with the energy of the crowd, and he thought better of beginning their new life with an injured family member or two. In addition to himself, his family comprised an old man with one arm, a wriggling toddler, a fussy and flailing baby, two small and easily distracted teenagers and two women trying to manage everyone else. Seeing the reality of this situation, he told everyone to wait until the shoving match was over and Elsje concurred that this was the best course of action for the moment. Gilles longed to run ahead, to push others out of his way and have a closer look for himself, but if he did this, he knew his family would be right behind him, fending for themselves as best they could.

While they waited, Elsje dispensed orders to everyone, including Jacomina.

"Hush, baby! Be good for just a little while longer! Corretje, take Bruinje over to relieve himself now, before we go, and Aafje, you stay with both of them. Father, you should go now, too, if you need to, we don't know how long a walk it will be until we get to the house. Don't get lost now, or we may never find you again! Heintje, stay with Gilles and don't go wandering off. Gilles, when you can, find out what we need to do next, where we need to go and how we will get our things."

It only made sense to make these preparations and be patient: They would still have to wait for the WIC's ferry boats to come out and get them. The ship had to remain out in the harbor, being far too large to pull up alongside any of the short docks that lined the shoreline. Gilles looked around, wanting to fix the picture in his mind so he would remember every single detail of the ship in the years to come. Although he was impatient to begin his future, he wanted time to stand still, just for a few moments. He wanted to keep this in his memory forever, a time when there were no known limitations yet and no pressing or immediate concerns that were sure to materialize as soon as he started living his new life. Right now, there was a wonderful, wide-open future in front of him, a banquet table prepared for the feast about to be served, his mouth watering in anticipation of what was coming. He lingered for a short time longer in his imagination, in a place where what lay ahead of them would always be

167

perfectly wonderful. For the moment, anything was possible in their future and everything was achievable.

He had always wanted to sail on the ocean and have adventures. Now he thought, a wry smile settling onto his face, that his wish had been granted. Gilles had dreamed about seeing exotic lands far beyond the place of his birth, thinking often of traveling to the orient or the new world. He had wished for a more exciting life than the one his father had planned out for him and this had come to pass, but he somewhat resented the fact that it wasn't completely his idea, on his planned timetable. He wondered if he would ever sail on a ship again, especially now that he knew some of the terrors that waited for men who ventured out on the open sea.

Soon Den Eyckenboom would be leaving New Amsterdam for her next journey. Before that time, repairs would need to be completed and reports would have to be filed. Trade goods, including tons of furs, hogsheads of harvested wheat and large quantities of golden-brown tobacco would be loaded on board for the return trip. The crew might get some extra sleep and hot food before they left, but they would not be allowed to go ashore. In addition to the frequently disruptive influence of sailors in the colony, the masters often ended up missing members of their crew, losing them to desertion, even in a land as hostile as this one. The memory of the orican storm might be enough to convince a sailor like Zufeldt that farming wasn't such a bad way to make a living after all, and a pretty face on the shore could be enough to clinch the decision.

The master of the ship had no time to rest. After all of the paperwork was completed and the repairs, new provisioning and future sailing plans were done, the ship did have a shallow enough draft to continue heading up the Noordt River, further into the interior of the new continent, to trade at Rensselaerswyck or carry supplies to the men at Fort Orange. Given the time of year though, they would probably not risk becoming icebound on the river for the winter. It was more likely that they would take the southern route back to the Netherlands, passing by the lower Virginia colonies before traveling through the West Indies and the Caribbean to do some lucrative trading there. Den Eyckenboom might even continue sailing further south to re-supply the embattled West India Company's Brazil colonies, now engaging in a struggle for control of the slave and sugar trades. It was definitely a battle worth fighting: The stakes were high, and when a country controlled those two commodities, it very nearly ruled the world. The master may not want to bring his ship into a war zone, but because he was contracted out to the West India Company, Gilles did not know if he had any say in the matter.

Gilles watched the flow of the refugees and fortune seekers as they began funneling up the two steep ladders, the one nearest to him on the family side and the one in the distance, behind the barrier in the single men's quarters. He thought he saw his man, Van Amsterdam, climbing the other ladder. His manservant would not know where he was going any more than Gilles did, so they would have to meet up with him later. It occurred to Gilles now that he had only spoken to the man once after leaving their home port, and he had much to tell him about how they were going to divide up all the work that needed to be done.

The new arrivals on the family side were pushing belongings and children before them or dragging them up behind them, much to the consternation of the passengers in the back of the line. The two dogs made it up the stairs, although one of them needed to be carried up by his master. The old people did seem to have a little more energy and moved a little faster than they had in the previous weeks. After the crowd had cleared out a little and the family was together once more after their last trips to the onboard privy, Gilles' family joined the line. Unfortunately, the mob had become impatient and soon a shoving match ensued. Two women started to fight, scratching and biting, pulling out handfuls of hair and shreds of clothing from each other. The fight had started next to Gilles' family group, driving the crowd back from the two wildcats and separating the family members from each other. Gilles already had one foot on the steps, and before he realized it, he was pushed up from behind to the upper deck. Heintje was right behind him, crushed against Gilles but still clinging tightly to the back of his shirt. In spite of their best efforts to make their way around the combatants and stay with Gilles and Heintje, the rest of the family fell behind in the crowd.

"I'll wait for you up on the deck!" Gilles shouted back down to Elsje.

He hoped she could hear him above the screeches of the fighting women and shouts from the crowd of spectators. The men down below were trying to break up the fight but were having little success, a testament to the ferocity of the women. On the upper deck, the excited travelers

169

continued jostling each other, only behaving slightly better than those below, mainly because they were now under the watchful eyes of the shipmaster. They, too, began arguing and fighting, this time over finding spaces in the little boats that had come out to bring them in to the shore.

Gilles was certain that they would all make it there eventually, so he stepped aside, back from the fray, to wait for the rest of his family to join up with him. He saw no sign of his servant Van Amsterdam so he supposed the man had already made it to one of the boats, possibly even arriving on the shore. As he looked over to the settlement, Gilles' eyes were drawn first to the tallest building there, a stone church with a magnificent bell that stood within the walls of the fort. He could tell this was a church by the bell that was ringing, apparently to announce their arrival, and by the large cross atop the structure. Another grand stone building stood inside the walls too, and Gilles guessed that it might be the WIC offices or a hotel. Gilles could make no sense of this at all: Most of the other buildings were modest in the extreme, and he had never expected to see anything like that over here. A flag situated atop a pole that reached high up into the sky, towering over all of the buildings, also seemed to be announcing their arrival.

Just in front of them and a short distance back from the shoreline, Gilles identified what was surely the weigh-house, the signage in front and the great scales to one side of it making this an easy conclusion. This was the place where the Westindische Compagnie determined the weight and value of the furs, grain, tobacco and other commodities coming in and going out, mainly for taxation purposes. Gilles noted, and it was surely not coincidental, that not so far from the weigh house and right at the edge of the water were the gallows, the final destination for those who did not comply with the law. It was an ever-present reminder of the penalties for theft, just in case anyone was inclined to cheat the WIC out of their due profits. Gilles was relieved to see that there were no bodies hanging on the gallows to welcome them today, but he wondered now if the dark souls of pirates and thieves lingered there, still haunting that location. He resolved to stay clear of the place, just in case it was inhabited by any lingering phantoms. For now, Gilles had a more immediate fear of the living than the dead. He was less concerned with past inhabitants than he was with the current ones, those he had heard about and those he might not know yet, both the settlers and the savages.

The rest of his family had still not succeeded in joining him on the upper deck so Gilles used the time to take in more of his new homeland. In the foreground he saw houses that were neatly laid out in rows, many of them golden in color, affirming to Gilles that they were constructed of imported Amsterdam brick. Each heavy little baked yellow block had been carted across hundreds of miles of ocean, ballast for the ships that brought them over. There were also a few darker houses that Gilles supposed were brick structures made with some local sand of a different color. Aside from the brick houses, there were a few houses made of dark gray stone, some of those with wooden-shingled or straw-thatched roofs. The structures ranged from a few larger, elegant brick homes with more than two stories, their leaded glass windows shining brightly in the autumn sunlight, to some plainer, even ramshackle wooden structures in the distance that appeared to be constructed partially of fallen trees. As Gilles watched, he observed some people emerge from these crude shelters. These habitations seemed more akin to underground fox dens or rabbit warrens, but they were homes for two legged animals, men who had probably once lived in civilized abodes back across the ocean.

He had heard that there were a great many wooden outbuildings and houses here, in spite of the Netherlanders' nearly inbred fear of house fires. Wood was no longer used for most construction in old Amsterdam due to the great conflagration that had nearly destroyed the city, although that had been nearly two hundred years ago. The Dutch did have very long memories, and Gilles knew how obstinate they could be. This willfulness seemed to be passed on to them in their mother's milk, but he knew the other reason why the WIC had been so insistent on using only Amsterdam brick.

Construction in New Netherland had brought the Amsterdam brickmaker's guild a new and protected market, ensuring even more profit for the masons in the home country. The WIC had initially stood fast behind the tradesmen, refusing to quarry the local stone or make their own brick here. Unfortunately, the need for shelter had quickly outstripped the colony's ability to get their hands on enough imported brick, and soon there was a serious shortage of housing for both people and animals.

The people in New Amsterdam quickly came to the realization that the climate was too harsh, and they couldn't just wait around for a few bricks to arrive, especially since the infrequent company ships didn't always come over every year. When the need for shelter was more urgent than the need to follow the regulations and maintain profitability for the brickmakers at home, buildings made from other materials started to appear.

As Gilles' eyes moved over the settlement, he could see that there were some stand-alone structures and additions to the existing buildings that were constructed of wood, including some new ones that were in various stages of completion. Now he could smell the new wood on the wind as he realized that the background noise he had been hearing was a cacophony of hammering that echoed from all directions in the town. At almost this same time, he realized that not all of the dark houses were made of a different color of brick, but were burned-out shells of houses, and there were a number of those. Gilles wondered how this great fire could have started and how it could have taken out so many of the buildings. Maybe the WIC had been right to insist on using only brick and stone for construction, but then why were they rebuilding with wood?

He hoped that his own house was one of the ones that was still standing. He did recall a paragraph in his deed stating that the structure was built mostly of brick and stone, and this had been indicated by the drawing of the building on the margin of the indenture as well. He felt the bulk of it now as he touched the inside pocket of his coat, validating that it was still there and had not been lost during the journey. The document had been carefully wrapped in another layer of paper and then sealed in a waxed cloth before they left so Gilles hoped that it had survived the trip and was still legible enough to be honored by the local authorities. Maybe it wouldn't matter: He was the new company clerk and could just write it into the record, legible or not. He would not take the deed out to look at it now though, not just yet. He would wait for the exact moment when they all gathered around him on the shore. Only then would he withdraw it from his pocket and consult the document. If the house had been burned or was not habitable in some other way, they would need to make it livable through the winter or find accommodation elsewhere. Gilles didn't want to begin his new life in this place as a beggar, and he didn't want to ask Elsje's brother-in-law for help, especially not with so many of them, and all of them looking so ragtag from their long journey. Ver Hulst was an important WIC man and introducing themselves in that manner would make for a very inauspicious beginning. Gilles was not going to let something as insignificant as a lack of shelter discourage him though; he had come too far and would not be stopped by the very first challenge he faced.

The rest of his family was going to see this recent fiery devastation of the town soon enough. They had already left behind burned-out homes on the shores they had left, and Gilles hoped the sight of it would not be too much for their weary souls. As he looked out over the patchwork of destruction, Gilles wondered if it been a lightning storm with high winds that had started and spread the fires. He doubted that all of the damage could have been caused by one chimney fire that had spread to other buildings. Back in Amsterdam, the sweeps tried to clean the chimneys frequently to prevent such tragedies, but occasionally one did see free-standing fireplaces on an empty lot or the gutted and burned-out shell of a brick home that was still standing. There had been rumors of trouble with the Wilden and this could explain the problem with the fur trade, the missing settlement on Staaten Island and the destruction he saw before him now. His anxiety resurfaced, but now it was more for the safety of his wife and children. He wondered how far his house was from the fort. Was it within running distance, even when they were carrying the children?

Gilles hoped that he wasn't seeing all of New Amsterdam that there was to see. Maybe there were more homes beyond the trees. The settlement was disappointingly small and impoverished-looking, at least from the perspective of justifying this move to his wife and father-in-law. After all, they were coming from one of the greatest and richest cities in the world to this shabby little backwater. There was wealth to be found here, as evidenced by over one hundred thousand tons of skins from a mountain of trapped and skinned North American creatures that had been reported each year on the WIC ledgers, but they obviously had not invested very much of it on this side of the ocean. This place appeared to have very few people but an excessive number of animals, trees and perils.

There was a cold wind coming across the water now, but Gilles decided to look around for something more encouraging about this place that was to be his new home. The respectable-looking houses looked fine, although there were not as many as Gilles had hoped to see. The heavy sounds of the numerous hammers at work told him that it was not Sunday and also that there were carpenters, skilled tradesmen living here, who were busily working on the homes and other buildings. As Gilles looked out to his left, to the west, the fort loomed large, covering the southwest corner of the island, encircling the church and the other great building he had seen there. Some movement on the grassy flanks of the fort's dirt-fortified ramparts startled Gilles, and he realized that he was looking at a herd of grazing sheep that had climbed up there to take advantage of fresh untrampled grass.

Gilles had never actually seen a fort up close before today. Now that he examined it with a more critical eye, the stockade walls did not seem very sturdy. He strained his eyes to see what was beyond the fort to the west, on the far side of the island, and he saw what looked like a windmill. These great machines, masterpieces and hallmarks of Dutch ingenuity and invention, did all kinds of work: pumping back water, sawing lumber and grinding grain. He puzzled as to why the windmill near the fort was not turning and doing its work on this breezy fall day, but then he realized that someone had built the great power generator too close to the protective walls of the fort for it to efficiently utilize the wind. Was this true of other things here, that they had not been properly constructed and were unable to function adequately?

Looking further out to the west, beyond the windmill, Gilles thought he could make out the tops of some very large ship's masts in the distance. That had to be the anchorage, where the ships already processed through the WIC customs house floated at anchor in the Noordt River, waiting for repairs to be completed, sailing orders to come through, or the winter to pass before beginning their next voyage. It made sense that they would be there, in a safe mooring place furthest from the assaults of the wind, the sea and any marauding pirates but still close to the protection of the guns in the fort.

Reluctantly dragging his thoughts back to his family now, Gilles looked around to see if Elsje was anywhere in sight yet. He heard his wife's voice coming up from the hold before he saw her emerge from the darkness. She was one of the last ones up the stairs, struggling with her baby and shouting over her shoulder to the others. Corretje followed

Elsje, carrying Bruinje like a sack of cabbages slung across one of her thin shoulders, securing him in place with one hand as she pulled herself up the stair railing with the other one.

"Gilles! Gilles, where are you? Get over here and help us!" Elsje called out.

There was nothing he could do to help them for the moment due to the unrelenting wave of humanity that continued to push forward between them, their hunger for this new beginning being almost as great a driving force for the crowd as terror in escaping a burning building.

"Over here Elsje! I have Heintje with me!" Gilles called back to her, hoping that his wife could hear his voice over the commotion.

Gilles reached out to grab Corretje and Bruinje as they were being carried helplessly past them in the stream of people pressing toward the ferry boats. Hauling them over to his side and pushing them behind him, Gilles looked around to make certain he had not lost anyone else in the crowd. Hendrick and Aafje had joined them, and they were all together now, just waiting for the opportunity to safely navigate their way over to the ladder leading down to the ferry boats.

The gray woman pushed past Gilles and he noted that she was all alone. The sister was nowhere to be seen, probably missing for the moment in the surging crowd.

"Get out of my way!"

She fired her fist toward Gilles' face, but he ducked just in time. Missing her mark, she only succeeded in landing a blow on his shoulder. Never even slowing her pace, she pushed an old man roughly aside at the top of the ladder and took his place, climbing down with amazing agility into the last spot on the boat that was just leaving.

"Can you believe that?" Gilles asked Elsje.

"Did you expect her to be any different? Just because we are in a new place, people don't change," Elsje declared, her chin set in an "I told you so".

"Get back!" one of the mates snarled at the crowd, pushing them all roughly away from the ladder with a capstan bar that he brandished. "The boats are all filled and we won't fish you out of the water if you fall over! You'll have to wait for them to come back and get you!"

"The babies! Be careful of the babies!" Elsje cried, holding Jacomina close to her and repositioning herself behind Gilles, alongside Corretje and Bruinje.

"Are you alright?" Gilles asked Elsje, now ready to go after the sailor.

"Ja, ja, we're fine, really Gilles, we just need to stay in a safe spot for now."

"Maybe we should have stayed down below," he said, relaxing a little when he saw that everyone was safe enough.

"Nee, the air up here is good, a little cold, but it is good."

"I've been telling you that for months," Gilles said.

The master interrupted their conversation by calling out to the crowd.

"Those other boats coming here without the WIC flags are looking for payment from you," he announced. "You are free to leave the ship with them, but if you do, we can't promise any help on payment negotiations or your safety."

The mercenary vessels came circling and jostling like hungry fish, but no man or woman had so far taken advantage of their calls and offers to take them ashore. Recalling the gun shot he had heard earlier, Gilles was still a little concerned. He felt like an exposed target on the open deck, and he wasn't certain that this feeling was going to pass very soon. As he looked around though, he saw that the sailors seemed unconcerned, even laughing and joking with each other.

The family stayed together, all except for Hendrick who stood off to the side behind them all, scowling out over the water toward the land. Unfortunately, now Gilles was reminded of another time when he had done the same thing, stood on a ship's deck looking out over a new and alien landscape. That venture in the Palatinate had not turned out so well, but this was going to be different, he swore to himself that it would be. Here he would make his stand and make a better life for all of them. There was no going back to any of his old lives, and he was running out of places to go in the world. He was definitely looking forward to sleeping in a place that was far away from men whose sole raison d'etre was to see him dead. It would be fine with him if his days were consumed solely with enjoying his family and caring for the crops he planted.

If the challenges were great, the opportunity here was great as well. The future was wide open. Gilles had to believe that the settlement would not be abandoned and that there would not just be opportunities for farmers, masons, shipbuilders, carpenters and joiners, but also for those who created items of a higher nature, in parquetry, leaded glass, tile, copper, and yes, eventually for goldsmiths and silversmiths like Alain Gagner. Maybe someday there would even be printers of books, musicians, writers and portrait artists. This might have just been fanciful thinking in the extreme, but Gilles wanted to believe those things would come to pass here in the future.

In this place there were many like Gilles, people who could never go back to where they came from. Even if the company did pull out one day, there were many who would continue living here. Gilles would almost certainly be one of those to stay on if it was safe, or, in a sudden wild thought that came to him now, he could join up with the Pelletiers, living in the woods and becoming part of a savage nation as he had heard one group of Virginia colonists had done. He shuddered at this strange thought and cast a glance at his young children. What did their future hold? He had no way of knowing. He only had his hopes for them: safety, food and shelter first, then beyond that, prosperity and education.

Now Gilles couldn't wait to set eyes on his own little piece of property in New Amsterdam. He pulled his cloak closer around him and looked out to the houses once again. He wondered which one might his. He hoped it was one of the nicer ones, the ones lined up further to the west, looking like they had been transported as a single piece from the Netherlands. They boasted two or more stories, elegant brick exteriors, beautiful windows with neatly painted shutters and welcoming double doors.

Gilles could see a couple of horses and one cow inside a fenced field, and he observed some pigs and chickens that were wandering freely in the streets. He saw none of the savages that he had expected to see, mixing in with the populace as the foreigners did back in the marketplace of old Amsterdam. It didn't look like there were very many shops though; in fact, it didn't look like there was much business of any kind that was being conducted here today. In spite of the sun, a cold breeze suddenly chilled him and he pulled his hat further down onto his head, pushing aside the feathered plume that had been broken during the journey in a mishap when Bruinje accidentally sat on it. The hat had looked fine when he left Amsterdam, but now it was as battered and bedraggled as the voyagers.

Looking up to a few clouds that had just started to gather in the sky above him, Gilles saw that a change was coming, but he could not tell what it might be. It could get warmer or colder, bring rain or maybe even snow. He had no idea what day of the week or even what month it was. It was probably sometime in November by now, the great storm and repetitive days of calm having completely confounded his sense of passing time.

"Elsje, there is a cold wind up here. Are you sure that you don't want to take shelter and wait below with the children?" Gilles asked again.

"I've waited for weeks now. We are good here," she replied.

She pulled the blanket closer around her as baby Jacomina snuggled deeper into the warmth of her mother's arms. Heintje was impatient as usual, but probably fearing Elsje's or his father's wrath, he didn't stray very far. Being as short as he was, and failing to get a better look at what was on the shore by jumping up and down in the same place to see over the crowd, Heintje located a spot at the rail where he could see a little more. Corretje, holding tightly to Bruinje's hand, shifted from foot to foot, perhaps to keep her feet warm, and Gilles noticed that she was wearing the new wool stockings that had been knitted on the voyage. Elsje had certainly prepared them all and thought of everything, including the last trips to the chamber pots. Aafje stood behind Elsje, at first holding the tied bundle of extra clothing, but eventually she lowered it to the deck as the wait grew longer and her arm grew fatigued. Gilles realized that her other hand, the injured one, was probably still causing her a great deal of pain. He was a little surprised that Elsje said nothing to the girl about their clothes sitting on the ship's dirty deck, but then he realized, as he was sure his wife did, that it no longer mattered. They had worn the same clothes for many weeks without being able to wash them out with soap. Gilles knew that clean clothing would be high up on Elsje's project list, right after finding food and shelter. He was painfully aware of his own gamey smell now too, and he wondered how long it would take to get rid of that. Maybe he could talk her into getting something large enough for a whole person to bathe in, but this was an eccentricity that he knew would be discouraged by Elsje and ridiculed by Hendrick. His wife would certainly think he had lost his mind if he suggested such a thing to her.

The entire settlement was definitely aware that a ship had arrived in port. The governor would already know that it was a WIC ship and the church bell, having alerted everyone within hearing distance, had finally stopped ringing. Gilles had barely been cognizant of it, but once the sound stopped, it occurred to him that it did have a beautiful, melodious sound. The ferry boats returned for another load of passengers, and the crowds were gradually thinning out on the upper deck of the ship. The boats filled up quickly once again, but thankfully, they had now removed the dogs that had left their smell and their fleas all around the ship. Gilles watched as this next boatload of people to leave the ship was rowed in and made landfall on the island. The crowd on the shore went nowhere and continued to swirl around in place. The local residents were probably waiting for everyone to disembark, curious to see if any of their family or friends had arrived on the ship, and the new arrivals were waiting for their belongings to catch up with them. Children on the shore chased each other around the harbor and adults came out from their homes to see the excitement and get a first look at their new neighbors. Gilles was reassured by the sight of well-dressed women and men talking to new arrivals who had just come from the ship. He took heart that there were at least a few signs of civilization and prosperity. Now Gilles wondered if his friend Jean would be there to meet them at the docks. He didn't see anyone who looked like Jean, but it was at too great a distance for Gilles to discern individual faces in the crowd, particularly under the large hats.

Gilles watched Zufeldt as he finished coiling up a length of rope. As much as Gilles loved sailing and the sea, the last thing he would want to do right away was to set out again on another journey across the ocean, especially if it was like the one they had just endured. The young sailor probably took Gilles' thoughtful look for confusion as to what to do next or apprehension about the future.

"It's all right, Jansen! We'll get your things to you. Go ahead on to the shore." Zufeldt pointed to a very small watercraft as it approached. "It's a company boat, but no one recognizes it because it's so small. See the flag? The seamstress made a special small one because a bigger one might take it over in a strong gale!"

Gilles thanked Zufeldt and wished him well for the rest of his life since he probably would never see him again. He was anxious to get to the shore, although he knew Elsje would have concerns about being separated from their belongings. They hadn't brought very much. There had been no family heirlooms to bring, no special chair that had been grandmother's,

179

no family crockery for cooking, not even very much clothing after the fire in Amsterdam claimed most of the family's possessions. What little they had was of no great value and had fit into just a few chests. Having lived with so little for the past few years, Gilles didn't know what he would do with a lot of possessions if he had them again.

With some help from Zufeldt and other members of the crew, Gilles and his family descended the rope ladder. They were seated in the little craft with just the ship's master, the young stowaway, and the mysterious heavy chest that had been loaded onto the ship back in Amsterdam. What was in this thing that it had such importance to the company? The WIC could not mint their own money over here so maybe it was filled with Florentine florins or Carolus guilders. It would be an ironic thing if a chest filled with gold sank the little boat now or if the weight of it slowed them down enough to become sitting targets on the open water between the ship and the shore. It was more likely that the box was full of official correspondence, documents to answer legal pleas, requested rulings from the courts, or directives from the company officers. The Nineteen Gentlemen, referred to as the Heeren, made their decisions and rulings back in the homeland regarding operations in this colony and others, sending their decrees out across the oceans and the continents. The organization seemed to run on paper, tons and tons of paper.

The dark young stowaway had been silent for the whole trip, even while he worked with the crew at whatever the master set him to, cleaning mostly, small compensation for his passage fare. He wasn't old enough, large enough, or strong enough to be of much use to the master. Gilles watched the boy, wondering what the child's future would be and if the child was pondering this same thing. His clothing and hair seemed to be the poorest of the poor, and yet there was something dignified, perhaps even regal about him. The shipmaster proclaimed loudly that this was his last chance, and if the boy did not speak now, he would probably be sold to a less than desirable master because of this defect, his inability to speak.

Maybe the boy could not hear or understand what the master was saying. Gilles doubted that he was weak-minded or entirely without hearing: His eyes seemed intelligent enough, and he looked all around in curiosity. Maybe the boy was silently contemplating his future and an indenture to an unknown master as a bound servant for seven years, eighteen years, or more.

The child might be one of the survivors of the war that had been raging across Europe for the past thirty years. He could be one of the Marranos escaping from Spain's ongoing inquisition, or a half savage, fathered on the African continent by a European sailor. Maybe he even had the blood of the Wilden from this continent and was returning home.

Over the past decades, a number of the savages had been captured and taken to foreign capitals across the sea, souvenirs of voyages to be put on display by adventurers who grandiosely gave themselves titles like "World Explorer". They brought these living exhibits back to impress a king or regent, and not coincidentally, as a showpiece to obtain more funds for future explorations. The kidnapped savages usually fell victim right away to the diseases that waited for them across the ocean, dying in the faraway European cities without ever seeing their homes again, but Gilles had heard that a few of these creatures were hardy enough, intelligent enough and resourceful enough to find their way back to their native lands. Some of them even traveled across the seas voluntarily, joining up with shipmasters as willing sailors.

Why was this small child traveling alone? Was he an orphan? Had he run away from so cruel a master that the unknown was better than what he knew? He could not guess what the boy's bloodlines might be, because Gilles depended mainly on his ears, on hearing speech, to identify the origins of the people he met. If the boy had spoken at all, Gilles was sure that he could have placed him right away, but the child never spoke a word and never uttered a single sound. Perhaps the fevers had left the boy a deaf mute as they had so many others. Maybe he hid this clue to his identity out of fear, with deliberate care as Gilles had done at times, hiding his own French accent. The child might have good reason to fear that he would be returned to whatever horror he had escaped. It was also possible that his tongue had been cut out; there were those who did this on other continents, even to children, for the crime of lying.

Gilles' curiosity about the boy had to move aside now. He had too many concerns regarding his own family and their immediate needs crowding in on him. The food, shelter and other requirements of the next few hours alone were more than enough to keep his mind busy, occupied to the extreme, first listing and then rearranging his most urgent priorities. The oarsmen made quick work of the distance between the ship and the shore, rowing swiftly across the bay. The oars dipped evenly into the water as the little boat was rowed in by strong, practiced, and expert arms. Elsje and the rest of the flock babbled excitedly together, pointing at things here and there. They were tourists for the moment, about to be left off in a place they had never set eyes upon before, in a world where they would soon have to quickly find a way to survive. Gliding across the water, they passed by the bigger ferry boat that was now returning to the ship for a last load of passengers, and maybe, now that it was almost emptied of people, some cargo as well. They pulled up alongside one of the docks that reached out from a rock-strewn strand of white beach.

The master's voice interrupted Gilles' thoughts.

"If you could wait for me ferryman, I'll need to get back to my ship very soon, but first I need to take care of some business. I need to see if Governor Kieft or Van Tienhoven is available since you have no schout or other lawman here."

"What do you need them for?" the oarsman asked.

"I need to ask them about repairs and compensation for the willful destruction of my ship by one of my former sailors. If my suspicions are right, this man, Tiedeman Pels, will soon be turning up here and the authorities will have their hands full. I hope your jail is not at capacity?"

"Is this Pels a dangerous man?" Elsje demanded to know.

"Don't worry, this is not a matter that will concern you, Mevrouw Hendricks. He will most likely get a crew together and try to steal a ship. For now, he has been left behind in New England, and it may take him some time, but I have no doubt he will turn up here eventually. I had neither the deck hands nor the space to lock him up and keep him confined for the remainder of our journey. He probably won't be a danger to others unless they try to stop him."

The master said no more but wrapped the rope around his wrist again, the other end tied around the little boy's neck like a rich old woman's small dog. This reminded Gilles of the old woman and her dog on the ship.

"The crazy woman, can you believe she pushed that old man out of the way just to get ahead of everyone else?" Gilles asked Elsje.

"I'm not surprised," Elsje replied.

"I'm sure she pushed her mother and the dog overboard during the trip. She probably did that to her sister, too."

"Her sister? What sister?" Elsje asked.

"Her sister, her mother and the little dog. They all disappeared during the trip. I know you were busy with the children and were not feeling well, but you must have noticed…"

"Someone went over the side?!" the shipmaster asked, alarmed at the belated report.

"Yes, the crazy woman's mother, sister and dog. They were all together on the berth across from us. You remember them, Elsje."

"I thought she traveled alone."

Gilles opened his mouth, dumbfounded at his wife's reply, but they were at the shore now and he had no time to discuss it any further with her: Their new life was upon them now.

The oarsmen helped them as they stepped out of the little boat, each one of them carefully testing their footing first before planting both feet on the dock. Having finally reached the land, they stepped out of their old lives and into new ones, holding on to each other, swaying and out of balance from living for so many weeks on the undulating sea. The wind had picked up again, although the sun still warmed their faces. One of the oarsmen called over to some men on the shore, asking them to help the shipmaster with the heavy chest.

"What will you do with him?" Elsje pointed to the boy.

"Someone will buy him," the master said.

"And if they don't?" she asked.

"I guess that is up to the governor. I'll be gone again in a few days."

"We'll take him if he has no place to go," Elsje offered.

Gilles should have known that this was coming, but he saw it too late. If the stowaway had been older, Gilles might have asked to take him, so the boy could work his patroon lands, but being so young, he wouldn't count toward the quota and would just be another mouth to feed. Gilles said nothing, but Hendrick, who had been quiet up until now, had a faster response.

"We can't take in strays now, Elsje!" he admonished his daughter.

"We have shelter and if that is all we can offer him, we will."

Gilles could see that he would be wise not to get involved in this discussion even if he was the head of the household. He had learned through past experience that it was best not to say anything at all when

Elsje's mind was made up. Luckily for Gilles, the master had a ready answer for her.

"There are good people here who can offer him more than you can right now. I know you will find these people yourself and will get to know which ones they are, after you have been here for a time. Do you trust me?"

Elsje looked at the shipmaster for a moment as if in thought, but his words had reassured her, so she let the matter drop.

"With our lives," Gilles replied for her.

The master smiled, tugged on the rope and hustled the child away with him, striding down the dirt path to the West India offices with the boy trotting along beside him like an obedient dog.

A young man came running up to Gilles.

"Is that the shipmaster?" he asked, pointing over to the master and the child as they were disappearing down the path.

"Ja, what do you want him for?" one of the oarsmen responded.

"I want to sign on with him. Do you know if he needs more crew members? I have some experience with fishing boats," the youth offered.

"Well, you can go ask him."

The young man turned on his heel, racing to catch up to the master.

Even though they had so little to start with, Gilles realized now that it was wealth such as few of his fellow travelers had. They had a little money and a little land, prospects for getting food and income, but most of all, they had each other. They had the experience of Hendrick's old age, the skills the adults brought along with them, the energy of the young people, and the future in the infants. They carried with them the determination to leave the misery of the old world behind and make their new home a good one, not just for themselves, but for their children too. Even though he was not sure what they would find here in the coming days, weeks and years ahead, they had brought with them hope and belief in a better future. Gilles decided that he was going to live long enough to see all of his dreams realized, even if it took him the rest of his life. It was a completely new world for them to explore, and though all of his dreams might not come to pass, Gilles was certain that he would not have to worry about being bored. He walked forward into the new day.

Printed in the United States
by Baker & Taylor Publisher Services